OBLIVION

the Masquerade

TONYA HOLLERS
& TODD HOLLERS

ISBN-10: 098540650X
EAN-13: 9780985406509

Library of Congress Control Number: 2012908944
Panic Girl Press, Plano, Texas

Panic Girl Press

Dedication

*For our son, Taylor Hollers—May all your dreams come true.
Thanks for the book title!*

Contents & Musical Playlist

One
Run Like Hell I
Pink Floyd

Two
I'm Alive 9
Kenny Chesney & Dave Matthews

Three
Awake My Soul 19
Mumford and Sons

Four
Invisible 27
Taylor Swift

Five
Dare You To Move 35
Switchfoot

Six
Rain 41
Creed

Seven
New Divide 47
Linkin Park

Eight
Crash Into Me 53
Dave Matthews Band

Nine
Breath 65
Breaking Benjamin

Ten
Piece Of My Heart 75
Janis Joplin

Eleven
Here It Goes Again 93
OK Go

Twelve
Tusk 103
Fleetwood Mac

Thirteen
Halloween 111
Dave Matthews Band

Fourteen
Soul To Squeeze 117
Red Hot Chili Peppers

Fifteen
Buried 123
Stereo Trigger

Sixteen
Welcome To The Black Parade 131
My Chemical Romance

Seventeen
Music Of The Night 145
Phantom of the Opera

Eighteen
Wicked Game 157
Chris Isaak

Nineteen
Kashmir 169
Led Zeppelin

Twenty
Dog Days Are Over 177
Florence and the Machine

Twenty-One
Silent Lucidity 185
Queensryche

Twenty-Two
I Don't Love You 197
My Chemical Romance

Twenty-Three
Wish You Were Here 207
Pink Floyd

Twenty-Four
Starts With Good-Bye 215
Carrie Underwood

Epilogue
I Miss You 221
Blink-182

Acknowledgements

We would like to send out a special thank you to our family and friends for supporting our secret pursuit into the unknown. We appreciate the insight you bestowed upon us to follow our hearts regardless of the trivial roadblocks, detour signs, and nose dives. Who said life was easy anyway? And if they did, it would have been a long, monotonous drive. Thank you, Panic Girl Press, for paving the way. A special thank you goes out to our son, Taylor, for believing in us and listening to our endless exchange of storyline ideas. And thank you technology, social media, perseverance, and chocolate...you are the necessary fuel to our fire.

Here's a special shout out to the hodgepodge of musical talents that embody a great source of spiritual muses, transporting our vision into reality. Just to name a few: Pink Floyd, Kenny Chesney, Dave Matthews Band, Mumford and Sons, Taylor Swift, Switchfoot, Creed, Linkin Park, Breaking Benjamin, (the late) Janis Joplin, OK Go, Fleetwood Mac, Red Hot Chili Peppers, Stereo Trigger, My Chemical Romance, Andrew Lloyd Webber's *Phantom of the Opera*, Chris Isaak, Led Zeppelin, Florence and the Machine, Queensryche, Carrie Underwood, Blink-182, 30 Seconds to Mars, Adele, Gin Wigmore, Goldfrapp, Muse, Avril Lavigne, Guns N' Roses, and The Rolling Stones.

Most importantly, thank you to our growing audience of YA readers and those forever young at heart and unbiased in age. Without you, our dreams would be lost and left idle in fairy-tale limbo.

The Masquerade

All the world's a stage,
And all the men and women merely players:
They have their exits and their entrances;
And one man in his time plays many parts,

——William Shakespeare

Countless costumes seem to cover every square inch, concealing my true identity.

My mask shields an overflowing mound of emotions that I hide, playing this perfect part of deception.

My role is to try to fit in against a mountain of odds while burying my secrets and sadness in a bottomless abyss.

I hide in the corridor, afraid to make my entrance, as opportunity tends to pass me by time and time again.

I make excuses for those who hurt me, leaving scars on my soul.

For the sake of my friends and family, I hide my true feelings behind this mask full of falling tears, for I am a teenager lost and alone in this world—this world that taught me to be something desirable and anything other than myself. I vow to never let anyone inside because I am the great pretender.

Until the day I met the boy behind the turquoise eyes, and then everything within my tiny world reels out of control. I begin to unravel, freeing myself from the suffocation of my life, the weight of this costume, and finally—the Masquerade.

OBLIVION
the Masquerade

Chapter One

Run Like Hell

December 23, 2012

The motel sign outside flickers a stream of red into the cool, dark room between the broken blinds, hanging in the window; a crazy Morse code entices me to find answers hidden within the pattern of lights, keeping me from sleep. Everything around me feels unfamiliar. We found this seedy hotel late at night after hours of driving and took the only vacant room out of desperation, hoping to catch a few winks of sleep. I miss my family, my friends, my school, and my life—my life, the way it was before.

On the flickering television, the media continues to report the failure of the great Mayan prediction, chalking the recent destruction up to a violent streak of freakish weather—if they only knew the truth. My bruises ache as I lie down against the hard mattress, and I want to drift away to another place...a place of familiarity and comfort. So I close my eyes and count my ballet steps in my mind. The silence transforms to music, and memories of my mother find me once more.

My concentration breaks as I catch a glimpse of him staring at me. He has given up everything for me, and I have no idea how to repay him. The weird thing is, I haven't asked for any of this—it just happened so fast.

As I close my eyes, a crashing sound jolts me to my feet. I peek out the window as cops in SWAT gear force their way into the next room, arresting a group of thugs. Paranoia sets in because we are two teens on the run. I sling my backpack over my shoulder, and we drive away from the screaming sirens and flashing lights. It's time to run again, and we run like hell. I close my eyes, and the memories come flooding back—back from a place where reality twists and bends only to be consumed by darkness—a place I only know as... *oblivion*.

(Four months earlier)

Camping in southern Oregon with its thick forests, rivers, and mountain terrain was a sight for any wildlife enthusiast. Evening quickly approached as a rusty blue truck pulled up to the campsite. It wasn't an official campsite, but a piece of land near the river with a small clearing to pitch a tent. The sunset perched on the horizon, turning day into night, and the majestic pines cast dark shadows onto the rough and rocky ground. Three men pulled items from the truck and dropped them near the sweet spot called out by the older man.

The full moon fell low on this clear and warm summer evening. Stars hung like diamonds above. On this calm night, three friends fell into the same ritual of setting up the campsite.

Afterward, the campers were surrounded by the glow of the campfire and companionship. They sat gazing through the intertwining flames while waiting for the final charred log to fall to pieces on top of cooling ash. They could only hear the soft crackle of the fire, blazing through the night.

The light from the full moon above competed with the towering pines, and then clouds rolled overhead, blocking almost all the natural light. A small lantern sat on the rocky ground several feet away from the men. An assortment of flying bugs lingered around it. If they listened closely, they could hear the soft tap of their wings against the glass.

As clouds approached and thickened the sky, the smell of rain carried with each passing breeze. The tents whipped against the empowering winds, tearing through the small clearing. Pinecones dropped like torpedoes. Large pellets of rain fell sporadically, and all three stood to collect their possessions. Lightning bolts zipped through the sky, creating patterns of blinding light. Thunder broke with a monstrous boom, making each man run for cover.

A dark figure broke from the forest line, knocking over one of the men, and the lantern spun on the ground until the bright light turned dim. Darkness covered the area as lightning bolts struck close to the figure, trailing it through the campsite. A slavering pack of wolves, too many to count, tore through the clearing, chasing the figure with fierce aggression.

One of the men grabbed a tree limb to protect himself. The dark figure ran through the campers and farther into the dense forest with the pack close on its heels. The last wolf turned and faced the shaken camper that clung anxiously to a broken tree limb. The wolf then sat quietly blocking any attempt for the camper to help the running figure. As the petrified camper held the broken limb like a bat, the wolf's golden-eyes stared deeply into the man's soul. The creature's sleek, gray fur was rain-soaked, but it sat guarding the forest confidently with its muscular physique. Saliva trickled down its sharp canine teeth. The wolf sensed the man's vulnerability and leaped, knocking him to the ground. Growling with its jaws apart, it exposed several sharp teeth and pierced the man with its gaze before finally running off into the forest.

The terrified camper slowly made his way to his knees with the help of his two friends. Claw marks had ripped his shirt, exposing fine lines oozing with blood. The near-death experience weakened his knees, making it difficult to take the next few steps toward the truck. Silence escorted the three down the dark, desolate country road. The wind calmed as the heavy rain turned to a fine mist. No one knew what just happened or how they had escaped it virtually unharmed.

The dark figure continued his journey running through the forest with lightning bolts, thunder, and wolves hot on his trail. Fear ran through his mind just as quickly as his feet ran across the rough terrain. The rain only made it more difficult to get a good footing. He saw a clearing about thirty yards ahead, and his feet ran faster toward the light. The sight of a road brought a small smile to his face as his steamy breath warmed his cheeks.

Sweat dripped from his brow and rolled down his face. He made his way to the road and stepped out in front of a small yellow Volkswagen bug.

The small car swerved as he ran across, and the tires screeched, skidding down the road. It struck two of the wolves, flinging them into the brush. But there were still far too many creatures on his trail; so the figure kept running and once again entered the forest. He wished he could have ran toward the car or stopped for help from the campers in the clearing, but something told him to run or others would be placed in danger.

As he made his way through the thick forest toward another clearing, the moon pushed through the clouds, shining upon the foggy, moist air. The rain had departed to a fine mist, with only scattered thunder. It appeared he was no longer under fire from the lightning. But the wolves refused to give up. Soaking wet with every muscle trembling in exhaustion, he slowed his step and turned to glance at the distance between him and the wild pack thirsty for his blood.

The beasts took great effort to separate, calculate, and contemplate their next method of pursuit. Backing away slowly, the young man kept a focused eye searching for the golden-eyed monsters waiting patiently for their final attack. Losing his balance, he slid gracefully at first, and then rolled down a steep cliff, bouncing against jagged rocks and boulders littering the pathway. Several of the wolves, afraid of losing their conquest, followed him down, beating themselves against the same bloodstained boulders while releasing sharp whines of misery. The fall ended in a shallow ravine; wolf and human blood flowed together, following the direction of the small spring-fed river.

One wolf fell on its stomach with its back legs twisted, exposing slivers of white bone through the thick gray fur speckled with blood. His tongue protruded forward and flopped to the side of his long stern snout. His golden-amber eyes opened halfway as the pupils dilated into a whirlpool of dark charcoal. Its last breath started with a pant and ended with a deep sigh. The ferocious creature died within an arm's length of the battered and bruised young man. However, he watched in horror as three other creatures stumbled up on their paws and staggered closer to him.

Strength came over him as an adrenaline rush, and he rose to his feet while pressing his broken ribs into place with the palm of one hand. He held out his other hand as if it were a weapon.

He yelled out into the forest, "What do you want from me?"

What he didn't expect in response was the comforting feeling of something he didn't quite understand, and then he realized the ramifications of the master plan. Calmness washed over him as he stared deeply into the eyes of one of the wolves. Then a sudden bolt of lightning struck him turning everything white, and he closed his eyes. The remaining wolves atop the cliff, observing their defeat, backed away snarling and scattered into the thick woods, howling to bring what was left of the wounded pack back together.

Ten minutes earlier, I was making my way down the country road with my little car's wipers on full blast. They still couldn't keep up with the extreme rain blocking my view. Wind gusts attempted to push my car from the road, but I kept a firm grip on the wheel. The radio station played a three pack of Pink Floyd; I turned up the third song, "Run Like Hell," and hummed along with a thumb drumming on the steering wheel. The storm had come on unexpectedly after I was already on the road. Otherwise, I never would have agreed to run out in this mess to get a pizza.

The skies turned gray growing darker by the minute. Pine needles blew onto the windshield, getting caught up in the wipers. The wipers groaned as they drug the dirty leaves and debris against the glass. My cell phone rang. I reached for it, but knocked it to the floorboard. With one hand on the wheel and the other searching aimlessly, I took my eyes off the road for only a moment. Glancing back up through the rain, I saw a dark figure cross in front of me. I swerved and skidded down the road, striking against something with a thud, and then spinning with a thump into something else, until the car came to an abrupt stop facing the opposite direction. Shaking with my hands covering my mouth, I let out a slow breath. Stunned, I couldn't move and feared I had hit someone. As I slowly stepped out of the car, the smell of rain and burning rubber circulated around me.

I stammered into the open air: "Hello, is—is anyone there? Hello…?" My voice began to crescendo, but without any response. Just another reminder of how alone I really was.

Walking toward the tread marks on the road, I looked into the forest line. Thunder echoed and grumbled in the skies around me. A bright lightning bolt hit something out in the forest, causing the sky to light up, and my ears popped. I closed my eyes and covered them with my hands. Thunder came next, almost knocking me off my feet.

Again I looked into the forest, scanning for the reason I almost drove off the road. Feeling a sense of something watching me formed chills on my skin. Low to the ground surrounded deep inside a thorny bush, golden-eyes peered out at me. I ran to my car, climbed inside, and locked the door. Franticly, I fiddled with my keys trying to untangle the assortment of trinkets, dangling in a cluster. I inserted the key and prayed the car would make it down the road without dropping important parts. A muffled voice came from the floorboard. It sounded like someone calling my name. The call must have picked up prior to the accident.

I snatched up the phone and hit the gas.

"Piper, can you hear me? Are you OK?"

"Dad?" Tears ran down my face.

"Piper—oh my God, what happened? I could hear you screaming."

I quietly cleared my voice and wiped the stream of tears with my sleeve. "I'm OK. I thought I saw something on the road and I swerved, but the rain must have caused me to slide. I don't know. I think I hit something, but I…Dad, I just want to come home."

"Do you think you can drive home? Patrick and I can come get you."

"No, I'll be alright."

Random thoughts kept me company as I firmly held the wheel with each curve. I fought certain thoughts from entering my mind, but before long I couldn't shake them. Last year's accident and the images of the crumpled silver SUV folded like paper haunted me. She missed my last ballet recital.

I danced a flawless performance as I searched for her through the audience. My heart pounded in my chest with each jump while she slipped away bleeding to death. I had a nagging feeling something was wrong... something was tragically wrong. Later that night on the news, a blue tarp blocked the view of the driver's seat, and police lights cast colors upon the forest trees. The boisterous anchorman reported another drunk had taken another casualty, but they couldn't report the dead young woman's name quite yet until her family was notified. It didn't matter. The only thing left untouched was the back bumper with the ballet sticker she had gloriously applied after my fourth grade recital. On the road below, shattered glass glittered like stars fallen from the night sky and scattered upon the pavement. My life was forever changed.

I shook my head to clear it of the terrible memories as my car rolled into the driveway. Dad was sitting on the edge of the front porch. He walked toward the car and motioned for me to drive up closer to the house. My brother, Patrick, flew out the front door with his cell phone in one hand and walked around the car. I opened the door and stepped out, trying to fight back the tears and feelings of helplessness. Dad looked me over with his piercing eyes to check for even the smallest scratch. Then he pulled me in for a hug as he stroked the back of my head.

"I heard you scream...and I thought that was the last time I would see you again." His voice trembled, and he cleared his throat to steady himself. I knew it brought back the memories of losing *her*.

"Dad, the most horrible thing happened. This storm came in, and I couldn't see anything. My phone rang and I dropped it. I reached down to grab it and when I came up...I...I...saw someone cross the road, and I swerved. What if I hit him and left him out there to die all alone?" I rambled on like a mad tyrant. "Dad, we have to go back. We have to take another look." I grabbed his hand, trying to lead him back to the car.

"It's dark out, Piper. We won't find anything. Besides, I don't think you hit anyone. Your car would definitely show signs if you hit a person. You couldn't have missed that even in this harsh storm. No one is going back out tonight," Dad firmly stated.

They looked over the car in the dim light. Patrick kneeled down beside the front passenger wheel inspecting a dent and a gash fraying the car's polish.

"Hey Dad, I think I found something." Patrick pointed to the sliver of weakened metal. "What do you make of this?" Patrick pulled a tuft of gray hair wedged inside the metal gash. He held the fur up to the light.

Dad pushed his glasses upward on his face to inspect the specimen. "Looks like it came from an animal of some sort—maybe a stray dog." Dad replied as he took the fur from Patrick placing it in the palm of his hand examining each strand; as if he could determine the exact species just from this particular hair sample.

Patrick reached up underneath the frame near the tire and felt a wet, sticky substance. He pulled his hand back surprised to see the amount of blood and fur pasted to his hand. Jumping backward, he almost fell from his immediate reaction to wipe the animal tissue onto the blades of wet grass near him. Dad turned on the water hose washing the red blood and grit from Patrick's skin.

The sight of the blood made my stomach feel queasy. I went inside and straight up to bed. All I wanted to do was sleep. I thought I felt Dad cover me up at one point, but soon I was sleeping too deeply for dreams or nightmares—a luxury I hadn't enjoyed in a very long time.

At the bottom of the rocky ravine, the fallen, handsome figure lay broken and weak. Cool water from the small spring rushed against his body as it rocked him gently from side to side, nursing him back to life. His eyelids fluttered in sleep, his muscles twitched slightly, and visions overcame him in a sequence of events—snapshots of a life he hadn't known. An old life's experiences, dreams, thoughts, secret desires captured and stolen found their way back into this *new* life.

His blue eyes opened, and his blurred vision gradually became crystal clear, as did his plan. He had to hurry because time was running out.

Chapter Two

I'm Alive

The next day, I woke feeling stiff and sore. Slamming on the breaks and skidding down the road had taken a toll on every muscle in my body. I gently moved from the comfort of my warm blankets to standing erect and blindly searched for my slippers. The house sat quietly, and I soon realized I was alone. As I pulled back the blinds, the sun hit my eyes. I struggled to keep them open. Peering out the window, I noticed Patrick and Dad tooling around my little yellow car.

My last weekend before school started, and I found myself without a car. I didn't expect to have it back anytime soon. Dad's favorite mechanic shop credited attention to fine detail, but not swift delivery. I had to face the facts; I would be spending my last free weekend without wheels.

I sighed and then reached into my closet to pull out a pair of jeans and a concert T-shirt. Then one of my ballet slippers fell from the shelf and caught my attention as the ribbon dangled the shoe in front of me. It sucked me into a place I didn't want to go. So I untangled the ribbon and tossed the shoe into the corner of my closet. I slammed the door shut, leaned against the wall, and finally slid down seating myself upon the wooden floor. Memories haunted me of my life before *she* was taken from me.

Marcella, our housekeeper, opened the door and popped into my room, dragging the vacuum cleaner behind her. She sang along with her iPod as I sat quietly watching her before she had a chance to see me. I smiled graciously, clinging to even the simplest thing that could pull me from this funk I fell into.

"Piper, I thought you were out front with your family. I heard all about the accident. Are you OK?"

"I'm OK. I should probably get dressed and go downstairs."

Marcella fiddled with the vacuum cord and then sat down beside me. "You know, I'm here if you ever need someone to talk to, Piper."

I nodded and gave a forced, but believable smile.

She stood, smiled back, placed her ear-buds back into her ears, and turned the vacuum on. I pulled my hair back into a ponytail. But instead my fingers began to form the ballet bun by habit. Realizing it, I shook it loose quickly, gathered my clothes, and headed to the bathroom to change.

Patrick followed us to the mechanic shop. Dad drove my car while I sat quietly in the passenger seat staring out the window. My mind was somewhere else, and I felt like I was living my life on autopilot—present, but never really there. I picked at the scattered details of last night's accident. Within the dark shadows, the face of an attractive boy flashed through my mind. I knew it occurred moments before slamming on my breaks, but where did he go? Lost in confusion only led me to think of my mom's accident, but I forced it away like I do everything else that hurts.

I listened to Dad's countless stories of Ashland as he recalled where he was in life according to the steady growth of our town. Dad always wanted to be an architect and held an astute fondness for building design and aesthetics. However, he fell into the trap of corporate law lost forever to overnight business trips.

Dad elaborated on places Mom loved. In particular, Lithia Park was her favorite filled with gardens full of life and color that called her back time and again to watch the seasons conjure up a new inspiration of splendor. They met at the Shakespeare Festival on an unseasonably warm night. A blind date set up by a couple of friends started a blessed adventure and soon after, a family of four.

Dad parked the car, and then we walked into the mechanic shop. A broad shouldered man with a blue handkerchief wrapped around his head approached us. He reached out to shake Dad's hand. I watched his dark locks of curly hair peak out from the head wrap. He spoke with a thick accent that reminded me of Antonio Banderas, and I quietly giggled at the thought of how far astray I allowed my mind to wander. Dad filled out the paperwork and handed over the keys.

We met up with Patrick sipping on coffee outside a small café near the mechanic shop. The patio area possessed a courtyard atmosphere. A floral arrangement of climbing vines overtook the wooden lattice, covering it with full foliage. The stone wall separating the café from the courtyard was decorated with vintage artwork and a sign with today's menu. People walked their dogs, and a few joggers trekked along listening to their secret music stuffed inside their ears. But everyone stopped and noticed the TV news van marked KBBO Channel 4 driving down Main Street.

On our way back to the car, I glanced into the garage taking one last look at my car. The mechanic washed the undercarriage of my car with a power hose. A stream of red fluid flowed across the cement floor and filtered down the large drain. Chunks of flesh and hair deposited on the cement, and the man continued to soak it with a steady and powerful spray.

I thought about the blood flowing from my car while Dad drove us home. Patrick took off to a friend's house, and Dad left to run a few errands. I sat alone in the house thumbing through Facebook and sending random texts. Bailey hadn't responded, and I worried over the probability that her mom may have revoked her phone privileges again. Bailey was my best friend, and I needed her madly.

I reached over and turned on the TV. It was live news from the Oregon Shakespeare Festival. "This is Victoria Carson reporting from the Oregon Shakespeare Festival. Since 1935 this production has been bringing you masterful pieces such as *The Merchant of Venice* and *Twelfth Night*. Others will soon follow, and audiences adored the creations, making the Oregon Shakespeare Festival one of the oldest and largest professional nonprofit theaters in the nation." I recognized my mom's friend, Fannie, on TV and turned up the volume.

"Today, I am standing here with Fannie Gerard. We are thrilled to have her with us. She has been living here in Ashland, Oregon for seventy-nine years and remembers the Shakespeare Festival starting out. Some of you may not realize this, but Fannie actually worked as an actress here in the late 1950's. What would you say is your favorite play?"

"Oh dear, I can't choose only one, Victoria. They have all been special to me throughout my life. Each one reminds me of how I experienced the world around me. These plays have a place in my heart that I will always treasure. If I had to name only one, then it would be my love, *Romeo and Juliet*."

"Somehow, I thought you might choose *Romeo and Juliet*. I believe it's my all time favorite too. Thank you for sharing your lifetime experiences with us on this gorgeous morning here in Ashland. It has truly been an honor to meet you, Fannie. We're standing outside the Elizabethan Stage here at the Oregon Shakespeare Festival—back to you Mike."

"Victoria, have you heard anything more on the fires that destroyed eight homes in Stone Bridge?" Mike lowered the tone in his voice to show compassion, and then he flashed his bleached teeth with a wide smile.

"It appears we have a copycat on our hands," the news anchor stated. "Forester Sledge was arrested back in 2010 for the arson in Cannon Bridge Court, causing the deaths of two people. He was sentenced to twenty-five years, and to this day states he was wrongly accused. The fire marshal couldn't elaborate, but he did believe someone was going to great detail copying the 2010 crime scenes. There will be more on this story tonight at ten o'clock."

Cannon Bridge Court wasn't far from my neighborhood and these unexplained fires continued to haunt our town. Forester Sledge's nephew went to my school and appeared to be just as messed up as his uncle.

My phone buzzed in my pocket, and I sighed with relief knowing Bailey was calling. I answered with a simple, "Hey." But she cut me off.

"What is going on, Piper?" she demanded. "Your brother posted this odd comment online last night."

I turned off the TV and sat down on the sofa. "Bailey, I've been texting you all day. And you haven't responded."

"Yeah, my mom took my computer and phone away. I didn't get it back until just now. What happened?"

"I wrecked my car. I hit an animal or something. It was raining so hard. I thought I saw someone, and I swerved. It really freaked me out." I felt tears surfacing to my eyes, but I held them back and cleared my throat. "It was on the same road where my mom crashed last year."

"Are you OK? I can't believe it. That road is so dangerous, Piper. You have to be more careful. I can't lose you." Bailey pleaded.

"Really, I'm all right—just feel banged up and sore. My car is at the shop. Who knows when I'll get it back? I'm pretty much stuck here."

"I'm coming over. I know exactly what will take your mind off it—shopping," Bailey replied.

I managed a weak grin. "Thanks, Bailey. I'll see you soon."

I opened the fridge and took out a bowl of fresh strawberries. Some juice squirted onto my white T-shirt, and I walked over to the sink to wipe out the stain. Looking up from the faucet, I caught a glimpse of a shadowy figure outside the window. Jumping back, I knocked the bowl of strawberries off the countertop, shattering the bowl into tiny sharp fragments. Startled, but uncertain of what I'd seen, I hid next to the adjacent wall, waiting for the figure to reappear. Feeling ridiculous, I walked slowly toward the window to confront my fears and disarm my creative imagination once and for all. A piece of ceramic pricked my heel, and I looked back at my blood on the floor.

I grabbed a towel from the drawer and dabbed at my heel. Walking down the hallway, I opened the front door and slowly stepped out. I held my phone tightly, and a cramp formed in my wrist. Every muscle in my arm contracted, but I still didn't release my grip—my phone was my lifeline. I heard a small noise from underneath the hedge. As I bent down to take a look, a gray cat charged out screeching and hissing. I jumped back, falling onto the ground.

Laughing at myself, I stood up and wiped the grass from my jeans. Something brushed against my ankle, and I looked down to see what it was. A black sack made of cloth was hung up on Mom's holly bush. I knelt down and picked up the sack, holding it up to the sunlight. The thick material blocked out the sun, and small black hairs woven into the cloth dispersed unevenly throughout. A putrid smell overtook me, and I tossed the bag back to the ground. The smell of death soaked into my skin, and I hurried back inside the house.

Last night's accident was impacting my thoughts. I was paranoid after such a close call, I decided. A day out with Bailey was just what I needed. When she finally knocked on the door, I ran to answer it and pulled her inside. "I'm so glad you're here."

She gave me a funny look. "Piper, I saw the most peculiar thing. I parked my car in your driveway, and this weird old man came out of nowhere. He was dressed like a homeless guy with all these different layers of dirty clothing and standing in *your* neighborhood. He was so out of place. He had this book in his hand and kept hitting it with his fist. It was like he was trying to tell me something, but instead, he really freaked me out. What do you think he wanted? I turned away for a few seconds to find my mace, and then he was gone. Have you ever seen this weirdo before, Piper?"

She sat down in the plush chair and continued working herself into a tizzy. "I think we should call the police, Piper. I mean, what if he's a thief or a crazy person, or what if he's that copycat pyromaniac the news keeps talking about…"

"Bailey, I have no idea who he is or where he came from. Maybe he's just some confused old man. Our neighbors down the street had several cars parked out front. Maybe he's a relative or something. What else could it be? I'm sure he's harmless." I had to convince her that we were both safe—or else she would be sitting in that chair until night came. "Look, I want to get out and enjoy sunshine and shopping. School is starting in less than a week, and I want to buy a few things from that new boutique downtown."

Bailey rose from the chair as the color came back to her face. Her eyes gleamed, and a quick smile broke across her face, "Shopping."

"That's right. Let's go." I continued to coax her out the door.

Bailey revved her black Jeep, and wind blew all around us as we traveled downtown. Bailey parked the car, and we walked until something caught our attention. One bag here and another bag there added up to a wild adventure of fun. Hours flew by, and our arms became sore from carrying the load of jeans, shirts, shoes, and boots. Before we realized it, our stomachs were having a conversation, growling back and forth at each other.

We forced the bags into the Jeep and went around the corner to the Standing Stone Brewery. An aroma of alcohol, garlic, and wood-fire-grilled pizza greeted us, and we sat at a small table near the window.

As we were deciding what to order, a man sitting behind us rose and casually handed us a flyer from his small messenger bag. "It's a new store. Stop by and take a look. You might find something interesting." He smiled and tossed his head to the side, flipping his long bangs away from his eyes. Then he headed out the door.

After securing his bag, he unlocked his bike from the rack outside our window and pedaled away. The back of his T-shirt displayed a magic wand and cards with the words "MAGIC GIFT EMPORIUM." I opened the flyer and read it out loud.

Magic Gift Emporium invites you to come and dabble in the mystical, magical world right outside your doorway here in the tranquil land of Ashland, Oregon. Careful, once you come in, you might never leave. Come and explore the world of exciting magical trickery, gifts, and costumes. Professional magician will be on site every afternoon from three o'clock to six o'clock. Halloween is only a few months away. Authentic costumes are available for rent or to own. Grand Opening Today!

"That sounds so awesome!" Bailey replied. "Do you want to go when we're done with lunch? It sounds like fun. I need a costume anyway."

"Sure," I agreed.

We ate in a hurry, and then traveled a block from the restaurant to a building that sat alone on a small wooded lot. The new magic shop was housed in an old warehouse transformed into a Victorian mansion complete with steep gables and pointed windows. The shop had great curbside appeal with green gardens and sculptures shimmering in the summer sun.

We entered through the wooden door, and it creaked, as did the flooring with each step. The owners were dressed in Victorian clothing, and the magician wore a period piece complete with cape and black top hat. It felt like we stepped back in time. To the left was a sitting room with Victorian couches and chairs. Against the wall, bookshelves covered three walls towering from floor to ceiling. Magic books composed most of the wall, but a bookcase enclosed in glass held a section of secured books—a darker side made of black magic and Wiccan guides bound in leather.

A lively gift shop full of magic kits, toy wands, capes, fairy sculptures, and old-fashioned rock candy stood near the right side of the emporium. Upstairs presented a fine arrangement of collectible costumes in various categories. Dressing rooms at each end of the second floor held decorative tapestries for privacy.

Bailey and I walked around exploring all aspects of the not-so-little shop of horrors. We gradually made our way up to the second floor to try on costumes, wigs, and accessories. Pretending to be someone else was an invigorating end to our long day. Each year a new costume, a new look, a new adventure—closets full of past costumes all await the new arrival. This year I selected Alice in Wonderland, a hit made more popular a couple years back by Johnny Depp. All these years, I thought

I'd made it through the fairy tales, but for some reason I always passed over Alice.

The gift shop shelves were full of magic kits and mounds of white rabbits—as if they bred all day long. Baskets and baskets of the soft white creatures, black top hats, and rickety rackety rotating racks of kiddy magic wands stranded customers into the center of the shop. I made my way through, purchased my costume, and waited for Bailey.

Along the far side of the shop near the windows sat a cluster of snow globes upon a small table. Magic globes replaced the snow with glitter, and magic wands waved around inside. I sat down captivated by one globe in particular, and I rotated it slowly side to side to watch the magic wand float. Something hard pressed against my thigh, and I pulled out a leather-bound book stuffed inside the cushy chair.

"The Book of Shadows," I whispered. As I flipped through the pages, quickly skimming the texts, a cold chill blew across my skin. I felt my hair gently lifted upward. A high-pitched squeal rang in my ear, and I felt a presence kneeling beside me. I jumped to my feet and spun around to face the unimaginable, but no one was there. I bumped the table, and a snow globe fell to the ground, shattered, and the liquid splashed into a puddle upon the wooden floor. Flecks of glitter floated on top of the puddle, and a small angel with golden wings rocked back and forth, fallen far from Heaven.

A girl with multiple facial piercings and purple hair walked over with a broom and dustpan as I apologized for the damage. "I'll pay you for it," I insisted. "I feel so clumsy."

She continued to sweep the fractured pieces placing the remnants into the trash. "No, it's totally cool. Don't worry about it. It was just an accident."

I scanned the store for the eerie spirit haunting me, but everything appeared normal. My skin blushed in embarrassment as a few preschoolers glared at me, pulled at their mom's shirt, and pointed my direction. I heard them scold me in a tattling sing-song voice, "She touched the breakables, and now she's in trouble."

On the drive home, I tuned out Bailey's ramblings and looked out the window, trying to recount the strange events from today: the black cloth bag soaked in the smell of death, the creepy old man wandering the neighborhood, the witches' spell book practically waiting for me, and the evil presence toying with my mind. Could this just all be coincidence? Call me crazy if any of this was real. A jazzy card trick at the Magic Gift Emporium had nothing over the nooks and crannies that darkened my deepest thoughts.

Chapter Three

Awake My Soul

Star light, star bright,
First star I see tonight;
I wish I may, I wish I might
Have this wish I wish tonight.

My mom once told me to make a wish on the brightest star in the night sky. Most people wish on falling stars, but she would say, "Falling stars lose their power too fast to make wishes come true. Why spend your time wishing on something dead when you can put all your energy into life?" I wished for her to come back to me night after night, but my wishes fell on dwarf planets and deaf ears. She was never coming back, and I couldn't spend the rest of my life pretending in fairy tales with happy endings.

Since her death, I had experienced countless nights battling sleep terrors or insomnia. I started seeing a therapist to help me deal with her death and the fatiguing combat with sleep, or I should say lack thereof. Therapy sessions, sorting feelings, and building coping skills added up to an endless assortment of how I *should* handle my life, but when it came down to actually living it—the answers seemed more overwhelming than I had energy to stand. It seemed the more I reached, the further my life fell out of focus. No caffeine after two o'clock, sleeping journals, and warm showers before bed became my daily ritual. However, each night was the same—nightmares of running tirelessly through a dark forest with a vivid account of monsters chasing me. With my heart racing and my muscles aching, I can't get away. They circle around me, and I'm trapped.

The bottle of prescription sleeping tablets rested in my hands. I gently rocked the amber bottle back and forth as the small pills rolled around. Hatred of the medicine briefly entered my mind. I resented my powerlessness and dependence on it. However, sleep deprivation could change your opinion and rationalization of everything. Closing my eyes, I tilted my head back and swallowed it down. I pulled out my journal and sketched the evil jesters that dug deep into my nightmares with their claws.

Trying to keep my eyes open had become more difficult each fleeting moment. I closed the journal and held onto a picture of my mom with her warm smile and sparkling eyes. I felt myself float off into...And then it started again. I knew it was just a nightmare, but it felt real. And I couldn't wake myself.

My feet hit the cool dirt, and I was running through forest terrain. The damp night held a thick fog close to the ground, and I stumbled down a rocky ravine, landing in a cool mountain stream. Motionless, I lay there looking at the stars above me. The childish poem crept into my mind. *Star light, star bright—First star I see tonight—I wish I may, I wish I might—Have this wish I wish tonight.*

I stood covered in mud and followed the stream one step at a time down the narrow pathway searching for a way out—a way back home to my family. Shadows lurked, casting darkness upon my uncertain world. A sinister figure with spikes and sharp edges stabbed at me, darkening my desire to escape. Giving up and surrendering felt easier just for a second, but I couldn't cave...It wasn't in me to submit. Prying its long appendages off was a struggle. I thrashed about, trying to free myself from its claws only to come face to face with the malevolent monster.

An unearthly black creature's pale skin cracked with fissures displayed tissue, muscle, and bone. Missing cartilage had melted away, and a waxy substance poured into clumps of thick mucus pockets oozing among the withered flesh. Its yellow teeth doubled in size and count; fierce and sharp, they shone against the moonlight. Golden-amber eyes sparked an electric charge around the center of its charcoal pupils emptying into a pit of a bottomless hell.

I didn't want to see it. Closing my eyelids tight, I pushed away the hellbound, rotten demon clutching me within his jagged claws.

Dangling in midair, I felt my last breath squeezed from my chest. Screams could not form in my throat. Silence echoed nothingness against the range of trees and mountaintops. Coming close to passing out, I stared up at the summer night sky. Twinkling stars flickered against the dark palate and swirl of the Milky Way. My last thoughts were about my mom, her beauty, and that annoying poem.

Memories tugged at my mind. Flashes of her smiling, gardening, or lounging on the beach clicked away like camera snapshots in slow motion. Something jabbed at me from the pocket of my fuzzy robe with each jolt from the decaying creature. It took pleasure choking the life out of me, and it was angry that I didn't plead for my life. Reaching into my pocket, I pulled out the heavy metal object, placing it by my side.

I opened my eyes, and the scenery changed to the inside of a small chapel filled with windows. Wooden architecture and sculptures of angels decorated the ceilings and walls. The angelic stained-glass glistened, cutting beams of light and distributing warm tones onto the wooden flooring and burgundy pews. The towering trees outside stood still to watch the tragic events unfolding inside.

Then I felt myself spinning, and the creature was back, choking me within the chapel. Broken and numb, I felt my last breath escape my chest. The dagger in my hand, sharp at one end and adorned with a ruby cross at the other, dangled. Then, with a force unseen, it led my arm upward, striking at the evil being. Its eyes glowed with hostility. As soon as the metal point entered its body, it burst into a billion pieces of black shattered glass. Falling to my knees, I forced in a deep breath. And the dagger disappeared as quickly as the wretched beast.

I stood up and slowly walked out of the small wooden chapel. Glancing down I saw the fuzzy robe I had been wearing had been replaced by my blue birthday dress—the last gift my mom gave me. A small pathway led into the forest, and I followed it. The sun gracefully appeared, leading me home—when I heard her voice.

"Mom, where are you?" I whispered.

"Piper, my sweet Piper, I've missed you so much. I need you to be strong. You will have to fight like you've never fought before. The darkness is coming to steal you. You will have to choose—and Piper, choose with your heart as much as your mind. Choose wisely. Once you step inside the darkness, it will overtake you. I love you, Piper, and you must…"

Her voice began to fade into the bright rays of light, and I hung on every word. "Mom, please don't leave me," I begged.

Her warning only confused me more. Questioning my faith and sanity revoked any positive aspiration for finding truth and understanding. This sadness ate away at me, turning me into a hollow ghost of a girl. I wanted forgiveness from her, but what I really needed was to forgive myself. The noose of my own resentment wrapped tightly around my neck. Feeling smothered, I gently released the ropes of self-punishment, freeing myself from my own tormenting thoughts.

I glanced back once more at the small chapel in the woods. The beauty compelled me to stop just a moment to gaze at its serenity. All of a sudden, a ball of flames sparked into the trees, ravaging the forest, setting it ablaze. The stained-glass exploded. The towering wooden beams caved into a pile of hot timbers. I thought of the angelic wooden carvings, the towering pines that guarded the chapel, and a God that could have prevented it all…just like he could have saved my mom. I felt my faith fall upon the dirt I stomped upon. Then I realized—I didn't just blame myself; I blamed *him*.

The forest faded into oblivion, and I felt myself slowly waking to reality. The nightmare was over. I was covered in sweat and couldn't even recall what it had been about. I stretched out in my bed, staring at the ceiling while clutching the picture of my mom.

It brought back painful memories, and I remembered in great detail the day of her funeral. People came forward to speak words of comfort, fond memories, kindness, and love. My words scrambled around in my mind. They raced to find a way out to tell the world how much I loved—love her. I couldn't see for the tears blurred my vision.

I made my way toward her. I didn't want to breathe or feel another emotion for the rest of my life. It hurt more than I could stand, but I was still standing, suffering for an eternity. I knelt down beside her closed casket and cried. Father Mannelli stood beside me speaking the word of God, but I couldn't hear him. My world was whirling out of control. The stained glass captivated me, pulling my mind away from my overwhelming sadness. I didn't understand how I could feel completely numb and ravaged with pain all at the same time. This emotional turmoil spun my soul unsteady.

Eventually, I looked back at the people sitting in the pews; my brother held my father up as he burst into tears, sobbing uncontrollably. Patrick had always been resilient to sadness and heartache, and he knew how to be strong for others. Family and friends sat with red eyes and white tissues in hand. My vision turned narrow, and sounds became distorted. I felt myself falling.

I remember waking up disoriented and then staggered down the hallway in the direction of voices coming from the family room downstairs. I had missed the rest of the funeral and was now back at home. People stood around whispering and hugging one another. Familiar faces greeted me with smiles, hands soothed my back and shoulders, and words of compassion filtered into my ears. But the only thing I could hear was the knocking at the front door.

"Are you Piper O'Leary?" the deliveryman dressed in brown questioned.

I nodded, signed the electronic board, and accepted the package. It came from New York, and my stomach tensed up. I took a breath and tore into the brown wrappings. The inner box exposed a shimmering silver hue of tissue paper with a sticker that held the two pieces together: *Diane von Furstenberg*.

Dad knelt down and handed me a pink envelope. I lifted it close to my face and could smell her perfume like she was kneeling there with me. But the accident—it had changed our lives forever.

"Piper, she loved you so much." Tears came to Dad's eyes, and his voice was scratchy. "She couldn't wait for this package to come. She said it was a special dress and knew it was for you the moment she saw it. I'm so sorry she's not here for you now."

"Dad, I can't live without her. I want her back. I want her to come back to me." Things were left undone. I needed to apologize. "If I hadn't yelled at her the night of my recital, she wouldn't have left. She wouldn't have been on that dark road, and that drunk wouldn't have crashed into her." I never told anyone what my last words were to her. One of her paranoid episodes trapped her as she ranted about wild ideas. I called her crazy and accused her of ruining our lives. "She drove off in her car and to her death. And it's all my fault," I revealed with regret.

"Piper, it was an accident," he whispered while wiping my tears. "You can't possibly blame yourself. She wouldn't want you to feel this way. She loved you so much. Please don't blame yourself."

Our family secret of mental illness was well hidden. Mom would go away on "vacation," as Dad called it, when she got out of control. After regulating her medications, she would come back to us as our mom. However, we never knew when the paranoia would creep back in. Dad lost faith in her treatment while juggling life, love, and all the secrets stuffed inside our home.

I remembered times when she lost reality and tried to bring us into her world. It gradually became worse with time. At one point, I woke with her standing over me with a kitchen knife, repeating phrases about saving me from evil. Afterward, she spent months in the hospital. But Patrick and I begged Dad to bring her back to us.

I opened the pink envelope and pulled out her card wishing me Happy Birthday.

Piper,
I saw this dress and knew you would make it beautiful. My sweet sixteen, I can't believe you are growing up before my eyes. I am blessed to have you in my life and can't wait to see what the future brings. You are special and I love you so much, my little angel.
Love always, Mom

I broke the seal opening the tissue. There it was, the winter blue dress folded neatly in the box. No more tears. My eyes were red, dry, and just couldn't shed another drop. I smiled, lifting it out of the box. I looked upward to follow the dress and saw several faces looking at me.

"Could I have a glass of water?" I whispered with a rasp. Everyone turned to get the water, clearing the room in seconds. Alone, I admired the dress and planned to save it for a very special moment—one that would make Mom proud.

I traveled back from my memories and placed the jewel-framed picture of my mom back on my nightstand. It was time to get out of bed, shower, wash away the residue of the past, and embrace a new day. The winter blue birthday dress waited patiently for me in the back of my closet. And when I reached in to grab a shirt, the sleeve gracefully stroked my hand.

Chapter Four

Invisible

Patrick pounded on my door, and his deep voice bellowed, "Piper, get up and turn that alarm off. You're going to be late on your first day of school!"

Summer was over, and this year felt different in some odd, undefined way. The thought of my junior year at Ashland High caused excitement and nervousness to twist into a chaotic knot inside my stomach. Cliques divided into an assortment ranging from losers to most popular. I desperately fought to find my place, but fell invisible to the world around me.

I silenced the alarm's buzzer by ripping the plug from the wall and crept out of bed toward the shower. Summer had disappeared too quickly. Hanging with friends at Lithia Park and sailing on Hyatt Reservoir east of Ashland was how we spent most of our summer sun. Occasionally, I saw Aiden around town or practicing football with the guys. I hoped my secret obsession wouldn't betray me. For now, I had to keep it all under control. Aiden was with Rachel, and no matter how much I wanted him, there was no way I could compete with the most popular girl at Ashland High. And sadly, he didn't even know I existed.

Patrick would definitely leave without me if I didn't hurry. On the way out of the room, I bumped the blue Tiffany vase near the door. It spun around a few times, coming close to tipping over. I caught it before it had the chance to shatter. The vase had gone without flowers for several seasons and now held a collection of watches, iPods, a few cell phones, and jewelry. Unfortunately, a skin allergy to metal and the frequent infuriation of botched electronics filled the vase along with the remnants of gathered dust. I pushed the vase against the wall and headed out the door.

"Patrick! Come on, or we're going to be late," I yelled from down the hallway.

He jumped out from around the corner. "Me...late? No way! I can't wait to get this year started."

Patrick, a year younger than me, had tested out a grade, placing us together as part of the graduating class of 2014. Everything always came easy to Patrick: academics, sports, friends, and relationships. For me, not so much. An introvert by nature, I took time to feel comfortable enough to come out of my shell. I had a small group of friends, but Patrick had a swarm. They flocked around him hanging on every word that fell naturally from his lips. Patrick was on the football team this year along with Aiden Sinclair, the quarterback, whom I couldn't seem to get out of my secret thoughts.

"Bye, Dad, we're leaving now," Patrick yelled as he trotted down the staircase with his suede backpack hooked over his right shoulder. But no response from Dad.

"Dad, hello, see you tonight. We will see you tonight, right?" I rebroadcasted.

Dad peered at us from around the corner of the kitchen. With his hand covering one ear to block the noise and his cell phone braced against his other ear, he motioned us away. Next his hand turned into a gentle wave and then finally a sloppy salute to his forehead. Dad was always at the office or bringing the office home. It seemed he never had a free moment or thought that didn't involve business.

We took the Karmann Ghia. She was Patrick's greatest love. He had named her Grace. She wore a metallic sky-blue coat of paint, and the motor revved like the purr of an exotic cat roaming on a hot African prairie. When we arrived at school, he circled around the parking lot a few times, calculating a space that would be large enough to park without the risk of a ding or scratch.

I reached into my pocket and pulled out my class schedule. "First up... chemistry," I grumbled.

"Catch ya later," Patrick sang as he caught up with a group of guys tossing the football chaotically about. Jake, a six-foot-two linebacker and close friend of Patrick's, greeted me with a smile.

I stopped and stared at the school in front of me. It was my third year here, but for some reason I searched deeply into the bricks, stones, and mortar trying to find meaning, or some sort of substantial plan for my life—I felt more alone than ever.

Patrick and the guys walked a few steps ahead. Jake turned back and glanced at me. "Looks like Piper had a good summer. It's like she's not even the same girl anymore."

I think he was trying to pay me a complement, but Patrick stared him down.

"What?" Jake questioned without regard. "She's kind of like a hottie now...I mean in a weird way." Patrick slugged him, tossed the door open, and tucked the football underneath his arm. The new school year started, and a suspenseful eeriness pushed me inside.

The first few days of school were always pretty lame. Rules, regulations, and expectations covered in monotone voices crushed my energy. What I wouldn't do for a tall café mocha from Starbucks with extra whipped cream dripping down the side of the cup! The intrusive sound of the stubborn wall clock's second hand *tick—tick—tick* only teased me with the ridiculous amount of time I had left trapped here inside these four walls. I leaned back in my chair and fantasized about Aiden.

The sound of school bell led us from class to class. I spent brief moments socializing in the hallways and kept my eyes alert for any Aiden sightings. Creative literature fell before lunch. Jordan Mitchell taught my class, and that summer each teacher sent out an invite for students to write a three-to-five-page essay on any topic for extra credit. I didn't feel it was too much effort on a sunny summer afternoon to earn a free A, but evidently I was only one of two people in the class who had taken advantage of the proposal.

"Who would like to stand up and read your essay to the class?" Mrs. Mitchell questioned as she lowered her glasses while looking at her student roster. I folded my essay and placed it underneath my right hip.

Kate, the infamous class meddler, butted in where she didn't belong. She saw my essay and raised her hand. "Oh, Mrs. Mitchell, Piper wrote an essay. Can she go?"

I turned around and gave her one ugly wide-eyed expression.

"Piper, please, we all would love to hear your essay." Mrs. Mitchell smiled as she popped her lime-green gum.

I pulled the folded essay out and stood from my seat. "My name is Piper O'Leary, and I have a Tiffany vase speckled in blue. When the natural light hits it just right, it shimmers with all the colors of the rainbow." For a brief moment, I wished I had written about something else—someone else. *I'm so pathetic*, I thought. I paused, took a deep breath, and continued reading my report. "It belonged to my mom, and it is one of my first childhood memories. I remember being three years old and looking up at the table. A big bouquet of roses, lilies, and carnations burst out from the vase in vibrant color and detail. But the vase hasn't felt the touch of live flowers in years. Now it holds a collection of assorted bracelets, rings, necklaces, and earrings that I'm unable to wear due to my bizarre metal allergy. The upper portion of the vase contains a variety of iPods, cell phones, and watches because around me batteries freakishly drain of power.

"Once holding beautiful garden life, now the Tiffany vase only contains poisonous metals and dead electronics. The light can no longer filter through, and colors cannot transfer to the walls and dance around. The vase is only one shade of blue, and the rainbow of cascading colors cannot break free…"

"…Once I fell asleep in my bed and woke the next morning with a red itchy impression of President Thomas Jefferson's face and the word "LIBERTY" posted to my right hip. A five-cent nickel found its way into my bed and transferred to my skin overnight…"

I looked up from my essay and glanced around the room at all the tired eyes. Sitting pretentiously in their new school clothes, they drifted in and out of consciousness dreaming about anything other than school. I could have stood here reading a passage from some cheap, trashy romance novel, and no one would have known the difference.

Mrs. Mitchell popped her gum and nodded her head, but it was obvious she had mentally joined the same lame bunch sitting in front of me. I shortened the essay and jumped ahead to the electronic failures.

"Over the past few years, I collected a small mountain of failed electronic gadgets. Researching the phenomenon led me to crazy chat rooms, government conspiracies, and secret Alien invasions jamming electrical waves. So I continued to collect the worthless pieces and place them inside the Tiffany vase. I remembered the vase once held fresh flowers and clear cool water while sitting in the middle of our wooden kitchen table. Now it sits on the wood floor of my room collecting dust and death, thirsting for the touch of flower stems and the shelter of blossoming flower buds."

Silence filled the air as everyone stared straight ahead in a mystical trance stealing student souls, and it was called—boredom. I sat down quickly, and Mrs. Mitchell suddenly stood to stretch her legs. "Piper, that was just lovely and, um, inspiring."

The only other student, who had written an essay, Johnny Sledge, stood and walked to the center of the room. He tugged the crumpled essay out of his pocket. Only he could decipher the scribbled words that were dug deep into his paper. The garbled mess also crossed over to his speaking abilities. He ranted about 2012 and how the universe, as we knew it, would come to a tragic and unforgettable end because planet Nibiru would quickly knock Earth out of orbit, bursting our planet into a ball of flames.

From memory, he preached from the pulpit of our literature room. All eyes were glued to him, and mouths parted open, hanging on every word. I couldn't figure him from a crazy nut, or a teenage prodigy prophesying the end. After all, his uncle, Forester Sledge, was the infamous arsonist of the Cannon Bridge Court murders. I was leaning more towards the crazy nut theory. I waited for hot Ashton Kutcher to walk in and show us the hidden camera because obviously—we've all been Punk'd. But no cameras and Johnny continued to explain the diabolical end of time.

The bell rang as everyone stared in deep thought. Mrs. Mitchell spit her bitter gum into the trash basket and dismissed the class. I met up with Bailey and Ryder as they stood in line holding their lunch trays. They had been dating before they even knew what dating really meant and believed they were long lost souls destined to find each other life after life. His older brother owned a T-shirt shop in downtown Ashland—Brody's T's and Coffeehouse. Ryder helped out in the afternoons to earn money and wore his own unique creations. Bailey spent every waking moment there in the back, drinking lattés, chatting online, and making out with Ryder. Anything really, just to be close to him.

Bailey and Ryder chatted while I ate my lunch in silence, unable to explain the emptiness I felt. I finally saw Aiden across the courtyard among the roughhouse games of his football friends. I watched as Rachel pulled him away with a single touch of her hand. He followed, watching her every move. Aiden pressed her against the small oak tree and leaned in for a kiss. The bell rang, and the crowd blended in around them, blocking my view.

"Piper, are you coming?" Bailey snapped her fingers in front of my face. "Didn't you hear the bell? Come on."

I tossed my half-eaten sandwich and crackers into the trash, and we marched like soldier ants from class to class with the sound of each bell. I couldn't concentrate; if I wasn't thinking of Aiden, then I was trying to make sense of Johnny's 2012 essay. Sitting through another roll call was excruciating, so I mentally escaped out the window to the warm sunlight and grassy courtyard until an unexpected silence caught my attention.

"Logan, is there a Logan Taylor here?" Mr. Fletcher asked in a monotone voice. "He must still be out enjoying his summer. If anyone sees Logan, invite him to class. He doesn't know what he's missing." Mr. Fletcher gave a dry chuckle at his own sarcasm.

Time froze and the blah-blah world of education felt like fingernails scratching down the proverbial chalkboard. Finally the last bell rang, and I bolted from my chair. The day was over, and I threw my books into my locker, slamming it shut. As I turned around, I saw *him* walking toward me, tossing the football hand to hand. I stood breathless, watching his every move—how he planted his feet on the ground with each step, how his football physique gravitated toward me like a heavenly body deep out in the middle of an unknown universe. His dark, wavy hair and warm, sun-kissed skin enhanced his turquoise eyes. My hands sweated, my heart raced, and my mouth dried up. I wished my eyes could speak for me in some sort of telepathic connection, screaming out—*See me, hear me, fall for me*. As he stood a foot away, I thought he would hear my silent cry, but *she* stepped between us snapping our connection. Rachel, dressed in her cheerleader uniform, swept around and pulled him in for a long embrace. I felt knocked out of orbit as I steadied myself against my locker. Johnny was right—and Rachel was Nibiru!

Rachel Hart, Ashland's cheerleader captain, had been dating Aiden for over a year. Her beauty defined her. The sunlight caught the auburn highlights in her hair, and the brightest blue sky only paled in comparison to her blue eyes. Every male quivered at her charming splendor; however, *she* only had eyes for one. Rachel fell hard in love with Aiden Sinclair, quarterback of the Grizzlies and Mr. All American.

Beyond them, I saw Patrick walking down the hall toward me. "Piper, can you get a ride home with Bailey?" he asked. "I have to stay. Coach wants to review a few plays in the locker room."

I shook my head. "No, she already left. How long will you be?"

"Maybe thirty or forty minutes…not long. Do you want to wait around?"

"I don't have a choice, do I?" I released a short sigh. "I wish I had my car."

He tossed me the keys to Grace. The building felt empty and deserted. It's crazy how fast a place can clear out. I sat in the car and rolled down the windows, allowing the sunny afternoon breeze in. I pulled my ragged copy of *The Flame and the Flower* from my bag and thumbed through looking for a good place to start.

I read the first page at least three times, but my mind raced with scattered ideas. I shoved the book back into my bag. And I questioned what was taking Patrick so long. The ear-buds to my newest iPod were tangled in knots. I passed some time untangling the snarled mess. Then I closed my eyes, dialed up the volume, and sang along to the brazen lyrics of Avril's "Girlfriend."

The sunny warmth of the day had filtered through my closed eyelids, but a shadow suddenly overcame my warm ray of light. I opened my eyes, and there he stood leaning into the window frame. His piercing eyes glittered in the sunlight with small flecks of gold within the turquoise center. I sprang upright, hitting my forehead on the visor. My skin turned three shades of red, and once again words couldn't find their way out.

"I'm sorry. I didn't mean to startle you. Patrick wanted me to tell you he's on his way," Aiden said as I sat starstruck. Speechless, I nodded my head. He released a small, innocent laugh, stood upright, and jogged toward a black Ford truck jacked up on four enormous tires. As he drove by, I slid back down in the seat, embarrassed.

A few minutes later, Patrick climbed in and started up the engine, tossing his football and playbook in my lap. "What's wrong with you? Why are you hiding out? You're so weird, Piper." He snickered and then pulled out of the school parking lot.

Chapter Five

Dare You To Move

I sat on the hardwood floor of my bedroom, staring out the window and watching the clouds travel across the dark sky. They drifted toward an undetermined destination, chased by other clouds as if competing in some cosmic race to an immeasurable finish line. The clock continued ticking away seconds of my life—time I would never be able to retrieve. Unaccountable minutes added up hours, and I knew in the back of my mind that I didn't have control over my life. A slave to my soul and tireless body, I wished I could fall asleep. Two in the morning, and the house was uncomfortably quiet—another late night with *Tom and Jerry* reruns. What an unforgiving night for cat and mouse games. I reached over and muted the volume while watching the debacle of Tom's tireless torture to conquer the small mouse.

An assortment of sketchbooks layered the floor underneath my bed. Each book spoke a different story, and pencil strokes brought the two dimensional figures to life. I grabbed the yellow book, flipped it open, and began sketching, falling into my own world—just me, my pencil, and the long piece of sketch paper in front of me. I controlled the pencil creating my own reality as I felt the power with each stroke, shadow, and highlight.

A plan between my mind and fingers took shape. The sketch of my sweet Aiden unfolded before me. His smile opened bright against full lips. His teeth bore pillars of ivory, strong and bold. His facial features sharply cut into the paper, breaking the pencil lead. I tossed the pencil aside and grabbed another without taking my eyes off the paper. His eyes, bright like beacons in the night, generated warmth, pulling me in. His dark hair fell in loose ringlets, anchoring natural beauty onto my page. I admired him and dreamed of countless possibilities of how my life would change, if I could just make him mine.

Mesmerized, I stared at the portrait until my eyelids felt heavy. My muscles twitched as I drifted deeper and deeper into the nothingness trapping me each night.

Flashes of light and memories carried me in and out, finally dropping me off at my front yard. The summer sun sparkled like diamonds all around. I caught the smell of hot apple-cinnamon pie and gravitated toward the open window. It was just a harmless dream for a change. My world had turned into a *Tom and Jerry* cartoon. Cartoon Granny placed another pie in the window to cool. As I walked closer taking in the sweet aroma, I heard her voice. I peeked inside the room. My mother stood in black and white, sketched into life. Fine pencil strokes had brought her back to me.

She was not alone. A tall man stood near her, and she began to argue with him. She whispered, "No, I won't tell her. You promised me she would be safe. You said they would never find her. I won't let them take her."

The man turned toward me, aware I was there listening to their secret conversation. He turned into a burst of brilliant light, blinding me. The dreams pulled me to another place. The smell of apple pie was replaced by pine and wet dirt. I glanced down at my feet wrapped in my pale pink ballet slippers. Once again, I was running through the forest. I knew every rock, tree, shrub, brook, stream, dry creek bed, fallen branch, and steep cliff for miles. My heart pounded inside my chest, and I woke with a gasping breath.

Sunlight hit the prisms hanging on my bay window. I heard Patrick and Dad downstairs. The smell of Dad's famous cinnamon-apple pancakes radiated through the house. The cinnamon tickled my throat, and my mouth watered. I flew from the covers.

"Did you save some for me?" I begged, rushing into the kitchen.

"We wouldn't think about letting you miss out on this masterpiece, if I do say so myself," Dad replied with a smile and a wink. "I've got a business trip this afternoon, so I took the morning off to spend time with the two of you."

Patrick sat at the table stuffing his face with pancakes after drowning them in heavy syrup. Dad placed the extra pancakes on the ledge near the bay window while he packed the dishwasher full of dirty dishes. Pieces of my dream came back. I looked out the window expecting someone to be watching us, but no one was there.

After breakfast, I ran upstairs to get ready for school. Dad gently knocked on the door. "Hey, Piper…you'll be glad to know your car will be ready today. I'm going to pick it up this afternoon before I leave."

I reached over and hugged him. He didn't quite know what to do with his hands, and then he gently placed them on my back. Time without Mom's embrace and living the cutthroat life of corporate law left him socially inapt in dealing with real emotion. He pushed his glasses upward to a comfortable spot and smiled at me to hide his sadness, but his eyes couldn't tell a lie.

Patrick sat in his car beeping the horn while searching for a station on his radio. I waved good-bye to Dad and jogged toward the car. Patrick zipped in and out of traffic. The car stopped suddenly, snapping the seat belt against my chest and jerked me from my secret thoughts. I cautiously scoped the area for Aiden as I nervously twirled a small piece of my hair.

I met up with Bailey and Ryder for a few seconds before the first bell sounded. They created their own chemistry conducive to a blistering heat wave. Just a few feet from the door, I saw Aiden coming around the corner. His tall frame stood solid, and I admired each step he took toward me. He tossed the beaten leather football up and down in one hand. Entranced by his rhythm, I fell captivated by his charm. When the bell rang, knocking me back into my senses, I turned around and walked straight into the door, with a *bam*. No one seemed to notice. I turned the knob, stepped inside, and took my seat.

Leaning forward against the cool lab table, I gently rotated the swivel chair side to side. I wanted to throw my hands up in the air and spin around in a feverish circle screaming at the top of my lungs, but instead I stared at the periodic table plastered across the front wall of the classroom.

The flicker of the safety film roughly ran across the screen. With the lights dim, students bowed their heads drifting away. I continued to watch the outdated film and dreamed of Aiden. I calculated the possibilities of encounters I could set into motion. I didn't want to miss out on a single opportunity to see him. Between classes, I dodged and squeezed my way through the hallways to find him. Hiding in corridors, lurking behind posters and banners, kneeling beside lockers, and sneaking around trees and bushes in the courtyard only ended in disappointment. Crowded hallways and obtrusive building structures prevented my plans. The cat and mouse games felt absurd; so I turned back toward my locker.

The stern combination lock twisted easily to the right and then stiffly to the left before opening. Unorganized clutter fell into a pile of text books, spiral notebooks, and an assortment of pens. I gathered the pieces of my ridiculous life, shoving it all back into my locker. The Grizzle Bear mascot stickers decorated the inside, and the small mirror vibrated gently against my locker door. I glanced into the mirror at the reflection looking back at me and knew the truth. I didn't have a chance; an impossible feat bellowed, dropping a ton of weight on me—I was forever *invisible*. One last glance into the mirror, and there he was walking toward me. I felt a sudden spark catapulting me toward him. Without hesitation, I stepped out into the crowded hallway to face him. Unfortunately, I found myself flying through the air in slow motion and landing at his feet. My books and papers scattered mid air, littering the hallway.

Brady James knelt down to tie his shoes just in time for me to trip, catch full flight, and approach my destination. Alfa—Bravo—Tango—without landing gear, I dropped like a brick at Aiden's feet. Blood trickled from my nose and blended into the red carpet honoring our school colors. Laughter erupted around me as papers fluttered to the floor. I wanted to disappear underneath a magical cloak, but instead I felt my skin warming to an embarrassing shade of crimson while I gasped for the breath that had been knocked out of me.

A hand reached down, pulling me to my feet. Aiden stood in front of me, released my hand, and then wiped my blood-streaked cheek with his thumb.

"Are you OK?" His voice resonated, and I stared into his eyes, watching the golden flecks dance inside the turquoise sea. I swallowed the blood trickling down the back of my throat, and then I nodded an unsure yes. My eyes filled with tears, but I held them back. Looking away, I saw Rachel kneeling beside my yellow sketchbook, which was flipped open to the sketch of Aiden. I could see the gears turning in her mind—it seemed my secret was out.

She closed the sketchpad with one swift motion of her shoe and slid it toward me. We locked eyes momentarily, and then she turned gracefully in her red-and-white cheerleader uniform and bolted through the double doors into the courtyard.

Brady James gathered my papers and books into a disheveled pile near my locker as the hallway continued to empty of students out into the warm afternoon air. "Piper, do you want me to walk you to the nurse?" Brady asked as he bent down to inspect me. His look of pity said enough, and I turned to glance into the mirror. A dried clump of blood had pooled just outside my left nostril, and smudged streaks of blood crossed my cheek and neck.

"Gross," I whispered. "No, I'm OK." But my voice trembled as I shuffled the crumpled papers and books back into my locker. I turned toward Brady, but he was gone—everyone was gone. The double doors slammed shut, and the building stood empty. I slid down the wall into a seated position, holding the yellow sketchbook in my hand.

Emotion and self-criticism exploded inside of me. I wanted to run, but couldn't figure out how to get away from myself. Finally, I jumped up and tore through the double doors and out into the warmth of the bright sunlight. I started to walk toward Patrick's car. But I realized he would be in football practice until five, and I was late for flag practice. My hands were shaking, and I felt sick to my stomach. There was no way I could possibly make practice like this.

Turning back, I reentered the building and hid in the bathroom. Standing in front of the mirror, I didn't recognize the weak coward glaring back at me through smudged makeup and dried blood. Wiping the black mascara away seemed pointless because a steady stream of tears continued to flow down my cheeks. I heard voices coming down the hallway and hid in the stall farthest from the door. Pulling my legs up just in time, I sat still, listening and wishing I was far from here.

Little did I know, things were about to get worse.

Chapter Six

Rain

Thunder echoed outside. The same storm rolled overhead and flirted with the ability to produce rain, but instead it just threatened the world below it. The next few girls entered in as the other group left. I recognized the voices of cheerleaders; one in particular was Rachel. At the sound of her voice, I froze. Hiding inside the bathroom stall felt ludicrous, but how could I come out now? Some things were not meant for hearing, but I was trapped.

"Did you see that stupid girl in the hallway today?" Rachel questioned, knowing full well they had. Fishing for information, she caught it—hook, line, and sinker.

"Oh yeah, did you see her fly across the hallway, crash into Aiden, and bleed all over his shoes?" I recognized the voice as belonging to a girl named Devin. "It was awesome...free entertainment in this lame place. Who is she, anyway?"

"Are you guys serious? You really don't know who she is? Wow, usually I'm the last one to know," chanted another girl whose voice I didn't know.

Rachel cut her off. "Spill it already, Kelly. Who is this girl—this stupid, stupid girl?" Rachel demanded anticipating a quick answer.

"Her name is Piper O'Leary. You know, Patrick's sister. Patrick who hangs out with your precious Aiden." Kelly continued to spell it out for Rachel. "Why so interested in this girl?"

"Um, no interest. I've just never really seen her before." But Rachel continued to gather more information. "So, are they like twins or something?"

"I heard that he's a year younger, but he advanced a grade, or maybe she was held back. I can't quite remember. Why do you care, Rachel? She's completely harmless." Kelly continued to press for Rachel's recent curiosity, but came up empty.

Devin broke into the conversation again. "Hey, guys, we need to get back to practice before it's over."

As the door closed behind them, I dropped my feet to the tiled floor and peeked through the crack again to make sure the coast was clear. Seeing no one, I made my way out of the bathroom and down the hallway into the warm afternoon air mixed with the strange scent of rain. The parking lot was cleared of cars, except for Patrick's. He was standing in the distance talking to Coach and a few other football guys. I found a comfortable position sitting near the front passenger wheel and hoped no one would see me. Eventually Patrick arrived and unlocked the car. Calmly, I stood up and climbed in.

"I heard what happened today, Piper," Patrick commented as he started the engine and pulled out of the school parking lot. "Are you OK?"

I stared out the window ignoring his concern and wishing he would stop the brotherly advice I feared was coming within seconds. One—two—three—it was like clockwork.

"Piper, I know you hear me. Why do you always keep it all bottled up? You won't let anyone help you. Why can't you...?"

I stopped him mid-sentence. "What? Do you mean why can't I be more like *you*? That's really what you want to know. Am I right, Patrick? God, don't you think I want things to work out better than this?" I felt my voice shudder and knew I was losing it.

"You're always putting words in my mouth, Piper. You have no idea how far off-base you really are. I don't want you to be like me. Since Mom died, you checked out. I just want my sister back, and I don't know how to reach you. This wall of bricks you stacked around yourself doesn't protect you. It only isolates you from life. Mom's life ended—not yours. She would want you to move on and not give up. Piper, you gave up. That's all I'm saying...and I'm here, if you ever need someone to talk to."

I held back the tears and shielded myself from the pain I felt rushing over me. My castle of stone and mortar was strong, the moat impassible, and my weapons lit and ready for immediate fire. My fortress would never falter. When I squeezed my hands together, my pain turned to numbness.

Patrick turned up the music and pushed down the gas pedal. He could easily change his mood from concerned brother to easy rider, pounding on the steering wheel in rhythm with his crazy music. I envied him, his life, his careless freedom. I wouldn't know peace if it walked up and slapped me across the face.

As soon as Patrick pulled onto our property, I threw my backpack over my shoulder, opened the door, and jumped out before the car was even in park. I ran into the house and climbed the stairs two at a time, hardly even noticing that my car was in the driveway, just like Dad had promised. After slamming my bedroom door shut, I locked it and turned up my music to drown out the annoyance of my life.

Bailey had been blowing up my phone with text messages, but I turned off the ringer while hiding out in the bathroom. Standing at the foot of my bed, I reached up and fell back landing on the soft pillow-top mattress. I reached over and grabbed my backpack, unzipped it, and pulled out the yellow sketchbook. It opened exactly to the sketch of Aiden, just like it had earlier, and I flattened out the ruffled edges. Part of a shoe imprint marred the right upper corner, and I knew Rachel had her mark on him as well.

I scrolled through all the texts and dialed Bailey's number. She worried when I didn't reply, and now, forty-eight texts later, I knew she was growing wild with concern. Thunder grumbled in the background, and the walls of the house vibrated. It must have hit really close, but still no rain. The weather was all bark and no bite today, and it cautiously reminded me that I, too, hold back—hold back everything. The phone rang once and Bailey picked up the call.

"What the hell, Piper! I've been calling you for the past two hours. Why didn't you pick up? Are you OK? I mean, I've been going out of my mind worrying about you. You haven't been acting like yourself. You've been infatuated with Aiden…and, Piper, he's not even into you. Piper, I love you, but you have to snap out of it! I've given you space and ignored your various moods since your mom—since she passed on. I don't know how to help you if you won't let me. Why can't you just let me in? I feel like I'm losing you." Her tone turned from anger to pity within minutes.

I didn't know what to say. "I'm really sorry, Bailey. I don't mean to hurt you. I don't know what I'm thinking anymore. I feel so lost…but then again, I'm not sure I want to be found. I don't know exactly how to explain it. I feel so amazingly empty—like I've poured everything out, but all this anger and frustration is left, and it's grumbling inside me. I just don't know how to get it out." Static crossed over the phone, causing the line to break up. "Bailey, can you hear me?"

"Pi-er, I can't he-- you."

"Bailey? Damn phone!" As I cursed it, the phone shocked me, and I dropped it to the floor. I used my nail-file to pry the case apart, removing the memory card and SIM card just in time. The case felt hot, and the black rubber melted, oozing onto my wooden floor. Grabbing a T-shirt from my drawer, I picked up the phone and dropped it into my vase of wasted things. *Can't wait to explain this defect*, I thought with sarcasm. Customer service knew me by name and was sure to drop my coverage. My mom's cell phone was tucked away in my drawer. I inserted my cards into it and turned it on.

I heard Patrick's wheels spin out of the drive. Dad was gone on another business trip. The house was quiet, and I was alone. Slowly, I opened Dad's bedroom door and peeked inside. All of Mom's things were still untouched, like she was moments from coming home. Her perfume bottles sat on her dressing table. Her silk gown was folded in half over the suede chair. Lipsticks and peach blush were scattered on a circular silver platter. I felt the silk, smelled her perfume, and caressed the lipstick cases. The one person, I knew I could talk to—couldn't even hear me.

She kept her jewelry box in her closet. I walked inside, closed the doors, and locked myself within. I reached up to the top shelf and pulled the jewelry box down. A chiffon scarf, my favorite, fell partway into view. It was caught up on a small wooden box, and I gently pulled it loose, accidently pushing the wooden box off the shelf. I wrapped the soft teal and lavender scarf around my neck, noticing that it still smelled like her—a combination of lavender and vanilla—and knelt to retrieve the box. It had fallen open spilling the contents into a pile: old love letters, fortune cookie notes, photos, gold coins, and an odd-shaped broken pendent with a black ribbon running through it. Carefully, I placed everything back inside the box and closed it, tracing the beautiful design on the cover.

Another crack of thunder startled me as I pushed the box back onto the shelf. I went downstairs and stepped outside onto the patio, watching dark clouds overtake soft, white ones. The sky grew dark within moments, and I turned on the fire pit with a small twist of the metal knob. The gas logs caught immediately, creating a warm light that cast out the shadows keeping me company. Still not a single drop of rain fell. Nothing else could be compared to the simple smell of rain as it lingered in the air, but its stubborn stalemate wouldn't even release fine drizzle. It had been like this all day. I stared up at the darkening skies surrounding me.

As the wind picked up, the scarf I was wearing rose up in the breeze and wrapped itself around me like a distant hug. The soft touch and her smell competed with the smell of rain. Suddenly, against my own will, I began swaying gently side to side. A simple melody played in my mind, and I realized I was dancing. I had given it all up after she died. No longer did I have anything to dance for. But it was coming back in burst of raw emotion. I held back at first, but then I couldn't control the power of my spirit. Ballet turned dark for me after her death, and now it all flooded back.

I traded my leotard and tights for a pair of black running shorts, black T-shirt, and Mom's colorful scarf. As I danced, the scarf swirled and the colors boldly fought against the palate of the dark skies. I wasn't alone. She was here with me—dancing with me as I felt the dry dirt underneath my feet. And I danced and danced, completing my Swan Lake performance that she had missed the night of her accident. Then the rain fell. It started from my eyes, and then the skies opened up and poured down in a steady stream soaking my skin. I hadn't realized how thirsty I really was until now. The dry earth opened up and let in the wet, nurturing moisture it needed. I continued to spin underneath the dark skies, but it felt warm, bright, and more like life than I'd ever felt before. I spun circles across the narrow wooden pier near our small pond until I reached the end.

The dark skies opened up, and the stars shined down. As the rain continued to fall, the dark stranger admired her from a safe distance. Time was ticking. However, it was okay because everything was falling into place; just like the rain had its purpose, so will the girl. Thunder grumbled off in the distance and weakened, but the girl—she's growing stronger.

Chapter Seven

New Divide

The school days seemed endless, and my time filled with after-school activities. When I wasn't participating in some school function, I was thinking of Aiden. I remembered how disgusting I looked the last time he saw me with blood gushing from my nose, and then I flinched in horror of reliving the scene. I studied him from afar watching his every move. Aiden's ability to throw the perfect pass calculated a fine transaction between strength, thought, and chance. Watching him brought me to a definite place…he would never be mine…it was almost like we were from two different universes, sharing absolutely nothing in common.

From the corner of my eye, I caught a glimpse of meddlesome Kate whispering something into Rachel's ear. They weren't friends, and I wondered whose pot Kate was stirring this time. Kate finally pointed in my direction, and Rachel's eyes followed landing squarely on me. Quickly, I looked away feeling guilty for my desire for a boy that would never know how I felt.

Then Johnny Sledge tore onto the field with a handful of pamphlets nearly knocking me down. "You must listen before it's too late!" He pointed to the heavens proclaiming the end was near. "The Mayan prophesies are true. Wake up, people! Open your eyes to the truth. Don't go quietly into the night. Stand up to the monstrosities soon to come our way. Choose wisely before…"

His tirade didn't go far because the coaches pulled him aside, forcing him off the field. His stack of papers flew through the air and scattered across the turf as Johnny put up a short, but entertaining fight. One of his ruthless propaganda pamphlets flew into my view, and I glanced down at it. It displayed a picture of Earth set ablaze by a cosmic collision with the words, "END OF TIMES," boldly written across the torched planet.

"The show is over, ladies. There isn't anything else to look at." Coach Jaggar snapped her fingers and waved her hands wildly to grab our attention, "Focus and get back to work."

Rachel and the cheerleaders practiced on the opposite side of the field, running a series of flips and jumps while chanting superficial rhyming cheers. They were there to entice the fans with their long legs, short skirts, and flexibility. Patrick called them eye candy, worth a few glimpses here and there during practice, but game nights were sacred.

I had memorized my flag routine, but the sight of Aiden running just a few feet away made my heart skip a few beats and my feet miss a few steps.

"Do it again!" Coach Jaggar yelled. "We'll be here all night until you all get it right! Now, repeat it from the beginning." Her voice growled against the thickening gray clouds hovering around us. She folded her arms, tapped her foot with the beat, and observed each move closely as our shimmering silver-blue flags waved gracefully against the growing wind.

An unusual storm was suspended above Ashland, holding out for something spectacular. Large raindrops hit my face and ran down my cheeks as the wind turned from warm to cool within seconds. Thunder grumbled in the dark skies.

Coach Jaggar shouted, "We're not finished, ladies! A little rain never hurt anyone. The game is right around the corner, and our presentation could use some work."

The football players didn't notice the rain and continued to run plays, splashing mud onto their uniforms. At Coach Jaggar's command, our flag line continued the routine, crisp and clean, stomping the mud in unison. The wind attempted to rip the flag from my trembling hands, but I held on.

Then lightning snagged through the black sky with a sudden force. I closed my eyes for just a second, seeing the negative image of the lightning on the back of my eyelids as a crack of thunder drew startled cries from the girls around me. I could hear Coach Jaggar yelling, "All right, everybody inside!"

In awe of the storm's rampage, everyone scrambled in different directions. I turned to take one last glance at Aiden. Without an open receiver in sight, he was running the pass downfield. Another bolt of lightning came down from the sky and lifted him into the air. As thunder snapped in my ears, I couldn't believe my horror. Aiden fell to the soaked grassy field, where he appeared lifeless—motionless. And I thought my world was over.

I ran back down the field as everyone else was running away for cover. When I reached his lifeless body, I knelt down beside him. He wasn't breathing. I lifted his head gently and gave him two breaths. I saw his chest rise and fall with each breath.

Someone yelled, "AED...incoming!"

I looked up in time to see the AED hurtling toward me, tossed by one of the football players. Snatching it out of the air, I opened both clasps and turned on the power switch for the instructions as two football players knelt beside me. Graham removed Aiden's mutilated football gear and jersey between the breaths and chest compression. Then Jake dried off his chest, pleading for Aiden to live. The mechanical voice, calm and focused, instructed placement of the electrodes. Graham placed the electrodes, and we all anticipated the next instructions from the small machine.

"Analyzing...analyzing," repeated the mechanical voice. My mind yelled, *Hurry up already!* "Shock advised. Clear—clear, all stand clear."

Time stood still as we waited for the power source to charge and fire. Distorted sounds came from the sidelines as people ran for cover. The rain turned to fine drizzle, but the wind kicked up blowing dirt and debris all around us. Next the metal bleachers fell, crumbling down onto stunned onlookers. Complete chaos captured those fallen and beaten down. I turned back to Aiden as the charge came complete and ordered another all clear.

The electrical current caused a jerking motion, but Aiden remained lifeless. His skin was taking on a blue tinge. Another shock came in a sudden burst of energy, as I heard the sirens of a distant ambulance screaming.

"Resume CPR," the voice instructed.

My palms pounded against Aiden's chest, willing him to live, but the cycle of CPR ended without any sustainable heart rhythm on the monitor. My arms felt tense and quivered as my fists pressed against his body. I fell across his chest and waited—watching for some sign of life. By now a huddle of football players had gathered around us, and looking up at them, I saw hopelessness in their eyes. But I refused to believe it was over.

I reached out for Aiden's hand and held it tightly. All of a sudden, I saw his chest rise and fall. *Is this real?* I thought. I closed my eyes and then looked at him once more, patiently waiting for another breath. I felt his fingers move, and the monitor caught a sharp heart rhythm across the small screen. The color returned to his face, and then he opened his eyes. Aiden's brilliant turquoise eyes flickered brightly beneath the ominous sky. He tried to talk, but his voice was too weak. Our eyes caught and spoke silently. He squeezed my hand just as it was pulled away by paramedics diving in for the final rescue.

The ambulance had arrived with its equipment, gurneys, and supplies. The paramedics placed a protective collar around Aiden's neck and rolled him onto the gurney. I noticed a scarlet colored mark across his back and shoulders in the form of a broken V. It must have been from the shoulder pads when he was struck by lightning.

Within the commotion, I was shoved, lost my balance, and landed in a puddle of mud. Half my face was coated in the thick muck. Fists full of wet turf kept me tied to this world—and I held on tight. Somewhere along the way I had lost all of my energy to move. I watched as the dying wind caught the remnants of Aiden's shoulder pads and blew the pieces around like a light snow flurry.

Patrick yelled for me one moment. And within seconds, he was kneeling beside me.

"You're OK, right?" Patrick questioned.

But I couldn't speak. Time played tricks on my mind; slow motion, blurred vision, and distorted sounds plagued me with false interpretations of reality. He reached down and picked me up. Sounds became unclear again, and my vision grew dark.

"We're going home. I'm taking you home. Piper, can you hear me?"

Darkness drifted in and out, and weightlessness followed as I released the mud from my fists.

I heard the familiar voice of Johnny Sledge ranting about the end of the world. He stood on the sideline hollering, "This is testament. I told you the end was coming, and now you can see the proof!"

I blocked out Johnny, the flashing lights, and pandemonium of people screaming. On the way off the field, I saw a few dark feathers scattered on the edge of the ground. The winds caught them too and strew them about the broken turf. A strong gust swept the feathers upward swaying softly, as if an invisible music conductor waved them about with his musical wand.

"I need a medic! Someone, please help me!" Patrick screamed. The darkness took over, and I felt myself fall limp in his arms.

Chapter Eight

Crash Into Me

Days fell off the calendar turning days into weeks since Aiden's injury. I watched Rachel chase Aiden around growing more volatile as she was unable to charm him back around her finger. She couldn't stand the subtle attention he tossed my way. Locking eyes on one another in a crowded hallway became our secret pastime. Since the accident and his quick recovery, something brewed between us. I loved the idea of playing with fire, but I was afraid of getting close only to get burned. I'd wanted him for so long, and now I didn't know how to handle all these intense feelings creeping into reality.

I had to constantly remind myself to stop walking around deliberately looking for stop signs, speed bumps, yield signs, U turns, and of course my favorite—dead ends, drop offs, and DANGER ahead. Convincing myself wasn't easy because I was definitely out of my league. But something supernatural happened when I allowed myself to fall into those turquoise eyes.

Patrick's birthday approached quickly, and he had planned a road trip up to Newport for an extended weekend. We would leave Friday after the game and return to Ashland on Monday afternoon. Dad had another business meeting, but would fly in Sunday for Patrick's birthday. Dad had bought a beach house for Mom as an anniversary gift years ago. We spent countless summers and weekends there, but none of us had been back since her death. Patrick wanted to take a few of his friends out to Newport to fish, relax on the beach, and just hang out. My brother thought it would be a good idea to conquer our fears together. I invited Bailey along for some girl time and support because I knew it wouldn't be easy dealing with all the memories locked up inside.

Friday night's game had ended late. Running around the house, I gathered my weekend essentials, stuffing them inside my duffle bag. My phone rang as I glanced around the room searching for it. The muffled sound came from my bag, and I emptied out the contents. I snatched the phone, but Bailey had already hung up. A few seconds later, Bailey sent a text.

Bailey McAllen:
Piper, I'm so sorry. I can't go with you this weekend. I had an argument with my mom. She took my car keys and is threatening to have my cell phone turned off. I begged her to punish me when I get back, but she's not budging. She's so freaking annoying. She thinks I have been spending too much time with Ryder and thinks she can run my life. I'm pissed! I feel like I've failed you, and I'm truly sorry.
Friday, 10:15 PM

Piper O'Leary:
WHAT? I didn't want to do this without you. I don't think I can do it alone. I can't go.
Friday, 10:19 PM

Bailey McAllen:
You have to go, Piper. Not only is it your brother's Birthday, but sooner or later you have to face your fears, making peace with your mom and her death. Go! I have faith in you. I only have a few seconds left before she unlocks my door and takes my phone.
Friday, 10:23 PM

Piper O'Leary:
You're right. I'm on my way. See you when I get back.
Friday, 10:30

Patrick slung my bedroom door open. "Piper, are you ready? We're leaving in ten minutes. Where's Bailey?" He was holding a thirty-two-ounce caffeinated cola to prepare for the drive.

"Um…I have a problem," I remarked with irritation.

"What kind of problem, Piper?"

"Bailey can't come with us," I groaned.

"Do you still want to go?" Patrick questioned with hesitancy.

I sat quietly listening to my conscious spin a certain sense of self doubt, and then the voices in my head hushed. "Yes, I want to go...I need to go. Do you think there is room for me to ride with you guys?"

"We'll make it work, but you have to hurry and get downstairs." He glanced down at my bag emptied out onto the floor. "Piper, seriously, we're leaving in ten minutes."

"Give me five minutes, and I'll be ready." I threw my scattered things back into my bag and met my brother in the living room. I flipped the blinds to see which car we would take. My eyes widened and my heart pounded an unsteady beat against my sternum. Aiden's black truck waited for us, and I blinked a few times to make sure I was seeing straight.

Slowly, I made my way through the doorway and watched Jake and Graham toss the football around in the darkness, reliving plays from tonight's game. Patrick continued to rearrange the assorted luggage in the back, making room for everything.

"Piper, hand me your bag. Piper...your bag!" he sharply ordered, but I felt frozen. Then Aiden popped up from behind the back of the truck carrying a tire gauge. My bag fell to the ground, breaking the silence, and the guys all looked over at me.

"Hey, Piper." Jake hurried over, picked up my bag, and tossed it through the air to Patrick. My brother placed it in the back, wedging it between the ice chest and the tackle box.

"Where's everyone riding?" Graham questioned as Patrick climbed into the front passenger seat. "Guess that answers my question."

I crawled into the back seat sandwiched between two defensive linebackers. I wiggled off my flip-flops and slid my legs up onto the console between Aiden and Patrick, trying to find some room for this five-hour trip. The pink polish on my toenails sparkled in the interior light. The truck started, and we were on our way.

"How have you been?" Aiden glanced back in the rearview mirror at me. Just like at school, walking one of those crowded hallways, we greeting each other with a glance and a smile.

"Good, I'm really good. When are they going to let you start playing football again?"

"Maybe next week, if I get released from the doctor," Aiden replied as Patrick turned up the radio.

Jake and Graham struck up conversation, talking over me as I sat between them. "Dude, last night I finally completed *Call of Duty: Black Ops*. It was awesome!" Graham boasted.

"Boring," I murmured. I pulled out my iPod, pressed song shuffle, and dialed up the volume. It was going to be a long drive. I closed my eyes, crossed my ankles, tapped my toes to the beat, and slipped off into sleep.

Awakening stiff and stuck between the two snoring boulders, I climbed out the front to stretch my legs. The truck was parked at a convenience store about an hour from Newport. Patrick and Aiden were inside paying for gas.

Aiden tossed Patrick the keys as he rubbed his eyes. Jake woke with Graham's head resting on his shoulder.

"Dude, get off of me!" He shoved Graham, who didn't even wake up. Jake jumped out and climbed into the front passenger seat, stretching out his long legs and releasing a sigh of relief.

Patrick climbed in and started the ignition as Aiden opened the door and climbed in beside me. Cozy this time, I didn't mind the back seat with him beside me. His eyes were red and heavy. He tilted his head and gently rested it on my shoulder. I wanted to stay trapped in this moment with Aiden forever, but I kept thinking about the beach house and—Mom. How could I prepare myself? I missed Bailey.

Finally the truck slowed to a stop, and the motion detector lights mounted on the house pierced the foggy air. White steps led up to the wooden deck sheltered by screens. The teal-blue paint echoed a tropical paradise surrounded by the sound of waves crashing against the shore. The smell of salt drifted in from the turning ocean and seeped into the truck.

Everyone slept soundly except for me and my brother; we both stared at the house searching for some sense of resolution—but nothing came.

"Guys, we're here." Patrick opened the door, causing the interior lights to turn on inside the truck. A tear ran down my cheek, and I quickly caught it. Patrick was already out pulling items from the back. It didn't take long before everyone slid out to unpack the luggage. Standing outside, I couldn't find the strength to walk through the front door. The screened porch was as far as I could go. I sat on the wooden swing listening to the surf roll in carried by the night's tide.

"Hey, is your sister OK? She's sitting out on the swing," I heard Aiden softly question from inside the house. Through the window, I could see Patrick standing in front of the entryway, staring at an assortment of family pictures neatly framed and placed on a wooden table nestled among seashells and bottles of sand.

"It's all these memories floating around. I'll go check on her." The door opened, and Patrick stood beside the swing, swinging it gently with his knee.

"Piper." A long pause followed before he cleared his throat and spoke. "You have to just walk through the door. It's tough, but I know you can do it," Patrick calmly encouraged.

"I will. I just want to sit here for a little bit. I'm fine, really," I tried to convince him, unable to convince myself. I shook it off with a smile, but it felt like a mask unraveling.

"Piper, I'm really tired. Can you come inside with me?" He rubbed his forehead and eyelids on his shirt, and then he leaned against the door looking up at the moon.

"I'm really fine. I slept almost the entire way here and you didn't. So go ahead and go inside," I insisted.

"Are you sure?" He opened the door, placing one foot inside.

"Yeah, really. Go to bed. It's going to be a great weekend. I'm glad I was able to come," I reassured him with a small smile.

He nodded his head, yawned, and carried his tired body to bed. "Good night, Piper. I'll see you in the morning."

I curled up on the swing, listening to the rhythmic waves crashing into the shore, and rocked with the salty breezes blowing in from the ocean. I closed my eyes for just a second and woke up to a pair of warm arms lifting me from the wooden swing. He carried me through the door my stubborn feet refused to walk through and into the room where I collected shells, glass bottles of sand, photographs, and countless memories from my past.

"Good night, Piper," Aiden whispered as he laid me down with the quilt my mom had bought a couple years back. His breath felt warm against my neck, his voice soft in my ear.

Morning came, and the house filled with light. We had planned a trip to the Oregon Coast Aquarium. The aroma of hickory bacon swept through the house, as I grabbed my light purple sundress and flip-flops. Temperatures usually ran in the sixties this time of year, but with this weird weather, the forecast predicted seventy-eight degrees, blue skies, and full sun.

Patrick stood in front of the stove turning bacon and jumping away from the grease splatter. Aiden stood to the other side, flipping pancakes hot off the grill. Graham poured orange juice into the tall drinking glasses while sneaking a slice or two of hot bacon. Jake sang in the shower as the warm water began to run cool; the pitch of his voice climbed higher as the water became colder. And I stood there silently taking it all in.

"Good morning, Piper," Aiden greeted me as I walked into the kitchen. I smiled back at him. "Good morning," I replied. "Did you sleep well?"

"Yeah, the couch isn't too bad." His sarcasm showed when he arched his side and rubbed his shoulder. "Just kidding, it wasn't bad at all."

Patrick chimed in, "Piper, I didn't even hear you come in last night. How long did you stay out there?"

"I don't know. I guess I fell asleep." I looked over at Aiden, and then back at my brother. "Then, the next thing I remember, I was in bed waking up to the smell of bacon."

"Huh," Patrick responded curiously, and then he continued to drown his pancakes in thick maple syrup.

The platters of food circulated around the table until nothing was left. The guys ravaged the meal, hungry from the fuel they'd burned in last night's game. Within minutes, the table cleared, and clean dishes found their way back to the cabinets. We were off to the aquarium. It had been years since our last visit and within minutes we were there.

The acrylic tunnel was filled with electric blue water that flowed all around us. Huge bat rays glided through the water, flying into the sunlit liquid. I identified three of the five sharks in the tank using the colorful information pamphlet. They drifted through individually with their sharp rows of teeth gleaming inside the saltwater room—a different world, lost from land, as I knew all too well.

Schools of little silver fish swam in one direction, darting through the water. Golden fish with gray scales stared at us through the glass with their bulging dark eyes, and then they swam back into the darkness inside the hollowed rock formations.

The guys drifted in and out like the big fish in the water. They circulated around the small tanks filled with jellyfish, sea anemones, and sea stars. A group of girls watched the guys closely while pretending to admire the sea life. They swam in using their colorful clothing, sparkling jewelry, and hair to lure the guys into a dark lair of rocks, cliffs, and artificial reef. But the guys were clueless.

"Piper, we're heading over to the aviary. Are you coming?" Patrick asked as the other guys gathered around. Aiden leaned against the tank quietly staring in my direction.

"I'll be there in a minute. Go ahead and save me a seat." I continued to watch the tiny jellyfish with their strange lights floating inside the dark tank.

A swarm of fish circled me with the stench of sweet perfume, tight clothing, and heavy make-up. "Hey, are those guys with you? You're not from here, are you? So, how well do you know those guys? They're all really hot. Do you think you could introduce us to them?"

The interrogation came from all directions. Their desperate attraction annoyed me, but I chose not to show it. "Yeah, that one there is my brother." I pointed to Patrick. "The others are his friends. We drove up here from Ashland, but we're just staying for the weekend. What about you?"

"We're here from Portland. What about that guy over there?" She pointed to Aiden. "Are you with any of them?" asked a girl with a short white skirt and spray-on tan. She continued to ogle him through her thick, clumpy mascara and blue eye shadow.

I paused as I continued to watch the flickering lights inside the tank. "Um…no, we're just friends."

Graham looked back and instructed the other guys over toward us. The giddy girls with their gleaming teeth glided over toward them, flaunting flesh and batting eyes. One pulled out an ink pen and wrote her number wrapped around a heart on my brother's wrist. I slid away toward the sea bird exhibit, and then followed the map, observing all the other ocean creatures. The sea otters played splashing around the pool of water. Water droplets beaded up and rolled off their pelted fur.

"Hey, Piper we're all getting ready to go. We thought we would drive out to Yaquina Head Lighthouse and have a picnic before they close," Patrick explained. The girls circled back around. "They're going to meet us out there. Ready?" he asked as he grabbed my hand, pulling me away from the furry little creatures. "You've met my sister, Piper?"

"Piper—that's an unusual name. Anyway, can we follow you guys out to the lighthouse?" The one wearing the white miniskirt eyed Aiden, and then she passed him a small piece of paper with her number on it.

I climbed into the backseat of Aiden's truck, not wanting to see him put it in his pocket. The obnoxious girls followed behind us in two cars, swerving all over the road trying to get the guy's attention by acting stupid. I cringed and wished they would just disappear.

The lighthouse stood near the cliff overlooking the Pacific. Ocean waves crashed underneath, and white sea-foam floated through the fleeting waves. Blue skies painted a beautiful backdrop; it was a trip inside a postcard a million miles from home. The green beach grass waved me toward the lighthouse. The guys pulled lunch from the ice chest, and the girls flocked around like sea gulls—I mean, vultures. I couldn't help but think about the tiny folded note crammed inside Aiden's pocket. I cringed again and walked closer toward the cliff.

The crashing waves broke against the rocky shore. I turned up the music, and the vibrations pulled me a little bit closer. Free falling through my life was tiring. Just for a split second, I wondered what it would feel like to hit the ground below me. It had to be better than living like this—not knowing which way was up anymore.

"Piper! What are you doing?" Aiden had followed me over, but his voice only sounded like a murmur against my music and the crashing waves. His shadow fell upon the ground, and I turned to see him. I pulled my ear phones out, and they dangled against the steady breeze at my side. "What are you doing?" He reached out for my hand, and I took his. "Are you OK?" he questioned and pulled me toward his chest.

"I don't want to keep falling down this rabbit hole," I whispered.

"What do you mean?" he gently questioned. "Don't you know by now, I'm here to catch you." And then he wrapped his arms around me.

"What if I knock you down with me?" I replied as I looked up into his eyes, which matched the color of the waves crashing into the shoreline below me.

"Are you serious, girl? I guess there's only one rational outcome. You'll just have to crash into *me*." Aiden slid his fingers down my arms, finding my open palms. The wind gust blew my hair across my face. He guided the free strands back and pulled me in for our first kiss. His lips felt soft on mine, and it wasn't hard to let him in. His hands traveled from my neck toward my waist. Before I realized it, I was lifted in the air dangling above the cliff. "Are you still falling?" he whispered as he placed me back on the rocky cliff.

"Just falling faster now." I smiled, jumped into his arms, and kissed him fervently.

"Your brother is going to kill me," Aiden remarked with sarcasm.

He took my hand and led me back to the picnic. By this time clouds were moving overhead, and large drops of rain had begun to fall from the sky—the same sky that was crystal clear just a few moments before. We ran toward the lighthouse. The girl in the white miniskirt sat alone apparently waiting for Aiden. Then she ran with the others back to the car after the rain fell harder. Patrick caught a quick glimpse, and his head did a double take when he saw Aiden holding my hand.

"We're riding back to the house with the girls, are you coming?" Patrick yelled as small streaks of lightning sprang across the sky. "What is with this weather?" he contested.

"We'll meet you back at the house," Aiden replied as we stepped inside the lighthouse.

A spiral staircase climbed up the white tower, and we followed the metal steps up to the watch floor. The rain poured, tapping against the beacon. We watched from the window as our rain-soaked clothes dripped onto the ground. The storm left as soon as it drifted in. Blue skies returned, and a small rainbow receded into the horizon. Small waterspouts sprayed across the ocean, dancing out to sea.

Aiden stood behind me resting his chin on my shoulder admiring the view of the ocean. His arms wrapped around my chest, and he spoke softly into my ear. "Are you ready to go?"

I nodded, taking one last look out the window. Then we made our way back to the beach house. Graham was cooking dinner on the grill, and the girls swam in the pool with Patrick and Jake taking turns pushing each other under. We ate dinner around the fire, tolerating the obnoxious chatter from the flock of girls we'd met at the aquarium. Aiden and I left the group to sprawl out on the cozy hammock, talking until the stars came out and the cool ocean breeze blew across us. But he was warm, the hammock swayed in the wind, and before we knew it we drifted into a quiet slumber.

We woke to the warmth of sunlight and the sound of the girls pulling out of the drive. Aiden stretched his arms above his head and softly spoke. "Good morning, Piper." He kissed my forehead and pulled the blanket over us.

I could hear Patrick inside the house shouting for everyone to get up. He had booked a charter boat to go fishing and rushed around the house getting things ready.

"Are you going with us?" Aiden asked as he carefully climbed out of the hammock.

"No." I pulled the blanket around me. "I think it should be a guy trip. I'll see you when you get back."

Leaning forward, he reached over and kissed me. "Is there any way I could convince you to come?" he asked, walking slowly backward toward the house.

I shook my head no, smiled at him, and crawled back under the blanket.

It was a beautiful day of sun, surf, and beach. The water ran cold across my feet, and the sand oozed between my toes. I found a couple of sand dollars, a handful of seashells, and one piece of shiny blue agate. I sat for hours just watching the waves roll in while listening to the birds squawk overhead, diving in for their morning feast of fish.

After lunch, I floated in the pool reading a trashy romance novel. I thought of Aiden, his kiss, and how I didn't want to be anywhere except in his arms. I tossed the book aside and rolled off the float for a quick dip in the pool.

Underneath the water, I could hear the guys returning home. I climbed up the ladder and out of the pool. Aiden appeared from nowhere, tossed me back into the water, and jumped in beside me.

"So, did you catch any fish?" I asked as I splashed water on him.

"I caught *you*, didn't I?" His arms pulled me under the water. We came up tangled in each other's arms and looked up to see Dad standing over us with his glasses lowered upon his nose and his fists on his hips.

"Piper." Just one word, but his eyes said everything else. He didn't approve of a boy being that close.

"Hi, Daddy. When did you get in?" I asked innocently.

Aiden had already climbed out, grabbed a towel, and greeted Dad with a firm handshake and football conversation. I slid out of the pool and dressed for dinner.

Patrick picked out a seafood restaurant for his birthday near the beach, and we spent our final evening dining, walking the beach, and lounging by the fire pit. Our mini vacation was over, and on Monday morning we drove back to Ashland. Dad had rented a car and requested that I ride home with him. He said he hadn't slept well and wanted me to keep him company. I knew he'd spent most of the night thinking of Mom and the memories tied up inside the beach house.

All I could think of was Aiden and our new memories. I had taken a few snapshots of our trip and had them printed at the swim-and-surf shop. Most of the pictures I packed to take back home, but I left one behind propped up on my desk with the bottles of sand and seashells I once collected as a child. I took one last look out the window, watching the turquoise waves crash into the rocky shore and knew at that very moment—Aiden was really *mine*.

Chapter Nine

Breath

It was Friday night, and the whole town was prepared for an away game against our rival team, the Richmond Red Devils. Our school colors were wrapped tightly around the trees and danced in the wind as we pulled away from our high school. Everyone had their game faces on and was mentally checked into the zone. But I couldn't get Aiden out of my mind. Memories of our trip to the beach house invaded every thought, and I couldn't wait to see him tonight. I only hoped he thought of me as much as I thought of him.

The crowds broke into applause as we escorted the Grizzly mascot to the center of the field for the coin toss. Richmond's Red Devil mascot tore onto the field with their cheerleaders dressed in fire red. The fury caused the crowd to turn their cheers into a blustering boo of unharmonious ridicule. Unfortunately, the Devils won the coin toss.

Grizzly points continued racking up the scoreboard. It was Aiden's first game back, and the team pulverized the Devils beyond recognition. The Devils, crushed and confused, looked on in an uneasy daze. It was like the accident had never happened; Aiden came back stronger, and the team couldn't miss. I held my breath as Patrick caught the last throw at the forty and carried it all the way downfield. The crowd roared and flew to their feet. The clock counted down, and the game was won. It was the first time we had defeated the Devils in fifteen years.

After the game, Bailey and I returned to my empty house to get ready for the after-party. At least Dad had left a few lights on this time. Bailey had brought a pair of killer suede pants and selected one of my shirts to wear with them. I grabbed a pair of jeans, but Bailey pulled out a short skirt from her bag.

"No way are you wearing those jeans tonight!" she exclaimed. Her tone was almost insulting, but I knew she was just looking out for me.

"Come on, I love these jeans," I replied.

She scratched her head and tapped her fingernails against the wall. "Not tonight. Trust me, Piper. Glam it up a little. You're celebrating Aiden's recovery, for heaven's sake."

As I slipped into the skirt, my cell phone rang underneath the mound of clothes piled up on top of my bed.

"Hey, I thought maybe you might want a ride. Are you ready?" Aiden asked. His deep voice made my knees weak. "Besides, it's not every day a guy gets to thank a girl for saving his life."

"So, is this just payback?" I remarked playfully.

"No. Just couldn't think of anyone else I wanted to be with tonight. Come downstairs. I'm parked out front."

"Hey, Bailey's here. Can she ride with us?" I asked.

Bailey shook her head in a violent no, and her brown hair flew in multiple directions.

"OK, never mind. I guess she has other plans." I awkwardly replied.

Bailey whispered, "Tell him I'll meet you guys up there." She raced downstairs and out of the house.

"Are you sure you don't need a ride, Bailey?" Aiden offered as her tires chewed the gravel, spitting it out into the air. "Guess not." He cleared his throat and fanned away the dust from his face.

Confidently, he stood out front with a single red rose in his hand. It was near his face, and he looked captivated by the aroma it released. With the sudden sound of the door closing, he turned toward me. The flower fell to the ground, and he quickly reached down to pick it up.

"Wow, you—you look beautiful." His words stumbled, but his feet pressed steady against the pavement between us.

"You were awesome at the game tonight," I tossed the compliment back to him. I felt uncomfortable in my own skin. And thanks to Bailey and her short skirt, I wasn't sure what look I was attempting to portray.

"I can't seem to take my eyes off you." He reached over, handed me the flower, and kissed me on the cheek. The flower smelled sweet and soft, but my nose caught the swift scent of his intoxicating cologne.

He took my hand, bringing it toward his lips, and gave it a warm, soft kiss. I smiled and looked ahead. I never knew it would feel like this. I hoped it wasn't apparent that I was out of my normal realm. I still didn't understand this strange dance between us. Was Rachel still his girlfriend? Where did I fit in?

We drove out to Shelby's clearing, once an old farmland and now an abandoned field. A bonfire reached into the sky causing smoke to soar high above the tall pines. The victory was on everyone's mind, as well as Aiden's return to the game. He was the star of the show, and I stood quietly in his shadow. Chants and cheers rang out welcoming him to the party.

We walked hand in hand to warm up by the fire. Girls flashed skin in petty attempts for attention. Most guys ate it up, but Aiden didn't pay attention to them. He placed his arm around my waist, pulling me closer to him. I caught a glimpse of Rachel passed out with empty cups scattered around her.

Bailey waved in the distance, ushering me over. "Go ahead," Aiden insisted. "I'll come find you." He leaned forward and tilted his head. His warm lips pressed against mine as his arms surrounded me within a tight embrace. I felt every muscle in his chest contract against mine and tasted his soft lips. I didn't want it to end. Then he rushed off to see some of the guys to talk trash about the Devils. And I floated across the grassy field, tripping on a small rock bringing me back to earth.

"Bailey, his kiss is amazing. I thought we had something at the beach house, but this just confirms it…a public kiss. Do you think we're really together now? What about Rachel? Do you think he broke up with her?

How will I ever compare to her?" I felt myself slipping back to that dark place.

"Piper, stop it. Don't screw this up. Every time something good comes into your life, you immediately start looking for the fire escape. You're happy now; don't allow self-sabotage to take over. I can't bear picking up Piper pieces again."

I took a breath, nodded in agreement with her, and glanced over at the guys passing the ball back and forth. "Bailey, I promise, I'll make this work. I need my life to change, and he's the one."

Time ticked close to Bailey's curfew, and we walked toward her car. "Are you sure you don't need a ride home?" she offered as she jingled her keys in her hand.

"No, Dad's out of town. I'm pretty much without a curfew. I mean, Patrick doesn't even come home half the time. So, why can't I stay out a little late?" I asked, wanting reassurance.

"OK. I'm cutting out. Be safe." Bailey climbed into her car and sped away, leaving me alone. Or so I thought—when I turned around, Aiden stood quietly behind me. I bumped into his chest, and he didn't even budge.

"Aiden, I didn't see you come back over." I shivered as the wind blew against my bare skin.

"Are you getting cold?" he questioned while placing his strong hands around mine.

I didn't answer. His turquoise eyes pulled me into a place where words stood silent, and then I nodded yes.

"Piper, there's a place I want to show you, and it will get us out of this wind." Aiden took my hand and led me back toward the truck. The field, nearly empty, left a smoking pile of ash from the once raging bonfire. Everyone was piling back into their cars to head back into town.

"Where are we going?"

"It's a surprise." The door to his car opened, and I climbed inside.

Dirt roads wove deep into the forest, and the headlights bounced against the dark wilderness. Off in the distance, I saw a steeple among the tall pines. Aiden stopped the car, opened his door, and walked around to open mine, but I'd already hopped out in awe of the stunning sight in the middle of nowhere.

"How did you know this was out here?" I questioned. "It's beautiful." I couldn't take my eyes off of it. I felt like I knew this place, but it was impossible.

"It's a church," I said in great wonder and amazement.

"Yeah, but more like a chapel. I knew you would appreciate its beauty," Aiden remarked.

"How did you know it was out here?"

"I'm not sure. One day, I stumbled upon it while I was out for a run," Aiden continued as we walked through the doorway. "Or maybe, it found me."

Bold wooden beams supported the structure. The arched ceiling, doors, and flooring were made of rich wood. Transparent glass covered everything else, allowing natural light and forest scenery inside. The largest moon I had ever seen hung low over the chapel, allowing the moonlight to shine through the stained-glass angels in front near the pulpit.

"Nothing could ever compare to this," I whispered.

"Not true. I can think of something that compares," Aiden remarked, staring at me.

I found a pew in the front and sat down. I could hear his steps getting closer, and then he sat down beside me. Silence filled the hollow room, and then he spoke.

"I don't know how to say this…It's really hard for me to say what I feel." He swallowed and took a deep breath. "So, I'm just going to say it. Something happened on that field after the lightning hit me. I woke up different, and you were there holding my hand. Now, I can't get you out of my mind. I'm consumed by thoughts of you. The more I think of you, the more I want you. Piper, I…"

I stopped him with my finger against his parted lips. "Aiden, I feel it, too," I whispered.

He touched my cheek and pulled me in for a kiss. It felt soft at first, and then his grip became tighter. The taste of liquor radiated from his mouth. I pushed him back, breaking the kiss.

"What's wrong, Piper?" Aiden questioned with an unfamiliar darkness in his eyes.

I wiped the alcohol taste from my lips. "Have you been drinking?"

"Just had a few with the guys at the clearing. You're not mad, are you?"

"No—yes—I just didn't think you drank. Aiden, you drove me here! You know what happened to my mom, and now it's like you made me part of it."

"Piper, I wasn't thinking. I got caught up in the moment. It's just alcohol hasn't ever affected me this way before. I wouldn't ever dream of hurting you." He pressed his fingers against his temples, and a look of excruciating pain crossed his face. He stood for a second, unsteady, and then sat back down beside me.

"Are you OK?" I questioned with apprehension.

Responding with silence, he leaned forward, his lips just millimeters from mine. His gaze felt like eternity upon my skin. I felt my chest expand, but I couldn't find any air. His lips gradually made their way back to mine as our passion ignited a dangerous flame, making the kiss rough. The rose dropped from my hand. Aiden's hands wandered in places that began to make me question sensible boundaries as the stained-glass angels witnessed my sudden fall from grace.

"Wait—wait," I whispered, expecting him to stop.

He continued to kiss harder and stronger, forcing my head into the pillow of the pew. His hands pulled at my shirt, trying to unbutton and remove it all at the same time.

"Stop! Please, Aiden. *Stop it!*" I could barely speak with his lips pressed hard against mine. His tooth pierced my lower lip, and I felt the warm blood inside my mouth.

I wiggled my arms free and pried his face away. "Why are you doing this? What is the matter with you? Get off of me!"

He looked at me, bewildered by his actions. Then he sat up and ripped at my shirt, snapping the buttons into the air. A dirty smirk crossed his lips—the same lips that a few moments ago kissed me gently. I struggled to get away and shoved him back, but he was solid as a rock. Speechless, he raised his right hand and sharply struck my cheek. Shocked, I felt paralyzed with fear; the only thing moving were the cool tears streaming down my cheeks. Numb, I looked for some resemblance of Aiden, but he was lost inside this drunken monster.

I calculated a plan and threw it into motion. I reached underneath his shirt and pulled it off in one motion. In the back of my mind, I wanted to wrap it around his neck and choke the life out of him. I kissed him forcefully and dug my fingernails into his skin. Another sickening grin crossed his face as I tugged at his waistline. He sat up higher to unbutton his jeans, and for a split second, I was free—it was my moment, and I took it. I forced the heel of my boot squarely into a place I knew would take any guy down. The strike knocked him to his knees. He vomited, and the smell of alcohol overtook the chapel.

I jumped from the pew, falling to the wooden floor. Looking back, I saw Aiden with vomit streaming from his lips. Bizarre, with all the tackles on the field, I never thought I could have knocked his six-foot-two frame down to the ground with one kick. I turned and ran for the door.

"Piper!" Aiden yelled from behind the strong wooden chapel doors.

The full moon was hidden behind thick clouds, and the romance quickly changed to darkness. Shadows covered me as I raced along the forest trails leading out into the unknown. I ran fast, snapping twigs and shoving leafy branches out of my face. I couldn't wrap my mind around what had just happened. That wasn't Aiden back at the chapel. Part of me wanted to go back to see if it was all just a nightmare—but I just kept running. In the distance, I spotted a clearing. *Almost there*, I thought. And then I tripped, hit the rocky ground, and knocked the breath from my lungs. I watched in horror as my cell phone bounced from my pocket and danced across the rocky terrain, falling into pieces of shattered glass and metal.

A soft voice resonated from behind me, and I flinched in fear.

"Are you OK?" The voice carried softly with concern.

I glanced down at my torn clothes and felt compelled to make up a wild story, but nothing came to mind—so I maintained my silence.

"Come and sit down." A teenage boy with blue eyes and a soothing voice motioned toward a chair sitting empty near a small campfire. A tent flapped in the wind, displacing sound in the middle of our silence. He removed his sweatshirt and pulled it over my head. I didn't even realize I was shivering until I opened my mouth to speak.

"Why are you out here all alone?" I whispered into the darkness of the brutal night. I turned toward the campfire and watched how it flickered and crackled against the growing winds. I didn't know if the bruises were beginning to come through or if the darkness covered me.

"I could ask you the same thing…why are you out here all alone?" The boy with the soothing voice tried to look into my eyes, but I was trapped inside the flickering of the campfire. It reminded me of Aiden's unexpected rage burning inside the chapel and my affliction of what to do next. I closed my eyes breaking the connection, and then glanced up at the boy standing in the middle of an open field.

"I was left behind." My voice shook with uncertainty, and I felt I needed some sort of clarity. So, I repeated the phrase, "I was left behind—accidentally." It didn't sound any better, and I allowed the silence to speak for me once more.

"Are you OK? Do you need a ride somewhere? My name is Logan."

I glanced over at the metallic-blue motorcycle with two white wings embellished across the frame. "You'll give me a ride?" I questioned, looking back expecting Aiden to stumble out of the darkness and drag me back to the chapel.

"Well, I can't leave you out here all alone. Of course, I'll give you a ride."

He fastened the helmet strap around my neck, started the motor, and then I locked my arms around the stranger's waist. I closed my eyes and braced myself against his back, hoping not to see Aiden or the stained-glass chapel. The helmet on my head bobbled a bit with the rough road, and I held on tighter with each gust of wind.

As we came closer to home, I pointed the direction to the lonely house standing like a fortress among untamed garden and trees. I unlatched the helmet, freeing it from my chin, and carefully touched my lower lip; I knew it had swelled twice its size.

"Is anyone here?" Logan asked, looking toward the dark house. "Are you sure you're OK? Do you want me to call someone?" He reached into his pocket and pulled out his cell phone.

"No, I'm fine." I gave him a small smile, but the pressure in my lip intensified and a sharp pain radiated along my cheekbone. I wasn't fine—I was far from fine.

"It doesn't feel right leaving you here like this." He walked a few steps behind me toward the front door.

"No, really, I'm fine now. Thanks for the ride. It isn't what you think." I paused, and then the lies flew from my lips. "It was just a misunderstanding. We were all celebrating tonight's win after the game. I misplaced my phone, backtracked to find it in the forest, and got lost. I was left behind and thought I could jog my way out, but I slipped on something and fell... face first onto the rocks." I found myself rambling my way out of shame.

He paused in silence, staring uncomfortably deep into my eyes. "So, what do you think I thought happened?" he questioned as if he already knew the real answer.

I heard steps walking away. And then the motorcycle started up again with a loud vibrating roar in sync with my quickened heart beat.

"Piper, I'm glad you made it home safe."

I froze for a second when he said my name out loud. The lock turned easily, and I entered into my darkness—alone again. The motorcycle ran rough into the distance. I turned on every light in the house, driving away the mad world outside.

Chapter Ten

Piece Of My Heart

I woke from my dreams only to find I was living a nightmare. My protruding lip throbbed, my cheek ached, and my mind whirled with visions of Aiden in the chapel. Rain tapped against my window, and small streams began to form against the glass pane. Bailey's voice echoed in my mind: *Piper, don't screw this up.*

I heard the door open from downstairs, and Dad's voice called out, "Guys, I'm home. Is anyone here?"

I wanted to answer, but instead I threw the covers over my head.

"Who left all these lights on?" Dad mumbled, carrying his luggage upstairs. I could hear him as he headed back downstairs, turning off each light one by one.

I found my wayward strength, pulled the covers off, and crawled out of bed. Downstairs, Dad sat at the table tearing into a pile of mail.

"Good morning, Piper. I'm sorry I've been out of town so much. I promise I'll make it up to…" Dad glanced up and caught a look at my bruised cheek and busted lip. "Piper, what on earth happened to your face?" He jumped up, dropping the stack of mail on the floor, and adjusted his glasses to inspect my bruises and lacerations.

"Dad—it's nothing, really. I tripped and fell. Remember, I'm training for the track team. I tripped and fell face first. It would have been really embarrassing if anyone had seen."

I couldn't tell him the truth about the party, that my new boyfriend had attacked me, and I'd found my way home with a strange guy on a motorcycle. No, it definitely wouldn't go over well. Therefore, the "I'm so clumsy" story would have to do.

"Where's Patrick?" Dad questioned while he kneeled down to pick up the mail strewn all over the kitchen floor.

"Don't know. I guess he stayed over at one of the guys'."

"I tried calling you last night on your cell, but you didn't answer." Dad continued.

"Yeah, about that, I seemed to have misplaced Mom's phone out on that run. I borrowed it after my last phone stopped working. I dropped it when I fell." A memory pulled me in as I watched her cell phone bounce across the rocks, breaking into pieces of glass, plastic, and metal. This forced me into another memory—my mom's wrecked car crumbled with scattered glass alone on a country road.

"So you were hurt *and* didn't have a way to contact anyone. This is serious, Piper."

"I'm sorry, Dad. I'll be more careful. I promise this will never happen again."

"Piper, I trust you to make wise decisions, especially when I'm not around. I need you to be safe," he expressed.

"Dad, it will never happen again."

"If you can't find your phone, let me know and I'll replace it." Dad reached over and touched my bruised cheek. I couldn't look him in the eyes, fearing he would see through my lies.

"I feel I have let you down, Piper. I spend too much time away on business, and Patrick is busy being Patrick. Maybe I should hire someone to live here and watch out for you guys. It isn't safe being here all alone. Your mom would be disappointed in what has become of our family." His voice cracked, and he reached up to clear a smudge from his small-framed glasses. "I only wish I could bring her back for you and Patrick. You know I would—if I could."

"Dad, it wasn't your fault. Mom was in an accident. You can't blame yourself for that. I miss her too. We all do. She would be proud of you. Please give us another chance. I will be careful and check in more often. You can't be serious about having a stranger living in our house."

The door opened, and Patrick strutted inside, soaked from the pouring rain.

"Hey, Dad, how's the case going?" he questioned, tossing the football up into the air. I turned toward him, and his eyes widened in response to my bruises and swollen lip. The ball fell out of his hand and bounced chaotically through the kitchen.

"What happened to your face? Who did this to you?" Patrick abruptly demanded.

"It's nothing. I went for a run last night. I tripped and fell face first into that rocky ravine. You know the one—next to Shelby's clearing." I tossed a small hint to my brother, who needed to catch a clue of when to be quiet.

"Patrick, why would you think someone would have deliberately hurt your sister?" Dad questioned and sat patiently with his arms folded, anticipating an answer.

"Don't know...guess I've seen too much television. But now that I think about it, it makes perfect sense. Piper is pretty clumsy."

"Hello—I'm still standing in the room. No one hurt me; it was dark and I tripped. And we don't need a baby-sitter!" I blurted.

"Wha-at?" Patrick lengthened the one-syllable word in astonishment. The thought of losing freedom formed beads of sweat to his forehead. "Seriously, are you thinking of hiring someone to watch us? Dad, are we three again?"

"Patrick, it's not good that you guys are home alone night after night. Business is taking me away more often now, than when your mom was here. It's not safe. Piper could have been seriously injured, and no one would have even noticed."

"Dad, I'm fine. It was a small fall. And it would have happened even if you were home. Please reconsider. It would be so weird having some stranger in our house," I continued to plead.

"Enough, you guys, I need to just think it through. For now, I'll have Marcella check in on you guys. She will be my eyes and ears while I'm away." Dad stood from the table as Patrick and I just continued to stare at one another. "I have a few errands to run, and I'll be back for dinner. We are going out to eat at Chateaulin as a family. I have reservations at seven, and both of you are going. No excuses!" Dad closed the door and drove toward town.

Patrick found his way to my room and swung the door open. He stood in the doorway biting into an apple. "How did this really happen, Piper?" he demanded between crunches.

"Well, I couldn't tell you everything with Dad standing right there, now, could I? It's really stupid. Aiden was toasted and reeked of alcohol. I ran to catch a ride with someone else and in the process was left behind. I took the trail through the forest hoping I could catch the last car out, but that didn't work out well. It was dark; I tripped and fell. I couldn't call anyone because I lost my phone. Luckily, I came across this guy, Logan, who was nice enough to give me a ride home, so I took it—end of story."

Patrick shook his head and continued to listen, taking bites from the apple. "I'm glad you made it home safe," and then he tossed the apple core into the trash. "But I'm pissed Aiden left you out there."

Another reason I couldn't tell my brother the truth—all hell would certainly break loose. A rift would occur between the guys, and who's to say anyone at school would even believe that Aiden attacked me. Not to mention the utter embarrassment of all the gossip and whispers around town. This was Aiden and everyone loved him...not a single person would believe he would be capable of such a violent act. It was just the alcohol... it had to be...what else would turn him into such a monster?

I dialed Bailey's number; the tales spun out of control and my secrets were buried deep. Not one soul would know the truth and before all was said and done—I would believe, too. Pretending was easier than confronting the darkness inside the chapel. There was no other way out.

"...what an ass! He left you there all alone. Does he even know you got hurt due to his egotistical ignorance?" Bailey ranted over the phone.

"No, he was wasted. I haven't talked to him since then, and my phone is lost somewhere. So, if he's calling me, I wouldn't know." I chatted with Bailey until Dad called us downstairs.

I sat through dinner with my family pretending everything was OK. Patrick and Dad talked football, and I faded in and out, picking at my plate of food. I missed Mom, and the empty seat in front of me only reminded me of her overwhelming absence in my life. I needed her more now, than ever before. I stared at her ghost in front of me unable to hide my secrets; she would have known within seconds that something was wrong—horribly, terribly wrong. I closed my eyes, forced the visions of Aiden from my mind, and jumped into the conversation. My family made me temporarily forget the pain inside.

My world continued on as expected, oblivious to Aiden's attack. Sunday came and we all met downstairs for church. Dad rushed us along, "Get a move on. We need to make it over to the café before all the good pastries are gone." He grabbed the keys and shut the front door.

The café bustled with the Sunday morning crowd hungry for hot chocolate, scones, pastries, and croissants. Dad ran inside to pick up his order. Patrick sat in the front seat changing the radio and thumbing through texts. I sat in the back waiting for Dad. He graciously opened the door for an elderly lady and her grandchildren while he juggled the assorted boxes of muffins, scones, and croissants. He had stuffed a few packets of my favorite raspberry jam into his pocket. And a gust of wind caught the napkins, blowing them into flight. He snagged them out of the air while clinging to the slick warm boxes. I watched the free circus act featuring my dad, the juggling clown. I wanted to laugh, but couldn't risk breaking my scabbed lip apart again.

"Guys, I could have used a little help out there," Dad uttered with annoyance in his voice. He placed the warm boxes in the back seat, and the car filled with the smell of sugar, butter, and mountain blueberries.

"Dad, why is your luggage in the car? You just got back into town." I leaned forward to hear his reply.

"I know, but something came up, and I have to fly out this afternoon. I need you both to spend most of your time between home and school while I'm away. Did you happen to find your phone, Piper?" He glanced up in the rearview mirror to see if I was paying attention.

"No, I really hadn't spent much time looking for it. I'm pretty sure it's ruined by all the rain and mud."

"I'll call for a replacement, and it should be in the mail soon."

Dad drove into the church parking lot and circled around to find a spot. The parking lot was close to full. It felt like Easter Sunday or Christmas Eve when everyone crept out of their day-to-day lives and packed the church to celebrate their devotion twice a year. I guess the upcoming Mayan apocalypse scared lost souls into finding faith in this uncertain world.

I distributed the boxes among the three of us as we headed toward the church. Coffee and hot chocolate sat at the far end of the table, and we placed our warm boxes among the other goodies brought in. I found the box of croissants, pulled the flaky roll out, and wrapped it inside a napkin.

I found Dad talking to the other parishioners, and I reached into his front pocket pulling out the raspberry jam packet. *Heaven*, I thought. I carried my delightful treasure and found Bailey with her lips wrapped around a chocolate donut.

"Hey, I'm so glad you came today. Do you want to sit by us?" I tore the packet open and smeared the jam inside the croissant.

Bailey replied, "No, I can't." And then her voice grew with intensity, "Piper, your lip—it's huge. People pay good money to have lips like that."

"Shh," I hushed and covered my lip with the napkin. "Are you serious? I thought it was actually looking better."

"Does it hurt?" She reached up to touch it.

"Yes, it does. Do you mind?" I swiped her fingers away.

"I can't sit by you guys today. My mom brought the *step dude* and wants us to all sit together like a nice, happy family. He's kind of weird, but she seems to like him. I wonder if this one will work out for her." Bailey contemplated.

I found my way down the pew and sat next to Dad. Patrick made his way in as the music began to play. He sat on the other side of Dad. The choir filed in singing a familiar song and took their place behind Father Mannelli in his white collar and black robe.

I was trying to pay attention, but Patrick was distracting me. His phone hid precariously underneath the leather Bible that sat open upon his lap. He was texting and in church—if Dad caught him, the phone would be history.

A text came across, and he glanced over at me. His eyes said it all—how could he get the phone to me without Dad seeing? The congregation stood to sing, and Patrick passed the phone carefully to me. I hid it the best I could and read the text.

Aiden Sinclair:
Patrick, can I talk to Piper?
Sunday, 10:34 AM

Patrick O'Leary:
Whatever, dude.
Sunday, 10:35 AM

Aiden Sinclair:
Piper, I'm sorry. I woke up at the chapel kind of dazed and out of it. It was insensitive of me to drink on our date. I let you down, and it will never happen again. I don't recall much of what happened. I hope you're not too mad at me. You're not answering your phone. So, I guess maybe you are?
Sunday, 10:38 AM

Patrick O'Leary:
Really, you don't remember anything? ~Piper
Sunday, 10:40 AM

Aiden Sinclair:
No. Can I stop by and see you today?
Sunday, 10:41 AM

Patrick O'Leary:
Can't. At church now and have family plans later. ~Piper
Sunday, 10:42 AM

Aiden Sinclair:
Can I pick you up before school tomorrow?
Sunday, 10:43 AM

Patrick O'Leary:
Can't. Meeting Bailey to go over yearbook pics in the morning. ~Piper
Sunday, 10:45 AM

Aiden Sinclair:
Are we OK? I have a bad feeling about what happened.
Sunday, 10:46 AM

Patrick O'Leary:
Didn't like the drunk you! ~Piper
Sunday, 10:47 AM

Aiden Sinclair:
Truly sorry. I'll make it up to you, if you'll let me???
Sunday, 10:48 AM

Patrick O'Leary:
See you at school tomorrow. ~Piper
Sunday, 10:49 AM

Aiden Sinclair:
Can't wait.
Sunday, 10:50 AM

Without Dad noticing, I deleted the messages and passed the phone back to Patrick.

Patrick O'Leary:
Dude, don't ever leave my sister stranded again! Enough said.
Sunday, 10:52 AM

Aiden Sinclair:
Never again.
Sunday, 10:53 AM

I sat through the remaining service wondering if I had imagined it all. Aiden was a good guy; I was lucky to have him, right? He wanted to be with me and sounded genuinely concerned, but visions inside the chapel haunted me—grabbing, slamming, twisting, and striking me down under his power burned in my mind. The look in his eyes and the smirk across his face made me feel nauseous. I wanted to forget. I didn't want to believe. Pretending it hadn't happened was easier. No one knew the truth except me. I could forget. It was just the alcohol.

In a way I felt relieved, but it didn't last long. I was angry at myself for dealing with every problem in my life by hiding horrible secrets— lies—within this daunting masquerade always dancing around the truth.

After church, Patrick stalked the leftover food from the table and had his eyes locked in on the last blueberry muffin. He swooped in like a crane plucking a fish out of the water. I passed by him and took a few sips from the water fountain.

Dad stepped up behind me and asked, "Is everything all right?"

I turned around and wiped the water droplets away from my lips. "Yes, everything's fine. I think my allergies are acting up again."

"Are you sure? You could be catching a cold. Maybe that run is bringing your immune system down," Dad replied.

"I'm fine, really. Can we go now?" I took his hand and led him toward the door where we saw Patrick flirting with a group of girls.

Reaching into his pocket, Dad pulled out his keys. "I'm going to get the car. Wait here and I'll come pick you guys up. You look like you don't feel well, Piper." He touched my forehead to check for a fever and then walked swiftly to get the car.

Someone touched my shoulder from behind, and I startled in response. "Father Mannelli, um—how are you today?" Small talk was the fastest thing that came to my mind.

Father Mannelli placed his hand on my shoulder once again as he spoke, "I'm well, Piper, but how about you? You seem—jumpy. Is everything going alright?"

I feared he would ask about my bruised cheek and busted lip. Lying wouldn't come easy standing in church. Spinning a web of lies to Father Mannelli, a godly man who had known me since I was an infant, was a choice I didn't want to make. Sweat moistened my hands, and my throat felt dry. "Everything is going well—now." *Could I give a more generic answer? He was sure to see through it all.* I thought. Then Kate appeared, butting into our conversation.

"Piper," she pointed to my busted lip, "what happened to your face?"

Father Mannelli stepped back, but took notice with a gentle smile. "Remember, Piper, I'm here for you." He excused himself, and I continued to shoot Kate with invisible mind bullets. I walked away with her barking more questions, but I was in no mood to give her any answers, nor did she deserve any.

Dad approached in the car and slowed to a stop, trailing a few cars in front of him. I motioned to Patrick that Dad was here and opened the glass door. The girls had stolen his attention, and he appeared pleasantly enthralled. I waited a few seconds outside and turned back to look through the glass. Patrick was clueless. I tapped on the glass and pointed to Dad patiently waiting in the car, blocking the drivers behind him. Patrick stepped out, and the girls dispersed whispering secrets into each other's ears.

"What?" Patrick blurted as he coasted into the front seat.

"You're unbelievable. All those girls were hitting on you in church, and you—you loved it," I preached in a high-pitched voice, and then I realized how ridiculous I sounded. So I changed the subject. "Dad I'm going to drive up to the museum at SOU. Is that OK? I know you wanted us to hang out more around the house, but it's a beautiful day. And I wanted to see all the new exhibits that just came in." I tried to convince him I would be safe, and he shouldn't worry.

"I think that's a great idea, Piper. Are you sure you're feeling up to it? I wish I didn't have to catch a flight out today. I would've taken you."

"Dad, it's OK. Maybe another time. You know me; I get swept away and tune out everything and everyone except the art."

"Hey that works out great," Patrick chimed in to our conversation.

"What does that mean?" I curiously replied.

"The guys are coming over around two. We're going shopping for dinner. Jake has his grandmother's recipe for homemade lasagna, and we're gonna try it out. So, Piper, if you're not here, then we won't find you looking over our shoulders snooping around the kitchen. I promise we won't catch anything on fire. You can even invite Bailey over if you want."

"Bailey's having dinner with her mom and stepdad," I replied. "Is Aiden coming over?" I questioned with hesitation because I wasn't ready to face him today. I felt myself wanting to run and hide.

"No, Aiden, wanted to go play a game of football out on Shelby's field today," Patrick explained.

I almost sighed with relief, but held it back. "I'll be here. What time is dinner?"

"Wow, don't know. How long does it take to cook lasagna?" Patrick mentally counted the length of time to shop, prepare, and cook. "Can you just be home and ready to eat by six?"

"Sure. Who's going to clean up the kitchen when you're done?" I knew it would be a hot mess before the jocks were done.

We pulled into the driveway, and Dad parked the car.

"I have to take off now. I already talked to Marcella, and she will be stopping by each day to check in on you guys."

"Dad, we'll be fine," Patrick and I chanted in unison. I knew Dad was thinking about how he wished he hired a nanny; so we continued to remind him how responsible we would be.

Dad kissed me carefully on the cheek. Patrick gave him a firm tap on his bicep and said good-bye. He reversed out and headed down the road toward the airport

"Are you serious about the Italian feast?" I emulated a chef stirring a big boiling pot.

"Very funny, now go and feast your eyes on some goofy artist's creation and leave dinner to us." He trotted off while texting the guys to meet up at the grocery store.

The road carried me to the place I treasured and admired the most. I made my way inside carrying my sketchbook and pencils, traveling to my favorite collection, but something held me at bay—a borrowed piece I hadn't seen before. A replica of Michelangelo's *David* stood life size in front of me. The sculptor of this replica was unknown, and it had arrived a few days ago from a museum in New York. I flipped open my sketchbook and pulled out a few pencils from my bag. The room emptied of art onlookers, and then it was just me and *David*.

My pencil took flight, and the lines formed into my very own creation. I glanced at *David* and back at my paper, angling lines to form his incredible physique. His toned muscles defined individually led to the next, serving as a remarkable example of perfection embodied in human form. *David* was the only man I'd seen completely, and he stood confidently unaware of his magnificent features.

I leaned back against the wall, removed my teal heels, and sat cross-legged as I pulled my chiffon dress between my legs to make room for the sketchbook resting across my lap. I glanced between the two *Davids* and felt content with the beginning of my sketch.

As I sat patiently on the bench mesmerized by *David*, I felt myself slip into an altered state—some sort of vivid daydream, but it seemed different—like an out-of-body experience. Something forced me against the wall and dizziness came next. Then I felt the breath knocked out of my chest. The museum faded away as my vision meshed into a haze. Weightlessness carried me through a bright passageway of brilliant lights and tossed me inside Aiden's steamy bathroom. I watched as Aiden showered away the sweat and dirt from his ritual Sunday afternoon football game. He couldn't see me, and I didn't want to be there. I closed my eyes, but that only made the dizziness worse. I gasped for breath, but no air came.

He lathered up, and steam continued to fill the room, making the air thick and moist. Fog covered the mirror, and the warm mist interrupted any vision of his true beauty. Beads of water trickled down the lines of his contoured features and fell onto the floor tiles below his feet. He wrapped the towel around his waist and wiped the fogged mirror with the palm of his hand, revealing his athletic frame.

He stood in amazement at the person looking back squarely from the mirror. His dark hair, wet and unruly from the shower, shone against the soft light. His eyes, turquoise with a flicker of yellow, sparkled brightly delivering a certain sense of animal magnetism, startling and stunning at the same time. His broad shoulders stood strong holding his defined arms as if they had been molded by the hands of God. Soft, supple skin covered his fierce, rock-hard chest. His formation was remarkable like the Romans sculpted a masterpiece with each muscle transparently in awe of greatness. His only flaw was the scar from the accident. It formed a V across his shoulders tapering to his waist—another sign of the miracle of life.

He stood exploring himself in the mirror with a bewildered expression across his face. I could hear his thoughts, and I tried to block them out. Unexpectedly, he felt an overwhelming sense of being trapped in this body that stood strikingly bold. *It will have to do for now*, he thought. He dropped the towel and walked out of the room in search of a T-shirt and jeans.

He walked through me as I stood invisible in the doorway. A rush of bright light blinded my vision. A power of unaccountable strength ripped through me. And then within my confusion, I heard muffled voices of a fearless man stomping out the desperate plea of a weaker boy—a boy I thought I knew.

I quickly came back freeing myself from an unknown place. I gasped for air and almost choked on my own saliva. I coughed and cleared my throat.

A museum patron walked into the room and spoke with concern, "Child, are you alright?" She patted my back as I looked at her with tears in my eyes.

"I'm OK now. Thank you." It took a few more small coughs to clear my airway.

She walked out of the room, glancing back a few times to make sure I was really alright. I nodded to reassure her.

Alone, I sat staring at the sculpture of *David*. I glanced down at my sketch that started out as David, but turned into Aiden standing in front of a mirror lost in deep thought. I didn't understand where I went or what was happening to me. I wondered if it could be a side effect of the sleeping pill I had taken last night.

Spellbound once, but now awake—I gathered my pencils and closed the sketchbook. The artwork and sculptures sat quietly, apart from the hustle and bustle of the world outside. Displayed on shelves and podiums they sit; some were intimidated by wondering eyes as others stood confident against unforgiving spectacles and ridiculing remarks. *Am I the same silent creature sitting behind glass walls beckoning for love and understanding?* I thought.

One of my pencils rolled out of my bag and led me closer to the door. Reaching down, I picked it up and tossed it into my bag. What time could it be? I passed a Gerald Murphy painting titled *Watch,* an oil-on-canvas painting designed with gears and numbers winding time down, ticking time from past to present and into the unaccountable future. It teased me. It knew time was never a friend of mine.

The drive home was quick, and I wondered if dinner would be edible and if the kitchen was still standing. I seriously thought about making a quick stop at a nearby drive-thru, but I needed to have some faith in my brother, and I'd promised Dad I would be home for dinner. Our fate was riding hard on the fact we could be responsible young adults.

I drove into our driveway and saw Logan on his blue Harley riding behind me. I parked the car and stepped out. I felt nervous to see him so soon, but at least this time I didn't look a ragged mess.

"Hey, what are you doing?" I asked as I walked up to him.

He leaned over and pointed toward my car parked in the dusty drive. "Did you know your left brake light is out? I followed you for a couple of miles, but I guess you didn't see me."

"My mind must have wandered. I didn't realize you were behind me, or that my brake light was out. My dad just went out of town, so I can't get it repaired until he gets back."

"If you want, I can fix it for you."

"You keep showing up when I need you. Do you know something I don't?" I inquired briefly. "My brother is cooking dinner, and you're welcome to stay. Maybe, we can run to the auto-part store tonight. Is it close by?"

"It's a few miles into town. It won't take long," Logan replied.

I opened the front door. The aroma was breathtaking. The smell of onions, garlic, and tomato sauce radiated through the house and made my mouth water instantaneously.

"Patrick won't mind if you want to stay for dinner. Especially, when he finds out you're the one who gave me a ride home. He's still a little pissed at Aiden for leaving me behind," I recalled as a cool shiver fluttered across my skin.

"He should be—I would be if someone left my sister out in the middle of nowhere," Logan remarked with irritation.

"He was wasted and didn't realize he left me. I'm the one who ran off thinking I could find another ride. So, if you think about it, he didn't leave me stranded; I took off on my own," I lied.

"His main responsibility should have been keeping you safe, not getting wasted with his friends, right?" Logan replied with sincerity.

I couldn't give him the response he was pushing for. We walked toward the commotion in the kitchen. Music blared from the speakers. I gently turned the volume down to introduce Logan. "Hey! This is Logan. He's new in town and will be having dinner with us tonight."

"So, this is Logan—nice to meet you, man." Patrick reached forward and gave a sturdy handshake. "You're the guy who brought my sister home?" Patrick questioned, even though he already knew the answer.

"Yeah, it was no problem. I could see she needed a ride. I'm glad I was around to help her out."

Patrick introduced his friends, and they greeted Logan with a nod and an inviting knuckle-bump.

"So, what time is dinner, Patrick?" I asked, attempting to get a word in.

"It'll be at least an hour. I hope you're not starving." Patrick walked over to the noodles untouched within the cardboard box.

"Logan discovered my brake light is out. He offered to repair it. So we're going to run up to the parts store near town."

"Cool." Patrick searched through the dishwasher looking for the wooden utensil to stir the sauce now boiling on the hot stove.

"I'll be right back." I ran upstairs and grabbed a pair of flip-flops to replace my heels.

Logan and I drove off with the blue Harley's motor roaring underneath us. "I want to take you somewhere," he stated loud enough for me to hear through the wind and the bobbing helmet fastened to my head. He pointed off the road where the pavement turned into gravel.

"Where are we going?" I questioned and waited for a response.

"It's a surprise. I think you'll like it," he expressed with a flicker of a smile.

"What!" I blurted out and pressed my flip-flops onto the ground while the bike was still in motion. I motioned for him to stop by jerking the back of his shirt.

The motorcycle came to an abrupt halt, and I jumped off. I attempted to take the helmet off, but couldn't unlatch the clasp. I felt I was hyperventilating and couldn't catch a decent breath to save my life. I finally unlatched the helmet and tossed it, hitting him in the chest.

"Are you OK?" Logan reached out to console me.

But I stepped back, tripped over loose gravel, and landed on my ass. I glanced around quickly, and this place looked all too familiar. Aiden had wanted to surprise me with the extraordinary architecture of the chapel prior to his attack, and now—now Logan wanted to surprise me with something he found fascinating in a forest surrounded by trees with no one else around within screaming distance. I refused to allow this to play out again. I wanted to run, but where could I go this time?

Logan looked baffled at first, and then confidently aware. "What you're thinking—isn't what I meant. I brought you here to see the butterflies. The Monarch butterflies are beautiful this time of year. I came across a swarm of them the other day. It's amazing—when you stand underneath the trees and look up, it's like seeing autumn leaves falling down all around you. And if you stand incredibly still, they will circle around, intertwining in a stunning pattern of hundreds captivated within the same flight. That's what I wanted you to see. Can I help you up?" He reached out and offered his hand.

I felt embarrassed and didn't know what to say. "It's just..." So many memories came back—memories I'd tried so hard to forget, but now they were beginning to affect every aspect of my life, leaving me terrified of a harmless butterfly. I sat upon the dusty ground with my toes bleeding from the jagged pieces of gravel. *Piper pieces—I was literally falling apart,* I thought.

"I'm really sorry. I just don't like to come down here anymore." My voice trembled uncontrollably with the rest of my body.

"Let me take you back home, Piper." He spoke softly, and something in his voice made me feel like I'd known him all my life. I felt stupid for thinking the worst—that *he* would hurt me.

"No!" I sternly stated.

"You're not going to let me take you home?" His question resonated through the silent air.

"No, I mean—yes, you can take me home, but I want to see the butterflies first." I dusted the chalky grit off of my dress and walked toward the trees in the distance.

Logan walked a few steps to the side of me, and I examined the trees looking for the butterflies. He took my right hand and then my left. We stood staring at each other on the grassy meadow surrounded by tall trees providing shelter above us.

"Look up." He gestured toward the sky above us, and then I saw something astonishing.

The Monarch butterflies fluttered around like falling autumn leaves on a windy day. The tiny winged creatures danced around circling between us and behind us, pushing us closer together. The warmth in his eyes and the tenderness of his touch took me to a place I'd known only as a child— a place without fear, without guilt and shame, without preconceived notions—a place free from darkness. In its simplest form—it was a place of *hope.*

"Piper, believe me. I would never hurt you. I know in time you will eventually trust me."

I didn't know what to say, and he seemed OK with the silence. He led me back to the bike and placed the helmet on my head. The engine started up and carried us back to the paved road ahead. I reached around him and held on once more as the sun parted past the horizon. I could see the store's flashing neon sign in the distance.

We reached the auto-parts store, and Logan walked in to pick up the fuse and extra light bulb. I stood next to the bike looking down at my feet. Dried blood crusted my toes, and my nail polish had chipped away. The glass door swung open, and I watched him walk out carrying a small bag. One thought captivated my mind, and I couldn't find any other way around it—*who is this Logan Taylor?*

Before he started up the engine, I apologized for my crazy behavior. "I'm really sorry for how I reacted today. I thought the butterflies were beautiful. I've never seen anything like it before."

He smiled and started up the motorcycle. "I knew you would love it," he replied. The steady vibration of the Harley rode smoothly against the mountainside country road leading us home. In the distance, I saw a cloud of black smoke rising. *Another fire,* I thought and this time closer to home. A group of thugs on motorcycles rode recklessly toward us while weaving back and forth on both sides of the road. Logan slowed and pulled off to the side. The last guy, decked out in tattoos, smiled a creepy smirk. Then he pointed toward me, made a gun gesture with his hand, and then proceeded to shoot. Logan allowed distance to fall between us and the motorcycle gang and gently patted my thigh as if to tell me I was safe with him.

Logan steered into the driveway and cut the engine. I opened the door, and Logan stepped in behind me. Candles lit the room in warm light as music played gently in the background.

"Wow, I mean—wow." Everyone was awestruck, silently admiring the beauty of the dinner spread out on Mom's table. "You guys, it smells delicious, and the table looks amazing. Dad would be proud." We all stood enamored by the table set with Mom's china and linens rich in red, gold, and orange, familiarly close to the brilliant colors of the butterflies.

We sat down and enjoyed each other's company. Dad's oldies played on the radio, and the sweet smell of tomatoes and onions spun the air around us. The mood was set with Mom's charm, Dad's musical style, Patrick's favorite Italian meal, and great company among friends—in particular my newest, most intriguing friend, Logan.

Chapter Eleven

Here It Goes Again

Monday came too fast. I walked downstairs to gather my books for school. An envelope of pictures for the yearbook fell to the floor, scattering the glossy smiles and perfect poses near my feet. Bailey would be here soon. Reaching down, I swept the pictures into a pile, and her face caught my eye. Rachel with her dark hair, tan skin, and bright blue eyes boldly contrasted my blond hair, fair skin, and green eyes. I couldn't take my eyes off her and wondered how Aiden could. Bailey struck her horn as she flew into the driveway. I placed the photos back into the envelope and rushed out the door.

"Hey, girl." Bailey greeted me with a smile. Then she slowly lowered her dark sunglasses to look at my face. "Wow, you weren't kidding; it actually looks worse today. You must have hit the ground pretty hard. I shouldn't have left you…"

After a fifteen minute drive with music blaring, she pulled up to the school and parked. We walked toward the library to discuss the photos for the yearbook. The picture of Rachel and her cheerleader friends surfaced time and time again pulling me back under the tide, tugging at my very own existence. Then, without warning, a sharp stake wedged deep into my heart; my eyes fluttered in response to a picture of Aiden and Rachel locked in an embrace near the courtyard. No matter how I tried to fight it, I found myself wanting him more and this frightened me.

Out of the corner of my eye, I saw him approaching swiftly. It was Aiden. I stopped and turned toward him as I greeted him with a hollow hello.

"Hey, Aiden. I meant to call you back, but…"

He stopped me before I could finish and placed his hands on my face. "What happened to you? Your face—it's bruised, and your lip is swollen. Did...did I do this to you?" he stammered. "I just can't remember what happened that night. I had this crazy dream and woke up Saturday morning outside my truck." He touched my face, making the same grimace as my father had earlier. I guess the makeup didn't hide it very well today.

"You were drunk. Like, *really* drunk. I left to catch a ride with some-one sober, but it was too late and everyone left. I ran into the forest to take a short cut to catch the last few cars, but I tripped and fell down. I lost my phone and..." I held back on the part where Logan gave me a ride. Aiden looked confused and lost. It made me feel like I could have just imagined it all, but the bruises told another story.

"I only had a few beers," he said. "I've never gone out like that before. It messed with my mind. I don't remember much, but these visions and hallucinations seem so real. Nothing makes any sense. I had these dreams about you and me, but it wasn't me. I woke up and couldn't find you. I called, but you didn't answer."

I didn't want him to say anything else. I didn't want him to recant the images because I saw it all firsthand. My pulsating lip and cheekbone reminded me frequently of the reality of it all. "My phone was lost some-where in the forest that night. I didn't get your messages."

"How did you get home?" Aiden asked.

"I found a ride." I kept my answers short and simple. I owed him noth-ing—I kept reminding myself.

"How long were you out there?" he questioned with worry.

"It doesn't really matter. I'm fine," I continued to lie.

"Are you sure? Are we fine? Because things seem different now." He continued digging for something—something more.

I blurted out, "Rachel still thinks you're with her. I don't even know how to define what this is. You...me...what are we really doing?"

"I'm not with Rachel. She just can't get that it's over." He took my hand in his, looked intensely into my eyes, and gravitated extremely close to me; I could feel his warm breath dance against my skin. I told myself to hold out, but I felt myself slipping, falling. Aiden spoke softly. "I don't want anyone else—I only want you. I thought you knew. Every thought, every moment of my life is tied up in you. Please tell me I haven't screwed this up."

My knees buckled, my heart raced, my mind soared, and I thought my body would take flight, but I held it all in, not allowing him to see that this was what I wanted to hear all along.

"Piper, do you think you can give me another chance? I promise you, I'll never hurt you again," he pleaded as I began to fall back under his charm.

I couldn't speak. I wanted to trust him again. I wanted to pretend it all didn't happen. Reaching into my back pocket, I grabbed a pin and jotted down an address on his forearm.

"What is *this*? Whose house is this?" Aiden questioned, holding up his arm to inspect the inscription.

"That's where I'll be if you want to see me." I ran off before the bell rang just in time to get my seat.

The day continued ordinarily without conflict or precedence. Bailey and Ryder wrapped each other within their own world. Rachel steered clear during practice, burning her anger with each strike of her pompom. And Aiden slammed his fist into his metal locker, leaving a lasting impression when he thought no one was looking—but I seemed to notice it all.

It was four thirty, and I headed over to Fannie's house. Fannie was a friend of my mother's. Her husband had passed away last year around the same time as my mom. She was a sweet old lady, but a little persnickety—OK, very difficult to please. Patrick and I would help her out once a month with various chores; Patrick had to earn his volunteer points for National Honor Society, but I just enjoyed her company.

She asked us to stop at the garden center to pick up a few willow trees and flowers to plant in her garden. Patrick came over to mow the lawn, and I was going to find something for Aiden to do. My car carried the flowers and the four small willow trees shooting out of the top of my little yellow convertible.

When I pulled into the driveway at five fifteen, Aiden's truck had already arrived. He was probably inside working on the to-do-list that she left hanging on the fridge. I let myself into the house carrying a bag of potting soil.

"Fannie, I'm here. I brought the trees and flowers you wanted." I continued to walk through the house in search of the two of them.

"Hi, love." She greeted me with a hug and kiss. She stood with a slight stoop in her back wearing a floral blue and green housedress. Her hair had grown winter white, and her blue-eyes pierced through the hearts of everyone near her. Her voice carried softly with Southern charm; even though, she had lived in Ashland her whole life.

Fannie began acting in her twenties and had traveled to California often for small movie roles. However, her true love was theater. She loved to talk about the different productions she played in. In particular, she adored the ones here at the Oregon Shakespeare Festival. She kept several props and photos. Her back room closet overfilled with dresses, gowns, and wraps she'd worn on stage. In the past, we use to sneak inside and play dress up. She made me smile when no one else could. And after losing my mom, that was quite the quest.

Aiden came out of the back bedroom carrying a can of dust spray, one unforgettable pair of pink cotton panties, and a facial expression like no other. He would walk through fire, a raging storm, and a warzone for me…and I laughed because he did it all without a water hose, supersonic umbrella, or bazooka. No, he carried a pair of pink granny panties and slid right back into my heart.

"This young man came here to help me. Do you know this boy, Piper?" she asked as she circled around and patted him firmly on his butt.

"Yes, this is Aiden, Fannie. He goes to my school. He's going to help plant your trees. Isn't that nice of him? He has a lot of time on his hands and loves to help out," I boasted.

"He's polishing my wardrobe first, and then I'll let him plant the trees. Isn't he doing a real fine job?" Fannie continued to check him out from head to toe, making Aiden a little uncomfortable and then followed with a question, "Do you want some lemonade, love?"

"Yes, that sounds sweet. Can I help you?" I offered.

"No, dear, I can manage." Fannie headed off to the kitchen.

"Really," he whispered. He pulled me to the side and explained, "She has been hitting on me every since I got here. And pulled these out of the drawer and handed them to a complete stranger to polish her furniture." He held up the pink panties with stretched elastic band and twirled them around his index finger. "It would be different if they were your panties."

"Why, Aiden didn't know you had a panty fetish," I flirted with a surprised smile.

He tossed the panties into her laundry bag and then chased me down the hallway toward the front door. Patrick had already arrived to mow the grass. Listening to music, my brother was transformed into another world.

"Fannie, I'm going to get the plants," I called into the kitchen. She stood in front of the sink squeezing the lemons to make her thirst-quenching lemonade. "Fannie, I'm going to get the stuff from the car." I spoke louder this time to get her attention.

"I hear you, honey; no need to yell." She continued to stir the juice as the pulp floated to the top.

I helped Aiden gather the bags of potting soil, plants, and small trees from my car. Patrick was mowing the front and moved on to the side yards. Fannie stood on the front porch with a cool glass of lemonade. I carried it inside and found Aiden standing in the kitchen holding his glass. He raised his glass in a silent toast of some sort. Fannie washed up the remaining dishes, talking about where she wanted her trees planted. She couldn't make up her mind. I took a big swig of the drink and forced it down; even though, it burned my throat. The sour taste bit me, and my eyes and mouth watered at the same time. Tears ran down my face as I secretly spit a few of the seeds back into the cup. Aiden had to turn around to prevent from laughing hysterically. I wiped the tears away and tried to lick the sourness from my lips.

Fannie poured herself a glass of the lemonade. She took a small sip. "Oh my, I forgot to add the sugar. You poor dears, don't drink that." She poured it down the drain. Sugar was added by the cupful to the remaining pitcher as she continued to talk about where to plant her little trees. "Seven, eight, nine," she counted and continued to stir in cupfuls of sugar.

"Fannie, we're going to go outside to start the flower beds."

"Sure, love. I'll bring the drinks out to you when they're ready, dear. Now, where was I...two, three, four..."

Aiden and I walked over to the shed and located the assorted shovels and garden tools. Patrick waved at us and turned up the volume to his music flowing into his ears.

"You should have seen the look on your face when you slammed down that sour lemonade," Aiden said. "I didn't think I could keep it all together."

"And you should have seen your face as you cleaned her wardrobe with her pink panties."

"Touché, I guess we're even." He leaned forward to take my hand.

"I'm glad you came."

"I'm glad you invited me."

"Let's start planting." I handed him the shovel and pointed to the spot to plant the first one.

"Here?" he questioned as he pointed to the ground. I nodded, and he began to dig.

I pulled the weeds out of the flower bed and used the hand shovel to remove the wilted flowers struggling for life. Fannie tended to overwater, drowning everything, or under-water, causing the plants to wither away and die. I kept looking back watching Aiden dig the hole for the little willow. The little tree was quickly planted, and then he moved onto the next. I pointed to the location for the other tree before he began to dig.

Fannie came out to direct us, occasionally changing the location of the little trees. Aiden pulled up the tree and started over again. He smiled and tried to accommodate her. The sky turned to dusk, and we continued to work within the dim light of the porch.

"Thank you, dear, it's just lovely. Do you think that little tree is crooked?" she contemplated and pointed to the first tree planted.

"No, Fannie, it's a perfect little tree. Don't you think?"

"Hmm, if you think so, dear. Come back and see me soon. And you too, young man." She hugged us both. "Where is that brother of yours?"

"He left a few minutes ago," I replied.

"Tell him he did a wonderful job; maybe next time cut it a little shorter."

"OK. Good-bye, Fannie."

She walked inside, turning off the porch light and left us in the dark.

"Are you hungry?" Aiden asked as he climbed into his truck.

"Famished," I replied. "Where can we go dressed like this?" We were covered in dirt and sweat.

"Can you leave your car here? I'll make you dinner at my house. It's the least I could do. Piper, let me make things right."

"Can you really cook?" I teased.

"Guess you'll never know, unless you take me up on my offer." Aiden's voice charmed me, and he pulled me under the surf with his turquoise eyes. I knew I couldn't refuse and climbed into his truck.

His house was about ten miles away. It was weird riding in his truck after what happened last time, but he was a different person. It was truly like nothing vile had ever happened.

"Here we are," he said as he pulled into the drive of a two-story house that stood like a fortress. A pond nestled to the side of the property, and a small wooden pier led up to the water. Trees surrounded the back, and a small nook curved around the side deepening into the darkness. A couple of red and yellow canoes sat upside down on the rack. The wooden paddles were strewn around on the white sandy shore. Warm light came from inside the house, beaming from the ornate windows and a large light atop a wooden pole reflected onto the pond.

"This is where you live?"

"Yeah, this is home. The pond is my favorite place to hang out and just think." We walked closer to the pond, coming near to the water's edge.

"Do you fish?" I asked as small bugs buzzed close to the rippling surface of the water, and small fish jumped out to catch the crunchy snacks.

"Uh huh, have you ever fished before, Piper?" he questioned with curiosity, smiling like the cat that caught the canary.

"Yes, Aiden, girls can fish, too." I gave him a slug to his right arm. "My dad took me fishing when I was little. It was fun, just haven't been lately."

"Looks like I'll have to make time to take you."

I nodded. "What about the canoes? Do you take them out much?" We walked over toward the boat rack, and he lifted the paddles from the stiff sand, dusting them off. When they were free of the caked-on debris, he propped them against the canoe rack.

"Not lately. I guess I was really busy over the summer, and now that school has started..." He just lifted his hands into the night air, reaching for an answer, but failed to find it. "Would you like to come over this week? We can take the canoe out if you want."

"I would like that. Now, didn't you say something about making me dinner? I'm kind of starving."

"Come on, let's go inside." He took my hand, leading me away from the peaceful pond toward the well-lit brick home. We followed a pathway of stone that wound through the front yard. Aiden pulled the keys from his front pocket and opened the door.

"Are your parents home?" I whispered as we walked through the foyer.

"No. My parents divorced when I was twelve, and my mom left. My dad works a lot, and he's not home much."

"Sounds a little too familiar. My mom, she's...you know...gone. My dad is always out of town on business. Just me and Patrick most of the time. At least we have each other. Do you get lonely in this big house?" I dug deeper, knowing we were more alike than what I first thought.

"Sometimes, I guess. But then again, I like the quiet sometimes, too. The guys came over all summer. It was like a free-for-all. I think it got to me. Then Rachel was always over... Wow, I didn't mean to bring her up. I missed being alone. But now that you're here, it's perfect." The tone in his voice changed, and he reminded me of why we were here. "So, you say you're starving."

We walked into the designer kitchen, and it was obvious that no one ever cooked there between the shine and flash of the colorful palate. Aiden scrambled around looking for pots and pans with a befuddled look on his face. Clanging of utensils and pans echoed within the hollow walls of the house, but I sat quietly watching his every move. He lifted my legs out of the way to find something underneath the cabinet. He pulled bacon, eggs, cheese, onions, milk, and strawberries from the fridge, and pancake mix from the pantry.

"You like breakfast food, right?" he questioned as he gathered all of the items and placed them on the countertop.

"Um..." I pressed my lips together, hiding my response. "I'm so sorry. You said dinner, and I thought you meant..." I bit down on my swollen lip, trying my hardest not to laugh and ruin it. But I couldn't keep up the charade. "I'm just kidding. I love breakfast for dinner. It's the best."

"You know you had me going. It's pretty much the only thing I know how to make."

"How lucky for me! So, what do you plan on making?"

"Bacon, omelets, and strawberry pancakes. How does that sound?"

"Yum, do you need some help?" I jumped off of the counter and grabbed the spatula.

"No, get back up there. I told you *I* was going to make *you* dinner. Uh huh, back…back…" He took the spatula from my hand and pointed toward the countertop.

I jumped back up on the marble. "OK, it seems you have all of this under control. I'll just sit here and watch you."

He continued to whisk, beat, blend, sizzle, and drizzle, making the best homemade breakfast-for-dinner that I had ever seen. He poured two glasses of orange juice and placed them on the table. I reached over and stole a piece of hot bacon sizzling in the pan. It was delicious, and I tried to consume it before he returned, but it was too hot.

"You really are starving," he commented.

"Yeah, let's eat."

He carried the plates to the table; we ate and continued to talk for hours. Afterward, he drove me back to Fannie's house to pick up my car. And then he followed me home in the darkness. My clothes were dirty from planting the flowers for Fannie, but the smell of bacon bled into my shirt, bringing back memories of the night with Aiden—good memories that covered the painful ones.

Chapter Twelve

Tusk

Tuesday morning arrived slowly. I watched for dawn and waited for day to come. Aiden invaded my mind with his soft smile, handsome looks, and warm touch. The clock couldn't tick fast enough. I dreamed of spending the entire day with him. Our class had planned a field trip to the Museum of Natural History. Our school had participated in a fundraiser for research and building construction after arson burned through one side of the building last year, destroying the west wing.

I punched the button on my alarm clock before it had a chance to go off. I was already dressed and ready to go. The morning sun shattered through the blinds. Downstairs, Patrick sat at the table eating a bowl of cereal and drinking a protein shake.

"Hey," he said, not taking his eyes off his book and last-minute homework.

"Is that what you're wearing to school today?" I laughed, reminding him he was still shirtless and wearing pajama pants. "Are you going to be ready soon? Because I'm about to be out the door." I teased.

Patrick slammed his book shut, swigged down the remaining protein shake, slurped the milk from the cereal bowl, and ran upstairs. A few seconds later, he swaggered downstairs and out the door looking like a million bucks. I didn't know it was possible, but then again—it was Patrick. He slid through every yellow light just a few feet in front of me; I struggled with each red light falling farther behind. The parking lot was full, and I traveled row by row looking for a place to park. Patrick's car had the perfect place near the entrance as I circled around for another trip to find a spot. Our Irish luck followed Patrick around layering the ground with gold and jewels; unfortunately, I was the lonely one tripping over his perfection. I found a spot, parked, and hiked toward the school.

Buses parked outside ready to load students for the short trip to the museum. I met up with Bailey and Ryder. Ryder, dressed in his usual black jeans, black boots, and a black T-shirt, stood quietly holding Bailey's hand. His shirt read, *Until Lions Have Their Historians—Tales of the Hunt Shall Always Glorify the Hunters*. Another fine proverb he'd found and screened into his plain black cotton shirt. Such a quiet guy, but he always had something to say through the process of free speech broadcasted across his chest.

I crept up on them. "Hey, guys." Bailey jumped and reached around to hug me.

Ryder lifted his shades and propped them on top of his head as he softly spoke. "Hey, Piper."

It wasn't even eight o'clock, and Bailey already began to interrogate me. "So, how's it going with Aiden? I hope you were able to work it all out. Please tell me you did. You guys are so cute together." She wouldn't give me the chance to answer.

"Bailey, I'll meet you inside," Ryder gently interrupted. "I need to drop something off in the media room." He kissed her on the neck. A small rose-colored welt peeked out from her neckline, and she quickly pulled her shirt up to cover the mark. Their eyes spoke a secret language, and a warm blush crossed her cheeks as she smiled at him.

As he left, I replied to her, "Everything is going great. We hung out at his house last night. I love being around him, and I just can't seem to get enough. Have you seen him around?"

"Well, speak of the devil. He's walking toward us right now." Bailey couldn't stop smiling; she turned me around and pushed me straight into his arms.

"Good morning." Aiden pressed his lips against my cheek and gathered me in his arms. I followed the sequence of muscles from his wrist up to his arms that intertwined with a few bulging veins. Then my eyes continued to examine his chest covered with a polo shirt and three open buttons, leading me to his broad neck. "Are you guys ready for the field trip?"

I nodded yes. Bailey shot off down the hallway and crashed into Ryder giving him a hidden kiss blocked by the crowd heading into the building. Aiden released my hand and placed his inside the back pocket of my jeans. He leaned in next to my ear, and I waiting for each word, but instead he kissed my neck. A tingling sensation zapped each and every nerve in response; I felt sparks in places I never felt possible.

"I'll catch up with you at the museum, OK?" I saw his lips moving, but the only thing I could think about was his hand on my ass. He jogged away toward his classroom. I entered mine, sat down, and tried to cool off before our next visit.

The teacher reviewed plans for the day. It started with a guided tour, followed by lunch, and the remainder of the day on our own as a self-discovery tour. The only self-discovery I was interested in was Aiden and whatever he wanted to grab onto next. I readjusted myself at my desk, but couldn't find a comfortable spot because my body craved Aiden. I watched the clock tick down until the bell rang.

Assigned buses parked alongside the courtyard near the flagpoles. Aiden and Patrick rode on the bus designated for football players. Coach couldn't pass up a spare moment and reviewed plays with the guys in route to the museum. A few cheerleaders filtered in with the football players, just because they could. My bus became crowded quickly, and Bailey found a seat with Ryder. Logan sat alone and slid over to offer me a seat.

"Your lip looks a lot better." Logan reached over and slightly touched my lip. "Does it still hurt?"

"No," I paused, looking forward and then back at him. "No, I barely know it's there, unless I look in the mirror and see it. Then it all comes back."

"What all comes back?" Logan looked puzzled, but I felt he already knew the truth. His eyes seemed to stare right down into my very soul, and I had to look away to hide my secrets.

He touched the hidden bruises left by Aiden's grip as the bus made its last turn. I slid into his arms with my face against his neck. I pulled myself back over, and he gently released his hands.

"Sorry, you see how clumsy I am. Remember, I told you I fell and that's how I bumped my lip," I explained.

"I'm glad I was there. Maybe next time, I can prevent your fall." Again, he stroked the place on my arm where the faded bruises hid underneath my shirt, but he seemed to know more than anyone should.

The bus came to a sudden stop, and the door shrieked open. Balloons were tied to a large welcoming banner celebrating the reopening of the Museum of Natural History. A small band played in the courtyard near the entrance. Plastered against the main atrium wall was a collection of framed photographs demonstrating the rebuilding process. Logan and I walked inside, admiring the photographs; our hands dangled aimlessly against one another. Then he took his hand and wrapped it around mine tightly.

"Piper…" His eyes looked intense as if he wanted to tell me something—something serious—something pressing, but…

Aiden walked over purposefully bumping into Logan, who stood solid. "What's going on?" he asked, staring down Logan with a go-to-hell look. Then Aiden turned to me and kissed my hand, flaunting his conquest in Logan's face. Logan turned and walked away. Feeling like a piece of meat, I pulled my hand back from his grip.

Our tour guide's voice echoed, and her heels clicked against the marble floor. "Can everyone move to the center of the room? We need to make room for the people out in the courtyard. Please, everyone move to the center. The tour is about to begin." She adjusted her small microphone and began the tour. "This room is dedicated to the mammoths and mastodons that roamed North America until the last ice age—about ten thousand years ago."

Fossilized creatures hoisted up by wires balanced steady in place. Skeletal remains roped off on display stood solid with a recreated background of their historic habitat. The building was full of ancient dwellers with tusks, horns, and ferocious appetites revisiting us from a foreign time capsule. The guide continued to explore the lands of the past as we walked from one exhibit to another.

The next room encased the land of the lost—various dinosaurs from the T-Rex to the Velociraptor and strange flying dinosaur, the Pterodactyl. Horns, tales, teeth, spikes, tusks, and claws carried their weight in weapons during a time when the world was without words. They stalked their prey and acted on that single primitive impulse to fight until only one walked away. Primal fear frayed the instincts of the smaller to survive in the struggle with everyday life—a constant battle plagued by intensity unconceivable by today's society; *and then again*, I reconsidered my thought, *we really haven't come that far from history. People today can be just as vindictive. The only difference is our words and fists strike harder than any horn, tale, tusk, spike, or bite ever could.* History relived—the dinosaurs had nothing over our sword and tongue.

Several hours later, the lunch line wound around the small café. Students stood in wait for food to pile upon their plate—an easy meal, an easy life, in an easy town, broken off from any sense of conquer or quest. The herbivores layered lettuce with chopped veggies, and cheese with croutons scattered on top. The carnivores loaded up with burgers, chicken, and turkey sandwiches. They attacked their food forcing a fistful of meat into their mouths as the herbivores mixed in casual conversation while picking at the greens with a plastic fork.

Aiden sat down beside me with a custom-built burger dripping grease down onto his plate with each bite. His lips glistened with the juices pouring from the butchered meat, and I had a sick feeling that I wanted to kiss him.

The tour guide interrupted, "The café will be closing in fifteen minutes. The remainder of the tour will be at your own pace. Feel free to walk around exploring the exhibits. Again, we all appreciate your time and effort in helping us salvage and rebuild our museum. We definitely could not have done it without you."

I finished my fruit platter and thirsted for cool water. "I'll be right back," I said.

Aiden tossed the last bite of his burger into his mouth and carried his tray over to the trash. "Where can I meet you?" he questioned, wiping the slick layer from his lips.

"I'm just going to get a drink. I'll meet you near the tusk exhibit," I replied and pointed toward the west wing. Aiden leaned against the wall talking with a few friends while watching me walk away.

The cool water became colder with each sip from the fountain tucked away in the small corridor. I drank and couldn't seem to replenish my thirst. Each drop just made me want to drink a little more. My lips felt numb from the cold rush.

Unknown to me, Rachel crept up behind me with her sharp nails dipped in red polish and took pleasure tapping them against the wall. Staring me down, her chest grew with each breath, her nostrils widened, and her pupils dilated slowly into a pool of darkness. Her lips parted, exposing pearly white teeth, and she whispered harshly into my ear: "I would kill before I let him choose you over me."

I wiped the cool drops of water from my lips with my wrist. No words came to mind. Cornered by Rachel, I felt stalked by a savage beast. An instinct arose—a primitive instinct. I shoved her into the wall she had tapped upon with her Velociraptor claws. She lost her balance and slid down with a twist to her ankle as I walked toward Aiden. Rachel glared across the room, unhinged by her loss.

Bailey and Ryder trotted off to a secluded area, admiring one another instead of the ancient artifacts surrounding them. Aiden met up with a few guys talking football, and I drifted away, mesmerized by the cases of life lost to time: tiny fossils pressed into rock for eternity, arrowheads made of prehistoric bone, and sparkling gemstones underneath a locked glass case. Logan walked just a few steps behind me without crowding or conspiring, and interestingly incapable of securing his own conversation.

He appeared complicated, mysterious, and remarkably handsome. He followed me through the exhibit hall winding into a small, secluded room. A glass case stood between us, and I couldn't help but smile at his charming subtleness. I felt a different form of attraction to him along with a strong sense of fear because I knew Aiden could show up at any second. It was clear—Aiden didn't like Logan's newfound interest in me, and Logan despised the way Aiden treated me. This dance with the devil was becoming a strange habit. And I had no idea why I continued to give either of them the time of day. But I did.

"You know, I could be your tour guide." Logan looked down at the glittering stones and then back up at me.

"A tour guide? What makes you think I need a tour guide?" I teased. For a moment I fell into his eyes, unable to turn away or even blink.

Beautiful stones placed on soft pillows filled the case. He studied each one, admiring their unique splendor. "Piper, you're like a precious stone lying in the rough waiting to find your way to shine. I have faith that you'll find it. You may not see it now, but you will."

I didn't know what to say. It was the weirdest pick-up line I'd ever heard. Not that I'd heard a lot. It just seemed like an odd statement. He reached for my hand, and just for a moment, the world felt safe. His eyes desperately wanted to tell me something, but I wasn't sure I wanted to know. I pulled away, just in time.

Aiden appeared with a wild look in his eyes—similar to what I saw in the chapel. Darkness consumed him as if he wasn't the same boy I fell in love with. It was like he had two different personalities. And I secretly feared the one standing in front of me.

"Why is it that every time I turn around you are trying to get with *my* girl!" Aiden shouted.

"Don't do this, Aiden," I pleaded. "Logan is just a friend. You're making a scene over nothing." A small crowd began to form around us.

"Seriously, Piper, you're going to stand up for this punk," Aiden remarked as he glared into my eyes. Then he turned toward Logan and yelled, "And you're going to let a *girl* defend you!" Aiden suggested while calling Logan out with a finger pointed inches away from his face.

Logan stood firm and fearless quietly observing Aiden's every move. And then he glanced over at me which infuriated Aiden more. I reached for his arm trying to pull him back. Within the commotion, Aiden knocked me to the floor.

"Don't even look at her!" Aiden shouted sharply at Logan with spit flying from his mouth.

"Yeah, and don't *you* ever hurt her again!" Logan got up in his face sternly, and then whispered the last phrase before he walked away: "I know what you are."

Aiden turned and punched his fist into the wall, cracking the newly finished paint. Memories of all the violence came rushing back as I pulled myself up from the floor. Backing away slowly, I panicked and ran for the bus. The memories served as a reminder—I didn't want to be the prey.

Chapter Thirteen

Halloween

Halloween was exactly a week away, and the festivities around the town square crept out of the woodwork. Decorations with ghost, goblins, and witches popped up all over town. Orange pansies bloomed in flowering pots, and the smell of autumn drifted in the air, turning all the leaves auburn. I drove downtown to pick up a blueberry muffin before heading off to school. Facing the window inside the small café, I watched as beams of sunlight burst through the thickening clouds. The wind rattled the glass and rocked the hanging flowers side to side, and then ultimately swung them in a circle, twisting their frayed ropes together.

I thought of Aiden and Logan. Brutal memories of the fight in the museum passed through my head in slow motion. The flicker franticly focused into sharp images of Aiden's dark transformation, raging out of jealousy. And Logan wasn't blameless. He provoked Aiden with his new found interest in me, driving my boyfriend mad. I was angry at both of them. The violence continued to torture my mind, and my head felt consumed with tension. I was close to snapping.

I wrapped up the rest of the muffin and drove toward school, where I found Bailey sitting on the front steps texting. "Hey, Bailey!" I shouted, waving my hands in the air to get her attention.

"Can you believe this weather? It looks like the sky is going to crack open at any moment," she exaggerated.

"Bailey, you're so dramatic." But then again, I also knew the horror of it all.

Streaks of lightning sparked through the sky, followed by thunderous booms in the distance. The smell of rain dampened the air. We all knew too well what horrible events could occur with a single touch of lightning.

"You see? I'm not dramatic. I told you it was coming for us," she continued to rant. Aiden's misfortune with the lightning strike only heightened her obsession for the weather.

"Have you decided what you're wearing to the masquerade?" I questioned.

"Yeah, my mom took me shopping over the weekend, and we found this black sequined gown. I think she only let me get it so she could borrow it." Bailey scrolled through her photos, showing off the dress. "What about you?"

"My dad bought my dress at one of the shops downtown. I have my new phone and will text you as soon as I see it. He's picking it up today. He's trying to fill in for my mom, and in a way, it's really sweet. I hope it's not a tragic mistake. He still sees me as a five-year-old. So, I haven't got a clue what he'll be coming home with," I replied with a sigh.

"Call me when you get the dress. Maybe your dad will actually come through for you. It can't be that bad, right?" Bailey's optimism was undermined by her sarcastic undertones.

"I'll see you at lunch." I waved good-bye and walked toward my first class.

In the hall, Rachel stood near the classroom doorway with a flock of her friends. I rushed through the hallway trying to avoid another conflict, but Rachel stuck her long leg out in front of me. I tripped and slid across the waxed floor, this time ending up at Logan's feet.

"Are you OK?" he questioned and then reached down to help me up. "I'm fine—just a little clumsy." Another fall at the foot of another guy; it was becoming an awful habit.

Her stare pierced my skin with imaginary spears. Rachel left the scene with a wicked smile as Logan gathered my books. I did not allow Logan a chance to discuss the museum fight as I abruptly rushed off to my classroom.

"Are you guys coming to class today?" Mrs. Langley chirped from the doorway as she adjusted her glasses further down on her nose.

The rest of the day drained into thoughts of the museum and Rachel's never-ending torment. The dance was ten days away, and I couldn't wait for it all just to be over. I didn't want to be anywhere near Aiden, Logan, or Rachel.

I drove home to see the dress Dad had promised to pick up. He stood in the doorway with a monumental smile across his face. After running inside, I went room to room searching for the dress.

"Well, Dad, where is it? Don't keep me in suspense! Show me the dress."

"Close your eyes," he said. "I want to savor every moment of this."

I peeked out the corner of one eye and saw him pull a camera from his pocket.

"Piper, close your eyes!"

My cheeks ached from squeezing them shut. "Please, Dad, can I open my eyes now?"

"Not yet. OK, now you can. Open your eyes!" Excitement in his voice nearly brought tears to my eyes; I honestly couldn't remember the last time he was this happy.

He flashed the pink, ruffled mess of a dress in front of me, and I smiled as I broke into a hysterical laugh. It was cotton-candy pink with ruffles everywhere. It had a built-in petticoat to make it fluffier, if that was even possible. I was going to the dance as Shirley Temple and surely to sink to the bottomless abyss on my *Good Ship Lollipop*.

"Dad, I love it. It's um—unbelievable. You did well. Mom would be proud. Thank you." Strangely, relief swept over me. The seriousness of my life was shattered, and I was done juggling the three crazy balls I held in my hand named Aiden, Rachel, and Logan. I was done with it all. Dad stood there, and I just kept smiling at him.

"Are you sure you like it, Piper? You know we could always return it and get something else."

"Dad, you have no idea how perfect it is." I kissed him on the cheek and carried the dress upstairs to hang it in the closet.

Interestingly, one dress would solve all my problems. Rachel would know I'm no threat, Logan and Aiden would turn and run the other way, and everything would be back to normal. I'd become invisible again, and life would return to a redundant pathway of nothingness.

I hung the dress on the door hook, but all the fabric and ruffles kept the door from closing. I forced it into the corner of my closet, but it fought back, covering all of my things with pink fluff. My skin warmed with the thought of embarrassment. The masquerade mask would partially conceal my misfortune, but definitely not my fate. I snapped a picture of the dress figuring words wouldn't be able to explain and went back to my room to call Bailey.

"Bailey, can you talk?"

"Yeah, so did you get it? What do you think of it? How did...?"

I cut her off in the middle of her calculative attempt to probe me for answers. "I just sent you the picture. Did you get it?"

Silence held me in suspense because I knew Bailey would soon freak out.

"You're kidding! *That* is the dress you will be wearing in public to a dance—a high school dance with guys? Please tell me you're not serious. Seriously, it looks like a really bad birthday cake. You can't wear that. I won't let you."

"Well, it would solve the whole Aiden verses Logan fiasco. They would both run scared from the pink paradox. And Rachel would win, and I would lose by default," I explained as I predicted my ridiculous future.

"Maybe it's a joke, and your dad is waiting for you to come to your senses. You should confront him and tell him you'll wear it another time, but not to this dance," she insisted. "Piper, come on!"

"It's not a joke, Bailey. He was so excited and took snapshots to commemorate it all."

Bailey interrupted, "I have to go. I won't let you spoil this day because of your desire to destroy yourself. Who does that? True happiness doesn't come along often, and you're just going to throw it all away because boys want to fight over you, and a girl—a popular girl—is jealous of you. Really, what are you thinking? Piper pieces—I'm picking up Piper pieces because you purposely tear everything good in your life apart. I won't allow you to do this again."

Later that night, I passed by my closet. Pieces of the pink dress pushed the door ajar, freeing the frilly fabric from the darkness. I refused to surrender to its annoying display for further acknowledgement and slammed the door shut again. I took my sleeping pill and couldn't keep my eyes open any longer. I climbed into bed and watched the pink ruffles escape once more before drifting off.

Then darkness dazzled me in the distance, and my mind followed deep inside the dream. It started with sparks of memories from my past, and then glimpses of what was to come flashed before my eyes. I fought inside my dreams as sweat pelted my pores from fright.

I woke from the nightmare only to find myself trapped as a ghost of myself. Standing across the room, I watched my body sleep. Doors and walls were no longer solid; I could see without boundaries. A monster crept outside my room, and I felt powerless to move. *Another out-of-body experience or a really messed up dream,* I thought. Dizziness came next when I attempted to move. Gasping, I couldn't find air or call out to warn myself of the danger coming from the other side of the door.

Dark smoke slid in from the night. It twisted, intertwined, and coiled up the staircase. Shadows scurried within the twilight and reached my room, feeding through the crack underneath the door. The smoke traveled toward the ceiling, hovering above my body as I slept.

Evil stirred the smoke into a solid mass of many intricate shapes anchored above me. I heard its thoughts and felt its feelings that oozed from the creature. My body slept unaware of its strange fascination for me, but my spirit saw the beast for what it was. The pieces became one strong force growing with hatred, envy, lust, and most peculiar—love. A different kind of love—it was dark, desperate, and untouched by any form of human love. A wicked desire, unable to seek without destroying the one thing it coveted—her. I mean—me. It was becoming more and more confusing.

As my body slept underneath it, smelling sweet and appearing soft enough to touch, it called out. My body was unable to hear the tone it spoke outside the nightmares, but his roar screamed a terrifying noise throwing my spirit back where it belonged. Awake now, I sensed how it wanted to taste my skin and open my eyes to its beauty.

The blackness glistened, changing into curly ribbons. It coiled itself quickly toward the ceiling unable to understand its own emotions; it growled above tangled with rage and desire. Then it swept down, whisking across my tender skin. Slowly, it wrapped around my legs, wound around my waist, and then carefully bound my neck. And then it flowed back up inside the darkness. Calmness only lasted a few minutes before it fell hungry for more. Venomous fangs held on tightly as it supported the creature. The frenzy festered again igniting its compulsion to take a little more.

A thick shadow slithered down the wall and across the floor toward the bed. Its craving couldn't be stopped. As I tried to scream out, my blanket was tossed to the other side of the room. Unable to scream, I felt the entity hold me down as the shadow grew in excitement. Sweat continued to leak through my skin, and the shadow soaked it up. It slid off as I turned wildly in bed, wrapping me within its wrath.

With a gasp aware of the evil stirring all around, I attempted again to scream out. A weak cry broke through my lips, "Dad." Then I called out a little louder, "Dad," but no one came.

Dawn approached outside my window shrinking the shadow with beams of light. The monstrosity began to dissipate into its original shape: thin dark smoke that slithered back underneath the door and out of my room. However, curiosity captivated the flow to turn feverishly, spiraling through one more time.

Crawling out of bed, I fell to the ground as blood trickled down my nose into a puddle onto the wooden floor. The stream of smoke caught the scent, and darkness turned rushing into the steady stream of blood. It found a pathway inside circulating with each heart beat. No longer smoke, it coated itself with the wet warmth immersed with each drop of blood finding its most useful form—becoming one with *his* love.

The smoke, tinged with blood, filtered out of my mouth as I struggled for breath. The darkness retreated back to the place it came, but I still felt its presence—for it acquired a taste it refused to do without.

Running to the toilet, I vomited. The strange entity was gone. My memories faded. I glanced into the mirror, splashed my face with cool water, and removed the bloodstains from my skin. Then I knelt down and purged the foul fluid burning me from the inside.

Chapter Fourteen

Soul To Squeeze

My head pounded with a force near explosion. Thursday came with a vengeance. Sunlight streamed between the blinds stabbing my eyes. Distorted sounds echoed as I smothered myself into the firm pillow. Breathing wasn't necessary at this point. I just wanted it all to go away; the rush of spinning left me dizzy. Saliva built up inside my mouth. My stomach quivered. My pulse raced. I ran and knelt beside the toilet again to throw up.

"Piper, I made some pancakes for you." Dad stepped into my room wearing Mom's flowered apron protecting his suit from bacon splatter. "Honey, are you OK? You don't look so good." He wet a cloth with water and draped it across my forehead.

"Dad, something's really wrong." I held the cool cloth to my face.

"Do you think you can get dressed?" he asked.

I nodded while pulling my jeans on.

And then he walked out pulling the floral apron from his waist. He yelled down the hallway, "Patrick, I'm taking Piper to the doctor."

I braced myself against the wall trying to find my balance. I watched as Patrick opened the door and saw steam in the shape of skulls and vilified faces escape into the hallway. I cringed, closing my eyes to the horrible hallucinations.

"What's up, Dad?" Patrick looked over at me and caught me as I began to slide down the wall. His voice became distorted and the hallucinations began to fade into the darkness.

"I'm taking Piper to the doctor this morning. Can you move your car out of the drive?"

Dad carried me to the car as I drifted in and out, uncertain of everything. Memories of dark dreams collided in my consciousness.

Ringing in my ears muffled Dad's words: "Piper, you're going to be OK. We're here now." Then a distorted sound exploded in my head and pulled me back under the darkness.

I woke with Dad hovering over my bed and slowly glanced around the small room painted blue and white with medical equipment secured to the walls around me. A shiny metal IV pole stood tall near my bed. I watched fluids drip into the clear tubing.

"Piper, you're in the ER. You're OK, just a little dehydrated. How are you feeling?" Dad looked worried, and the lines across his face displayed the countless hours of concern for his family. It had aged him, and I didn't really realize it until now.

"Dad..." My mouth felt dry, and I tried to swallow a few times before speaking again. "I'm OK." The ringing in my ears had ceased, my stomach felt settled, my pulse was calm, and my head was clear.

"You really had me worried. I don't think I've ever seen you that sick before." Dad scooted his swivel chair toward me, reached out, and took my hand. "Do you remember any of it?"

"No, not really. I was feeling sick to my stomach." I paused trying to recall what all had happened, but couldn't. "I guess I remember just bits and pieces. What are you *not* telling me?"

He rubbed his temples, and I continued to watch as his fingers traveled back and forth across his forehead. He folded his glasses and tucked them neatly into the front pocket of his dress shirt. With his elbow braced against the bed and his hand covering his mouth, it appeared he wanted to keep the words from spilling out. "Piper, you said things that..."

I interrupted. "What—things, Dad?" I questioned with hesitation.

He swallowed, and I watched his Adam's apple rise and fall. "It must have been the dehydration causing you to talk out of your head. It's just that it reminded me—of one of your mother's paranoid delusional attacks. But it was just the dehydration and fever that caused the hallucinations," he proclaimed, trying to convince himself.

"Dad, I'm not like her. You don't have to worry about that."

He stared down at the blanket unable to look up at me. I continued to count his gray hairs underneath the mirrored light pulled down from the hospital ceiling. If her paranoid schizophrenia was genetically handed down to me, his balancing act was over. I refused to be the spark that ignited his tightrope—the only thing he had left to cling to.

"Dad, I'm feeling better. Do you think they'll let us go home now?"

The doctor walked in with a clipboard, reviewing labs and the discharge instructions with Dad. I smiled, nodded, and pretended all was well; all the while, I knew something was watching, waiting, and whispering in the darkness. Dad signed the forms, the nurse pulled the IV from my hand, and before sunset we were home.

Almost immediately, Dad fell asleep in his leather chair upstairs in his office, Patrick was at football practice, and I sat up on the wooden fort in the backyard watching the sun fall against the horizon. It cast an amber glow onto the mountain range, and lavender-pink clouds floated by unaware of the miseries spread upon the grassy-green lands and rock, making up the world I called home.

Logan's motorcycle sputtered into the driveway, startling me. His footsteps carried him around the front of the house and over the iron fence. The garden greeted him with green foliage, bright buds, and fallen autumn leaves that crunched underneath his feet. I greeted him with silence barricaded within my childhood fort, still upset over the fight at the museum.

"Piper, can I come up to see you?" He waited patiently for an answer while holding the wooden ladder in his fists.

I waved him up. Quietly, he sat next to me looking up at the sky. His biceps twitched as he spun his helmet in the palm of his hand. "I'm sorry about the fight. The last thing I want—is to frighten you away. Are you alright?" He paused in deep thought, looked up at the sky once more, and changed the subject. "I didn't see you at school today."

"I didn't feel well, but I'm better now." I changed the subject back. "I hate that you two can't get along. It seems you guys bring out the worst in each other. I don't want anyone to get hurt."

"Have I hurt you?" he questioned softly. His concerned eyes scanned me for any sign of emotional havoc.

He had a way of seeing right into my soul; I quickly looked away and broke into a smile. "No, you didn't hurt me. I don't think it would be possible for you to ever hurt me," I responded. "Why is it I feel like I've known you all my life…like you're just a piece of me? But then again, you're this distant stranger wrapped in seclusion, not allowing me to find the real you."

With his arms folded, he gave a deep sigh and looked up to the night sky searching for answers he couldn't share with me. He was protecting something precious, something mysterious, something that time would only foretell, and it wasn't my place to yank it out of him.

"Hey, I have something for you. It's sort of an early birthday gift, but you can't open it until the morning of your birthday," Logan teased. I couldn't stop my desire to frisk him for the hidden item. "I don't have it on me." He caught my hands in his, not allowing me to continue my search. "It's not here."

"Then where is it?" I inquired. He continued to hold my hands in his, and I knew we shared some kind of bond not recognized by language alone. It was an invisible connection, threaded deep inside not confined to walls, windows, or of this world; I didn't even try to comprehend its significance. I just allowed him to walk me down the wooden ladder and onto his bike.

"I'll show you." He placed his helmet over my head, and I couldn't stop my cheesy smile from breaking through. He gently tapped on the helmet like he was knocking on a door. "You have to pay attention so you can find it again." His seriousness only made my cheesy smile cheesier, and he responded with a cute chuckle. The motorcycle jerked forward as I held on tight copying the route in my mind, counting the lefts, rights, hills, trees, and every other landmark leading up to his final destination.

Darkness covered the forest as the moon coasted in and out of the clouds. I counted the steps leading into the edge of the wooded area. Towering evergreen trees stood around us, but one was different. Two trees tangled as one stuck out among the others. The strange tree had a distinctive scar darkening the bark. Then I noticed my name carved lightly into the tree.

"My gift is a tree with my name carved into it?" I questioned with a little humor and a lot of skepticism.

"No, Piper, it's not the tree, but what's inside the tree," Logan vaguely replied.

"Is this a riddle? How do you expect me to get it out?" I continued to run my fingers over the discolored bark, looking for a way inside.

Logan smiled as he watched with great satisfaction, "Piper, you're missing the whole point. You won't be able to get it until your birthday. I just needed to show you how to find it. It's very important for you to remember this place no matter what is happening around you. Then you have to meet me at that chapel in the forest."

"Why do you want to meet there?" Flashbacks of Aiden and the wooden chapel flooded back. My heart sank from the secret shame. I was physically healed, but emotionally wounded. Without the covering of a scar, my heart was just left open to tear apart and bleed again and again. I hated that place. The place my mind would carefully tiptoe around—desperately, trying to avoid; I hated that place and hated feeling powerlessness even more.

"You'll know, soon. You said you trusted me. So tell me you won't forget," he demanded. Logan led me back down the pathway covered with pine needles and fallen leaves. I glanced back one more time taking a mental snapshot of the twisted tree, knowing I wouldn't see it again for a couple of months. "Piper, tell me you won't forget," he repeated with a sudden sense of seriousness.

It was definitely more than just a birthday gift. "I won't forget," I reassured him, but I wasn't sure I wanted to know what secret the tree held for me. The motorcycle's wheels spun up some of the loose dirt, and we traveled out of the forest.

In the distance, smoke clouds were forming, choking the starlight from the darkening night sky. "What happened?" I called out and pointed toward the smoldering debris, but Logan couldn't hear me over the motorcycle's engine. The burned smell in the night air filtered around us. Fire trucks and ambulances flew down the road with lights and sirens screaming. I turned back to watch as the lights scattered out into the distance. I wondered who was behind all the random fires breaking out around town.

Forester Sledge was locked up. I began to question if he was really the cause of the 2010 fires, or if he was set up like Johnny insisted. In the back of my mind, I speculated the possibility that the motorcycle thugs may be involved. These thoughts kept me company until we rode into my neighborhood.

Logan pulled up to my house and killed the engine. "You must think this is odd…me asking you to find your birthday gift inside a twisted tree?" he asked as he walked me toward the door.

"I wasn't thinking it odd. I was just thinking it's pretty amazing that you have that much faith in me to figure this birthday riddle out." I opened the door and started to walk inside. Then I turned back and called out, "Logan."

He stopped, turned, and answered with a smile.

"How did you know my birthday was coming up?"

He didn't reply, just started up the engine, waved, and drove off into the night.

Chapter Fifteen

Buried

Friday, Saturday, and Sunday came and went without precedence. I ignored Aiden's multitude of calls and texts. I spent my time napping away the minutes of my life counting down toward, Halloween, my favorite time of the year. Monday followed, and Aiden was there—everywhere at school apologizing, pleading for forgiveness.

Aiden Sinclair:
I'm sorry I upset you at the museum. I don't know what has come over me lately. The last thing I want to do is frighten you away. I would never hurt you, Piper. I hope you can forgive me.
Tuesday, 8:30 AM

Aiden Sinclair:
Come on, Piper. Meet me somewhere. I have to see you. I need you.
Tuesday, 10:15 AM

Aiden Sinclair:
I lost control and I'm sorry. I'm an ass. I'll never do it again.
Tuesday, 12:30 PM

Aiden Sinclair:
I looked for you at lunch. Where are you? Please talk to me, Piper.
Tuesday, 2:00 PM

I erased the messages and placed my phone back into my pocket. Aiden caught me off guard, and I startled when he approached me from behind.

"Piper," he whispered, and I felt his warm breath on the back of my neck as I stood at my locker.

I turned around and fell mesmerized by the amber flicker, dancing inside the turquoise center of his eyes. He touched my cheek, and I froze, forgetting the reason for being angry at him. Then it came back—his wild aggression.

"Aiden, you have to stop this. You can't lose your temper anymore. Sometimes, I don't even know who you are. You frighten me. It's like you're two different..." He placed his finger on my lips.

"I'm sorry. I'm so sorry, Piper. Please forgive me."

"You can't attack Logan. He's just a friend," I continued as I gathered my books from my locker, slammed it shut, and turned around once more to face him. "Don't you know by now—that all I ever wanted was you?" And then I walked away leaving him with something to think about.

Aiden yelled from a mere distance, "So, can I see you at the parade tomorrow?"

I nodded, "I'll be there," and then I disappeared into the sunshine outside. Before Tuesday was over, his beautiful turquoise eyes swallowed me up, charming me back to a place I knew I couldn't resist. I was lost in love and dazzled by his beauty.

Halloween fell on Wednesday, and I decide to skip school. A bitter sweetness stung deeply because it was my mom's birthday—I missed her madly. I wanted to visit her at the cemetery. It tended to freak Bailey out, but for me the cemetery felt like a tiny piece of heaven.

In my backyard, I sat swinging in the autumn morning breeze, anticipating the Halloween parade. The long branches above me swayed, and the leaves fell sticking to my hair. I drew lines in the sand with my toes. The cool sand reminded me of Mom and all the trips we took to various beaches collecting samples to take back home. Different textures and colors of sand mixed together with a few scattered shells, most of which had broken over time.

Ashland's Halloween parade and carnival was starting around five o'clock. I planned to spend a little time at the cemetery before going to the parade. Alice had inspired me to play a little in Wonderland.

Patrick was sleeping underneath a pile of covers on the couch. The TV cast an eerie blue glow upon the walls. I picked up the controller and changed the channel; it was a news brief of the mysterious fires sweeping through the surrounding towns, mimicking the Forester Sledge case. But the endless search for information was still unsuccessful.

He continued to snore underneath the mountain of blankets. I didn't wake Patrick, just wrote a note on the pizza box lying on the table near the couch.

Patrick,
Bailey is picking me up for the parade. Meet you at the Plaza. Don't eat the rest of the pizza in this box or you'll be SICK! Going to see Mom.
Piper

I dressed as Alice. It was fun being someone else, even if it was only once a year. Maybe Wonderland wouldn't be as bad as my so-called-life. I grabbed the quilt from the closet and headed out with a small picnic brunch packed into a basket with my sketchbook and pencils. I drove with the windows down allowing the crisp country air to circulate throughout the car.

The streets bustled with pedestrians in search of making a full day of the event. Crowds would flock the downtown area before the end of the night celebrating the fall festival. Patiently, I drove toward Ashland Cemetery dreaming the lazy morning away as I anticipated how the day would transpire.

My memories took me back to my seven-year-old self dressed in a blue Cinderella gown as I walked downtown holding tight onto my dad's hand. Crowds of smiling people playing dress-up surrounded me. Dress-up was my treasured passion as a child, and I hadn't yet outgrown it. I enjoyed the costumes flowing and jingling downtown at the Plaza. Dad tossed me up on his shoulders, and I sat on top of the world, free to see everything. My crystal ball revealed my world to me as I tapped my fairy wand into the glittery harvest air; I realized at that very moment—I had it all.

Little scruffy dogs and big dogs joined in wearing comical costumes led by their decorative leashes. The sweet smell of cotton candy and kettle popcorn wisped through the air with each passing breeze, and I tried desperately to find the source of the sweet vendors.

I made my way back to reality and through the arched entrance of Ashland Cemetery. The quilt and picnic basket were awkward to carry, but I managed to maneuver my way to her gravesite. The dirt settled and sporadic blades of grass broke through the earth in vibrant shades of green since the last time I was there. Tall trees stood all around me, proceeding over the passage of time. Branches with rustling leaves danced in the wind. I held onto a corner of the quilt and tossed the other end up into the air with a *snap*, and then I lowered it slowly to the ground near her. The picnic basket held the quilt in place as I sat down staring straight up into the blue sky above me. Wonderland encompassed me, and I silently soaked it all in.

Footsteps crunched dried leaves in the distance. The sunlight beamed down, and its brightness took my sight temporarily. My eyes squinted against the warm rays of sunlight. Someone was walking into the shade under the covering canopy of trees. I blinked trying to bring my vision back into focus.

"What are you doing out here?"

I recognized his voice. "Logan, how did you know I was here? Shouldn't you be at school?" I scooted over and offered him a place to sit on the quilt.

"I didn't feel like going today. It was a nice day for a ride, and then I saw your car. I drove by at first and then turned back." He placed his helmet down and found a place to sit. "Do you want company?"

I nodded and smiled. "Are you hungry?" I opened the basket and pushed it toward him. "I have some grapes and a sandwich if you want to share." I tore the sandwich in half and handed it to him.

"Thanks, Alice." He smiled, bit into the sandwich, and pointed to my dress.

"Oh yeah, I forgot I was dressed like this." I tugged at the dress to straighten it against the wind, and then I realized how dusty my black Doc Martens lace-up boots really were in the sunlight. "Are you going to the Halloween parade and carnival today?" I popped a couple of grapes into my mouth, and the bitter sweetness pinched deeply into my jaw.

"I heard it's a big event in Ashland," he raved. "I thought about checking it out."

"You should go," I announced and then paused, remembering the friction between the two. "I'm meeting Aiden up there; otherwise, I would invite you to come with us. Bailey is picking me up after school, and we're meeting up at the Plaza." I thought about the fight at the museum. "I talked to Aiden. He saw you as a threat, but I made him understand that...we're just friends. We are just friends, right?"

He hesitated, broke into a soft smile, and dodged my question. "How 'bout I keep some distance between us for now. Maybe I'll see you around town?"

"The parade gets crowded. You can still go *and* keep your distance. There's no reason for you to miss out on our town's celebration." I tossed the bag of grapes at him, and he caught it with one flawless swoop of his hand.

"Oh, don't worry. I don't plan on missing out."

"You never really answered my question, Logan," I fidgeted with my Alice dress and stared deeply into his eyes. I didn't want him to get the wrong impression—I was with Aiden and could only offer him my friendship. The silence, awkward at first, propelled me closer to him, and I felt an unplanned attraction between us.

Again he dodged the question, plucked the plump grapes from the small withered vine, and tossed them upward into his mouth, catching each one until the bag was empty. I admired his accuracy and welcomed anything to take my mind off the nightmares and visions haunting me.

He quickly changed the topic. "What's up with you today? You sit here surrounded by graves and tombstones having a picnic with death, dressed up as a character that's more lost than most fictional characters can become...Why are you here all alone, Piper?"

He looked more deeply into me than usual, and I felt compelled to tell him about the darkness consuming my mind. I took a breath, twisted my fists into the glittery fabric of my dress, and let the words flow like sand through an hourglass. Secrets fell from my lips, and the weights dropped one pound at a time, freeing me from their bondage. He silently listened to each word, taking it all in without judgment—without interruptions.

"A drunk driver killed my mom last year in a car accident. He took her away from me—from all of us. Sometimes, I pretend she's still alive, and when I start to forget the sound of her voice, I come here. I feel her all around me and can hear her—feel her. If I try really hard, I can see her off in the distance waiting for me."

"Times were dark after she died, but times were darker before…My dad kept it all a secret. I was the keeper of their secret, and now I feel like I'm asking you to be the keeper of mine. Once, my dad found her standing over me with a butcher knife chanting something strange; she claimed it was evil she was saving me from while I slept unaware of it all. She was hospitalized a few months after that and diagnosed with paranoid schizophrenia. She was fine for a while, but it always came back to take her. My dad hid this from everyone else to protect us, but now…" I paused and then whispered, "I think it's happening to me. I see things, hear things, and feel something breathing down my skin. I want to run from it, but I know it's impossible. How can I run from myself? It's hereditary, you know. I think, maybe, she passed it down to *me*. It would kill my dad; I can't possibly tell him."

Tears had built up in my eyes, and I fought to keep them from ruining a perfectly good coat of mascara, but I was unsuccessful. Large drops rolled down my cheeks, streaking my skin with darkness. My beautiful stranger listened quietly, and I continued where I left off.

"I believe something evil is after me. It sounds crazy to hear it out loud. I feel it growing closer. So, I just sit and wait for this inevitable darkness to snuff my life out with one quick blow. I'm scared all the time. Either way, it can't be a good outcome. I'm either going mad or—I'm way out of my league and can't possibly outwit these shadowy demons. I sit here as Alice waiting for the Mad Hatter to appear at my 'picnic of death,' as you call it. Do I go to the doctor and request some sort of magic potion to make this all disappear? Will this magic potion only make me smaller or more pathetic? I'm just looking for my rabbit hole, I guess, or maybe I've already fallen and don't know it yet."

He sat quietly, staring intensely into my eyes. I broke the stare and glanced down, but I could still feel him. The silence tortured me slowly, and my cheeks warmed in utter embarrassment of spilling my soul and serving it up as the picnic's main course.

"I don't think you're crazy," he whispered into the silence of the cemetery. His warm hand reached out and took my sweaty palm. "Evil is and has always been lurking around, waiting for a soul to twist. You're strong, Piper. Evil would be crazy to think it could outwit you. You're the strongest person I know. You don't have mental illness. You're a girl who lost her mother to a tragic accident and is hanging on desperately to life and memories while trying to make sense of it all. Alice isn't a silly little girl anymore. She's the young woman that slays the dragon, regaining her power. I have faith—when you find your dragon, it won't have a chance."

"Really, you don't think I'm crazy?" The tears welled up again and I sprang forward, embracing him.

"No, Piper. I don't believe you're crazy."

The songbird flew free from its rattled cage. But the darkness, it lurked in waiting as it has and always will.

Chapter Sixteen

Welcome To The Black Parade

"Will I see you around?" I asked Logan, but I already knew the answer—just needed a little confirmation that I hadn't scared him away. I wouldn't blame him for jumping onto his bike and riding far away from me—away from crazy, but he did the opposite. He leaned forward and gently pressed his forehead against mine. For a moment, I felt all my worries disintegrate into the quiet of the cemetery.

"I'll find you. Don't worry, Piper, I promise not to cause you any harm."

He walked away, fastening the helmet into the same worn notch, and then he was off. I stood for a few moments waiting for the dust to settle, and then turned to take another glance at the cemetery. Unknown to me, a small group of people had gathered around a fresh grave, and silence turned to sobbing. I was so wrapped up in my own drama that I didn't recognize the pain of others.

I sat in my car and reached for the drawing paper and pencils. Quickly, I sketched the lady kneeling by the grave, reaching out, begging and pleading with all the uncertainty of life, death, and everything else in between. A man with dark sunglasses shielding his eyes held her tight preventing her from falling onto the turned earth recently disturbed to bury the small child. The pencil stroked the paper, and lines created people in their most vulnerable state. They say time helps mend, but the hole never disappears. It just sits empty, hollow, and yearning for something to fill it up, but nothing will ever take the same shape. I glanced in the mirror and wiped the streaks of black from my cheeks.

I arrived home to an empty house. Bailey peeled into the driveway a few seconds later. "So, what do you think of Little Red Riding Hood now?" She toyed as she stood strikingly beautiful with a red hood covering her sleek black bodysuit. "We need to get going, Piper. Are you ready?" She examined me and then added blue hair gloss to a few strands of my hair, proclaiming it was almost like the costume was taking over...turning *me* into Alice.

We raced down the staircase, and her long black stockings sprinted ahead of me. It wasn't a competition at all; she was already down by the door before I reached the middle of the banister. I caught a glimpse of my drawing out of the corner of my eye. The front cover of the book was folded back exposing the sad cemetery lady, crying out for her child. I looked down at my Alice dress and wondered if that child ever had the chance to play dress up with Halloween costumes.

"Piper, are you coming? Didn't you hear me? I called your name like ten times."

"Yeah, I'm on my way." I grabbed my keys, closed the sketchbook, and headed out the door.

Bailey's Jeep trekked toward the plaza as crowds gathered in the street. Community spirit filled the air with homemade jack-o'-lanterns, goblins, and the sweet aroma of cookies and cupcakes. Halloween was definitely my favorite time of year. Costumes jingled and glitter dazzled us as Bailey and I creatively scored best in show for horror, funny, cute, and skanky.

"Piper!" Patrick stood tall in the crowd, waving us over.

We made our way through. All the guys had congregated nearby, talking football and girls. Ryder leaned against a small stone wall scrolling through his music with his ear phones pressed firmly into each ear. He wasn't into football or male bonding. His main interest, or I should say *only* interest, was Bailey. He tolerated the guys, and they always included him, but there was an invisible divide between them.

When the jocks parted, we saw a desperate looking Ryder digging through the crowd searching for his one true love. Bailey ran into his arms and kissed him openly. I'm not sure how because large, pointed, blood-stained fangs erupted from his lips. His costume was simply the fangs and a T-shirt that stated *WOLFMAN*. It was one of his favorite movies.

"Baby, I missed you," Bailey whispered seductively as she wiped her lipstick smear from his lips. He grabbed her around the waist and positioned himself closer to her.

Seeing Bailey and Ryder together only made me want Aiden more. I burned for him in a way I had never felt possible. I wanted to unravel allowing him to see me—all of me. I no longer wanted to hide behind the mask I carried. This sudden freedom sent chills down my spine. I wanted to tell Aiden everything—my feelings for him and my fears. I was no longer afraid of the blemishes in my life and refused to allow anything or anyone to stop me.

"Have you seen Aiden?" I asked my brother. "I thought he was coming up here with you guys."

"No, he said he had something to take care of first and would meet up with us later."

"Did he say what he had to take care of?"

"I'm not his mother, Piper. He didn't say, and I didn't ask," Patrick snapped.

I wanted to smack my brother across the face. Didn't he know how important it was that I find him? Patrick's sarcasm drove me over the edge, and *this* time I wanted to run him over. I sent a quick text to Aiden and then waited impatiently for a reply. I called, but it rang over to voicemail. The parade started, and the crowd roared, ready to go. I felt the back of my dress moving, but the wind wasn't blowing. I turned around, thinking Aiden had arrived teasing me, but when I spun around Jake stood there grasping a handful of my dress.

"What are you doing!" I yelled in disbelief, disgusted by the groping of one of Patrick's friends. I pulled the blue Alice dress from his overgrown paws and turned back around. All of the guys quietly stared at him in amazement.

"What?" Jake shrugged his shoulders.

Through the crowded streets full of fairytales, goblins, creatures of the night, and movie stars, I saw him staring straight into my direction. Aiden was nowhere to be found, but Logan stood patiently waiting to maneuver across the street. I waved at him, but I just looked like everyone else waving within the interactive crowd. A large group of Elvis impersonators blocked my view of Logan. Jailhouse Rock Elvis danced around with White Glitter Pantsuit Elvis and Blue Suede Shoes Elvis. Fat Side Burns Elvis waddled in front of me, and I jumped up and down in attempt to find Logan.

I felt something brush against the back of my dress. I reached around to slug Jake and his relentless stupidity, but lost my balance when I saw Logan standing in front of me.

"Hey, it's you," I babbled in surprise. "I saw you across the street, but then I lost you in the crowd of Elvis'. How did you get across so fast?"

"Piper, I told you I would keep my distance, but when I saw you standing alone—I had to stop by and see you." He smiled and glanced away, looking at the parade.

"What do you think of it all?" I questioned.

"It's interesting. Are *you* having fun, Alice?"

I nodded and answered with an unsure, "Yeah." Disappointment crept from my voice as I quickly checked my phone again for a text from Aiden—but nothing.

"I'm going to get a drink. Do you want something?" he asked as he pointed to the downtown shop with a long line waiting outside.

"Sure. I'll take a lemonade."

After Logan left, Bailey came to stand beside me. She was swaying side to side, obviously hiding something epically notorious. Anguish spread across her face.

"You don't want to see this, Piper. I know I can't keep it from you, but I thought I could soften the blow a little." I kept trying to break free to see what all the upset was, but she was faster than me.

"What are you saying? What's wrong?" Over her shoulder, I caught a glimpse of Aiden with Rachel locked inside an indescribable kiss. The crowd filled in around them, and I turned away in disbelief.

"I thought they were over," Bailey remarked. "This doesn't make any sense."

"He asked me to the fall dance, and now he's kissing *her*. How can he do that?" To my horror, I then saw Aiden making his way through the mob toward me. Blinded with rage, I wanted to run and hide, but I quickly decided to play along.

"Hey, beautiful. I'm sorry I'm late. I just had something I had to take care of."

"I bet you did," I muttered under my breath.

"Did you say something?" he questioned as he glanced around, probably looking for his precious Rachel.

"No, I'm glad you're here," I pretended, but Rachel's kiss ruined my plans of breaking free, offering myself up to a guy that continues to disappoint me. He reached down and held my hand. My mouth felt dry like the desert, and I couldn't think of anything except Logan and my lemonade.

Logan appeared carrying the plastic cup of lemonade, and the ice floated alongside the slices of lemon wedges. Cool beads of liquid condensation dribbled down the slick surface of the cup and dripped onto my boots. I finished it in fifteen seconds flat, and the straw caught a pocket of air between the ice cubes letting out a slurping sound.

"Wow, you're really thirsty," Logan replied as he sipped from his soda bottle. He offered me some of his, but I didn't want to come across as a real lush; so I motioned I was good. I watched as Aiden clenched his teeth and tightened his fist one at a time. I waited for him to explode, but he did the unthinkable—the opposite.

Aiden gave a weak smile and followed it with a difficult sounding, "Hey." He was keeping to his promise.

The parade continued down the street until it traveled out of sight. The sound of the marching band escorted the witches, ghouls, monsters, fairies, and other mystical creatures downtown. It was over, and I had to wait an entire year before I could see it all again. It didn't matter; the only impression left in my mind was the kiss between Aiden and Rachel.

"Oh my God, do you smell that? It smells incredible," Bailey remarked. She closed her eyes and inhaled the scent of all the fried carnie goodies.

Street vendors fired up their grease and began to prepare corn dogs and funnel cakes. Kettle corn popped inside the warm glass box, and the sweet and salty smell escaped each time the door opened to scoop out a box of the crunchy goodness. Fajitas, old-fashioned hamburgers, and gyros sizzled as they cooked atop hot grills down the street.

"I'm starving! I think I want one of everything," exclaimed Jake, and Patrick agreed.

After dinner, the sun settled in the night sky, turning day into dusk, and then the neon lights of the carnival lit up the night. Bright colors danced across the framework of games and rides, inviting patrons to exchange dollars for tickets. Game attendants beckoned people to come and win by tossing balls, shooting balloons, and throwing rings.

"Everyone's a winner!" they preached, and then enticed. "Don't you want to win this pretty lady a prize?"

The guys lined up and took aim at the targets, firing until every last balloon popped and was left to dangle against the pegboard. Prizes were awarded and small stuffed pets were collected. Somehow, they all ended up in my arms—and then I saw her. A young girl dressed as Cinderella reached out to touch the stuffed animals, and I kneeled down to offer them to her. She squealed in excitement.

"Come on, Ryder just bought a book full of tickets for some rides," Bailey replied as she grabbed my hand, leading me toward the roller coaster with sparks flying against the metal rails.

"Tell me again this is perfectly safe, Bailey." I tried to pull back, and then kept a watchful eye for any violations. But she pulled me harder toward the crazy, crash-worthy atrocity powered by a multitude of tangled cords taped to the ground.

"Stop being such a baby. Have some fun for a change!" Bailey chanted as she buckled me in. Up and down we rode the coaster as it clattered down the track, rattling the entire way. Bailey remarked how great it was and how she wanted to ride it next with Ryder. I couldn't wait to get off and have my feet back on solid ground.

Patrick and Jake were waved over by a couple of girls. Bailey and Ryder held hands and walked a few steps in front of me. Aiden walked to my right and Logan to my left; both competing in some strange attempt to lure me away from the other. The kiss between Aiden and Rachel seared inside my mind, leaving me burning with jealousy. I didn't think I could pretend that I was okay when my world was falling apart. I knew it was only a matter of time before I would erupt. My heart pounded in my chest, heat radiated across my skin, and my voice screamed out, "I saw you, Aiden!"

Bailey and Ryder turned around, stunned with wide eyes. Logan jumped to my rescue, but this time I wasn't in need of being saved. Bailey pulled him away allowing me a chance to confront Aiden about the *thing* he still had with Rachel.

"I saw you kiss Rachel. I don't understand. Why are you playing me?" I shouted into the noisy crowd, filtering in around us. Aiden reached for my hand, and I shoved him back.

"Piper, it's a huge misunderstanding." He paused for a second as if he regretted the answer that would come next. "I know it sounds weak, but she kissed me, and I pushed her away. You didn't see everything. I swear. I promised that I would never hurt you. She means nothing to me. You—you are *my everything*."

With tears in my eyes, I replied, "That is your answer: You're blameless—it was all a misunderstanding! Really, do you think I'm that stupid?"

"Piper…" He reached out again to hold me, and I reacted, hitting him in the chest over and over. He didn't even budge. "Please believe me," he pleaded.

"I don't know what to believe or trust anymore." I stepped back allowing the crowd to come between us and ran away blending in with the carnival surrounding me.

A flickering light caught my attention, and I walked toward it. A glass box stood underneath the light with one of those antique porcelain fortune-tellers inside. The creepy doll dressed in Gypsy clothing stared at me with eerie green eyes—knowing something, but refusing to tell. I leaned against the box decorated in brass and gemstones and searched through the packed carnival for my friends, hoping they wouldn't find me. I desperately wanted to lose myself for a little while. The box rattled at first, and then the doll moved into animation; even though, I hadn't put in any money. Awkwardly, the jingle of her fringed outfit with ruby beads clashed against her porcelain body. Then her deep voice carried through the small slits within the glass.

"You have come to me for your fortune. *I* am Madame Esmeralda. Are you ready for your fortune to be foretold? Happiness or sorrow—I bestow upon you—your fortune." She laughed a harsh, wicked laugh that repeated and paused erratically.

Then the small window opened, shooting my fortune card upon the ground. I knelt down, to pick up the card and watched Madame Esmeralda's face as her eyelids fluttered. The box blinked off and on, and then her distorted voice slurred into a sudden stop. I glanced down at the card.

I sat quietly on a bench under the cover of darkness, trying to hate Aiden. But even after that—it was impossible. It crushed me into pieces, allowing this guy to have so much control over me. I dried my tears, took a breath, and waited for something to save me.

Madame Esmeralda's

Fortune Telling Cards:

Do Not Fear The Darkness.
Let The Darkness Fear You.

SECRETS STAB AT YOUR SOUL.
FIND A WAY TO BREAK FREE!

Another flickering light caught my eye about ten feet away. An attendant sat near the entrance of the hedge labyrinth. It was a garden maze with twists, turns, and narrow passageways that puzzled most and frustrated many. Currently, it was closed due to a lighting problem. A soft voice came from behind me, calling my name. A child's singsong voice called out to me: "Pi-per." I walked toward the entrance and stepped inside while the attendant, covered with tattoos, drank coffee and flirted with a few girls.

The lights flickered off and on, casting shadows onto the hedge. I walked inside the darkness, listening for the small voice. Lacy white socks and shoes exposed themselves underneath the green hedge along with the light blue hem of her Cinderella dress. I called to her, but she ran into the maze. I followed close behind. Two of the stuffed animals sat to the side of the pathway, and I knew it was the same little girl.

The maze led me farther into darkness as the moonlight fell upon us in fragments. The carnie sounds and lights drifted away, and I found myself in dark silence. The end of the maze opened into a quiet field. To one side was a tractor with hay to pull people back to the carnival after finishing the labyrinth. The field was surrounded by trees, and the smell of carnie foods was quickly replaced by pine, spruce, and recently baled hay. I called out to the little girl, but she didn't answer.

I walked toward the bales of hay that sat on the ground near the tractor as she played a secret game of hide-and-seek. A small field mouse ran in front of me, and I jumped back, releasing a terrified scream. Deep, jarring laughter reverberated across the field. Out in the middle of the meadow stood a tall man dressed in black pants and an unbuttoned black dress shirt. His dark hair fell in natural waves to the top of his shoulders. His chiseled facial features were strikingly beautiful, but the darkness in his eyes sold him out. Evil—irrevocable malice embodied in human form stood before me, and I could only shiver secretly as I felt compelled to walk toward him.

Out in the middle of nowhere, the little girl stood wearing the blue Cinderella gown. I watched in shock as he squeezed her arm tightly in his fist. She struggled to get away, but it only made his grip stronger and his facial expression more violent.

"Let her go!"The words came out of my mouth fierce and empowering. I couldn't believe it came from me. But within seconds, my black Doc Martens seemed to shiver as I walked right into combat. I looked down, realizing how silly I looked with my blue locks intermingling with my blond hair and the Alice dress shimmering against the moonlight. How was I going to free this child? I didn't know, but I kept walking toward them and stopped just a couple feet away.

"I said, let her go!"This time my words trembled a little, and my vulnerability displayed itself for his mere pleasure and opportunity.

He opened his mouth and a horrific roar bellowed from his throat, shaking the ground underneath my feet, "PERDITUS!" The beautiful man quickly transformed into a beast. Then he unfolded his unearthly long finger, pointing it right at me as he repeated with a wicked whisper, "Perditus."

"Piper—run!" A little voice carried from the lips of this small child broke the silence and angered the man. He forced her in front of him, covering her mouth with his large hand; it practically covered her entire face. As he lifted her off the ground, her feet dressed in patent leather Mary Jane's madly kicked at the fogging air. With no grand plan, I lunged toward them, grabbing her from his hands. We rolled to the ground, holding on tight to one another. The eyes of the beast turned golden-amber as he dispersed into a million dark fragments, vanishing into darkness.

"Who was that? And how do you know my name?" I demanded, but the little girl sat still and without response. Physically shaken, I made my way up off the ground and took her by the hand. "Where are your parents, and why did you come out here all alone?"

"But I'm not alone, am I?" she confidently answered.

"We have to get out of here before he comes back," I instructed.

"I can't go with you, Piper. I have to stay on this side." She pulled away from my sweaty palm and spun around like a ballerina in her glittering blue Cinderella dress.

That's when I noticed it: a small stitch repaired a torn area to the hem. I knew this dress. I'd had a Cinderella gown with a tear near the hem. My mom had cross-stitched it multiple times in the same location. With my finger, I felt the stitching from the hem upward. The little girl watched in anticipation, wanting me to figure it out. I looked into her eyes, and it finally knocked me back a few steps. I realized it, but how could this be true? She was...*me*.

"There's not much time. You have to follow your heart and find your way. Everyone is counting on you, Piper. Love isn't ordinary; it transcends even the smallest of creatures. Tonight you stood up for yourself— for me." She reached inside my pocket, pulling out the fortune card and handed it back to me. And then the little girl dressed as Cinderella pulled me down to my knees and whispered into my ear, "Don't go into the darkness."

"What does he want with us?" I questioned.

"He said you're lost—that you don't know who you are. And he doesn't understand why you don't know him. That makes him really angry." She spun around, pirouetting as the blue gown flowed with each movement, and then she disappeared.

"Wait!" I yelled out as I spun around searching for the little girl.

A sudden howl pierced the night, jerking me back into reality. And within seconds, others joined in. A pack of something was charging through the forest toward me. I turned and ran into the labyrinth, praying I would find my way through. It seemed I traded my Mary Jane's for a pair of Doc Martens and knew a battle had begun. The sound of wolves or wild dogs stampeded the soft ground behind me. Darkness slowly transitioned into small moments of light. The flickering light overhead damaged by the faulty transducer propelled me forward. The carnival sounds whispered in the distance, and I ran toward them. The aroma of battered and fried carnie favorites poisoned my nose, but I continued to breathe it all in. *Almost there*, I thought.

Out of nowhere, sharp claws punctured the hedge slicing into my arm. The wolf was trapped on the other side, but it continued to jab its large head into the hedge, trying to find a way through. Plunging forward, I threw myself out of the labyrinth, knocking over the attendant. My landing caught him off guard and blasted his black-framed glasses off his face. I was out. I was alive. Fear stricken, with his eyes wide with trepidation, he got up slowly. I handed him his glasses and assisted the jostled man with tattoos and piercings to his feet as the transducer kicked on, forcing a steady bright light onto the labyrinth.

"Looks—looks like we're back in business," he stuttered, and customers began to line up with tickets in hand.

I stood speechless, waiting for the creatures to find their way out of the maze and back into my life. Bailey called my name from a distance, and before long she was standing beside me. "Piper, where have you been? I've been looking all over for you. Didn't you get any of my texts?" She paused for just a moment to catch her breath, and then the interrogation began again. "Where's Aiden? Did you get an answer about what he was doing with Rachel?"

I stared into her eyes unable to speak. Blood dripped from my arm and fell onto the ground. Bailey jumped into action when she saw the puddle of blood pooling near my feet.

"What happened to your arm?" She inspected the claw marks. "We need to get you cleaned up. I have a first-aid kit in my car. Hey, Patrick, tell Ryder we're going to get Piper a Band-Aid." Patrick nodded and continued talking among his circle of friends.

"How did this happen, Piper?" Bailey questioned again as we walked to the car.

We passed by a few men, preaching about the end of the world. With their Bibles lifted, they pleaded for people to ask for forgiveness and prepare for the end. Curiously, I walked toward the shouting men. I wasn't sure if it was out of hope or sudden desperation, but I felt compelled to find answers.

Bailey pulled me back, and I stumbled toward her car. She repeated and emphasized each word, "Piper, how—did—this—happen?"

My raspy voice mumbled, "I must have brushed against something sharp in the hedge."

"Did you already go into the labyrinth? I thought it was closed because of the jacked-up lighting." Bailey continued to talk as she cleaned my arm. Her lips kept moving, but I couldn't focus on what she was saying. "Are you OK? Hello, Earth to Piper! Are you even listening to me?"

I nodded and whispered, "Yeah, I'm fine. I think I'm ready to go home now."

Bailey yelled out to Patrick as he stood nearby in the parking lot, "Patrick, I'm driving Piper home." Bailey then waved at Ryder and gestured that she would call him later. She tossed the small box of bandages in the back, and we drove off. I sat quietly in the car looking into the edge of the forest for the darkness hidden within the shadows and wondered if the secrets would someday set me free or drive me mad.

Chapter Seventeen

Music Of The Night

A couple of days had passed since the carnival. I forced the kiss and Aiden's explanation from my mind just in time to get ready for the fall dance. It was tradition in Ashland for this dance to take place the Saturday following Halloween. It was crazy busy with everyone running mad putting together the last-minute preparations. The art students designed backdrops creating the mood of an old opera house with a Victorian setting. Several props had been saved over the years from previous plays and fit into our scene well.

It felt good to be busy. I didn't spend all my time focused on Aiden, Logan, and the craziness inside my head. I ran from one place to another helping with art design, music, lighting, table decorations, and any other final touches. The caterers came and unloaded shiny silver buffet carts, heating elements, and boxes of sorted supplies and food. My nose caught the aroma of rosemary potatoes and wood-oven-roasted chicken, awakening my stomach from a state of starvation. I threw the thought out of my head, swallowed the accumulating saliva watering my mouth, and continued my work.

"Piper, can you help with the tablecloths and centerpieces?" Mr. Gables handed me a box of white starched tablecloths and pointed over to the cart with vases of flowers near the corner of the gym.

The teachers and staff dressed like fancy waitstaff from a classy restaurant to serve our dinner. Mr. Gables, my calculus teacher, was a tall, thin man with large black-rimmed glasses weighing heavy on his face. He actually looked handsome apart from his usual loose Dockers, striped shirt with pocket protector, and gray Nike's. I guess he was functional in his world of numbers, equations, proportions, and statistics. Comfort must have been his one and only quest, and he pulled it off inconspicuously.

I covered each table with the stiff white cloth. Black, white, and red satin ribbons were tied around each chair back, and the vases were filled with black marbles, white calla lilies, and deep red roses. The catering company set each table with china, silverware, and glasses. Time got away from me, and I still needed to get dressed. Patrick had dropped off my festering pink frock in the girl's locker room since I wouldn't have time to get ready at home.

While I completed the table arrangements, Bailey called my phone and left a vague message.

Piper, if you haven't started yet, then you need to get ready. I had to leave early to get one last item. I'm sure everything looks great. Just make sure you put in the same amount of effort getting yourself ready. I picked up something for you. I'll meet you in the locker room at 5:45. Don't leave without seeing me first.

It was already five o'clock, and people one by one vanished from the scene to get ready for tonight. I placed the last vase on the table and turned around to take it all in. The seating area shimmered against the warm, flickering candlelight. Burgundy carpet covered the gym floors to prevent scratches and damage. A golden carpet led the pathway toward the dance floor. Small trees wrapped in twinkling white lights turned the gym into a magical experience. A small area near the dance floor was set aside for the band. Our school had hired a band from Southern Oregon University.

I rushed off to the locker room to take a quick shower. My stomach felt queasy at the thought of the pink dress. And my heart pounded an unfamiliar beat inside my chest. Aiden and Logan would be arriving in style, and I felt fear digging holes through my vital organs.

I reluctantly stepped out of the shower and wrapped the warm towel around my body. I noticed my iPod lying on top of the countertop with a small note instructing me to push play. I scrolled through my playlist and noticed that *Phantom of the Opera* had recently been added to my collection.

"Bailey," I whispered into the silent room. I sheepishly tiptoed into the dressing room and jumped out to surprise her. She wasn't there. No one was.

I placed the ear-buds in my ears, pressed play, and "Music of the Night" began. I passed a black satin bag hanging on the hook in place of my white bag. *What is this?* I thought. Before I could unzip the zipper, a small pink note fell onto the floor. I knelt down and picked it up. Bailey's handwriting marked the front of the envelope. I tore it open and read it out loud.

Piper,
I told you I wouldn't let you show up in that awful pink dress.
Love, Bailey

The garment bag was marked as property of OSU Theater Company, and I continued to pull the zipper down, holding my breath in anticipation. It was the dress Christine had worn while singing "Think of Me" from *Phantom of the Opera.* Beaded starbursts of silver and gold decorated the flowing gown. It was beautiful like a fairytale falling to Earth, right into my locker room. I felt time breathing down my neck, and once again I rationalized my ability to get myself together in time to pull this off.

The door to the dressing room creaked open slightly, and it caught my eye. I wasn't alone anymore. "Hello," I called out. "Bailey, is that you?"

The door swung open wide, and there she stood, strikingly glamorous as always. The black sequined gown fit her curves as if it had been made just for her. She looked out of place standing in bad lighting graced by dingy lockers chipped of paint. The stale air had turned to jasmine and soft roses from the subtle scent of her perfume.

"You look amazing!" I exclaimed. "And I love your gift. I can't believe you got it. You outdid yourself this time."

"Uh, why aren't you dressed? It's almost six o'clock, Piper. What have you been doing?" Bailey continued to dramatize as she ran around the dressing room, plugging in the hair dryer and curlers. Then she gathered makeup and hair spray from my bag. Her black stilettos tapped against the tile floor as she glided like a fashion model on a catwalk.

Bailey blew strands of my hair from the root outward, adding volume. I'd never known I had this much hair. She pulled it all back into a clip to work with later. Magically, she blended in my makeup and finished off my features. My eyes sparkled, surrounded by the golden color she'd painted onto my lids. She dusted my cheekbones with a peachy-pink powder. Satin lipstick rolled across my lower lip first and then across the top. I pressed my lips together and checked the color in the mirror. The reflection looking back at me was impressive. Maybe I could pull this off.

Everything was completed except for the gown. Saving the best for last, I guess. I slid into the gown and heels, feeling like Cinderella at the ball. Hopefully, it wouldn't fall to pieces at midnight. I slowly stepped out and stood in front of the mirror waiting for her to recognize me. I patiently watched as Bailey packed up the beauty supplies. She dropped the brush in the sink, and it circulated a few times before hitting the drain stopper. Other than that, silence filled the room. When she turned around, her mouth dropped open, and then she broke into applause with her two dainty hands.

"Logan and Aiden will be stunned when they catch a glimpse of you," Bailey proclaimed. "I actually feel a little sorry for them." Bailey paused a moment and then gently spoke, "*Such stuff as dreams are made on.*'" If there were ever a time to quote Shakespeare, then today would be the day.

"*To be or not to be,*'" I returned with hesitation. "I'm so nervous. What am I doing? I'll never be able to pull this off. I don't even recognize the girl staring back at me through the mirror," I worried. "My outside doesn't match my inside. They'll see right through me."

She reached out and held my hand. "You know, you look just like her."

"Who?" I questioned too quickly, and then I knew she meant Mom. I missed her, and she was missing all of this—my life.

Bailey pulled out her masquerade mask and flashed it in front of me. "Where's yours?" she asked, digging through my bag with her back turned.

"You mean—this masquerade mask?" I held it up to my face and winked at her.

"Are you ready to make your appearance?" she asked as she squeezed my hand one last time. I nodded because the words felt trapped in my throat, swelling from fear of the uncomfortable awkwardness of being on display for everyone to see. My skin felt tight. I wanted to unzip it and crawl out.

We walked to the gym. Bailey opened the door with a quick push, and a cool breeze blew across my skin. The room was lit by soft candlelight, and couples danced swaying to the beat, with their feathers, masks, and gowns waving in a stunning array of colors. Aiden and Logan eyed me through the crowd of masqueraders. Their strides were equally steady and swift as they approached from opposite corners of the room. Aiden, dressed in black as the Phantom of the Opera, held his eerie white mask in one hand, and Logan wore a Victorian era black tuxedo; surely, picked out by Bailey.

In the center of the room, I caught a glimpse of Rachel standing with a dumbfound look upon her face. Her jaw parted, and her hand fell to her side, dropping her glass of red punch. The glass fell and rolled toward me, but I didn't take my eyes off her. It was obvious she wanted me dead a thousand ways and would steal Aiden's kiss to provoke me.

The guys appeared simultaneously before me and then realized they would have to share my attention. However, all I could see was Rachel's piercing stare as she gathered her dress in one hand and ran out of the room in a violent tantrum.

I glanced at Bailey as she danced close to Ryder with her head resting softly on his shoulder. Then I smiled and took a deep breath, bringing me back to the two guys standing in front of me. Suddenly, Coach Sheppard appeared and pulled Aiden aside to run over a play or two for the next football game. He pulled a small, crinkled book from his back pocket, coerced Aiden in friendly conversation, and led him away to a well-lit corner of the room. Aiden kept glancing up at what he was missing with a displeased expression written harshly across his beautiful face.

The band began to play "All I Ask of You" from *Phantom of the Opera*. Logan took my hand and led me to the dance floor without words. The floor cleared, and only a few couples remained, inspired by this classic piece. Bailey and Ryder held each other tightly and melted into the music. Her black gown looked glamorous against Ryder's quirky tuxedo paired with one of his original black T-shirts with the words *This Is It* written across the front. And he sported it with one white sequined glove.

I reached my arms around Logan's broad shoulders and touched the back of his neck with my fingertips. Again, I had the feeling of knowing him from somewhere in my past. I looked deep into his eyes and felt his yearning to tell me something—something important, but his words seemed trapped in a secret. Time felt frozen, and his touch felt warm against my skin. A small piece of heaven must feel a bit like this. The song ended too soon, and Aiden cut in for the next dance, "Phantom of the Opera." Logan bowed out graciously.

Aiden's dance was different—harsh, emotional, and passionate. The dance floor crowded with people, pushing me closer to him. The lighting turned red, and the fog machine thickened the air around us. As if a supernatural spell trapped me, his mystery enticed a dark desire in me that I couldn't fight off—nor did I want to. His grasp of my hand felt firm and controlling as he led me forcefully around the dance floor. I didn't understand the intensity of my feelings: desire mixed with fear. I felt danger like I had when I was with Aiden in the chapel, but at the same time I was more attracted to him than ever. I felt his allure overwhelming me, forcing all my previous doubts out of my head.

My beaded mask had untied itself during the powerful dance with Aiden. It fell to the floor, knocking off one of the rose stones. Aiden reached down and retrieved the stone and the mask. The irresistible connection he held over me snapped when he released my hand. I felt dazed, dizzy, and somewhat confused.

"Thank you for the dance," I whispered into the foggy air. And then I stepped back trying not to look into those turquoise eyes that would only pull me under again. "I'll be right back. I'm going to glue this back on." He reached out for my hand, but I pulled away clinging to my mask and stone.

"You don't really need that mask. Stay with me," he whispered.

The boy I knew had grown into a powerful man overnight, it seemed. I couldn't think straight or make any sense of these extreme feelings, leaving me blinded and out of control. "I'll be back," I shyly stated and headed out the door before I had the chance to fall back into his wonders. I walked by Bailey and Ryder sitting at the table. The servers were carrying food out on large silver platters.

"Piper, where are you going? Dinner is being served. Come sit down." Bailey patted the seat beside her.

I shook my head. "I have to glue this bead on my mask first."

"Dude, did you see Rachel pour punch all over the place when she saw you come in?" Ryder reviewed. "Spectacular! It was priceless. Some guy overheard her friends talking about the ugly dress you were going to wear tonight. Something tells me you selected something else to wear. I think she would have swallowed her teeth if they weren't attached to her gums." Ryder continued to laugh, reliving the whole event in its entirety.

Weird—for such a quiet guy, he had a lot to say about Rachel and her misfortune.

Bailey didn't make any comment, but winked at me as I walked toward the art room to find some glue to repair my mask.

The door to the art room was locked, but the janitor's closet was open, and I peeked inside for something to attach the stone. Then it happened. A blow to my head knocked the tiara out of my hair and onto the ground. I reached back, touching my scalp, but it felt numb. Something ran down my back, and I reached back again to see what it was. Bright red blood covered my hand.

My vision went hazy, and I turned to see a fuzzy image of Rachel. She had a crazed look in her eyes, and then she knocked the light out with the bloody broomstick. Pieces of warm glass sprinkled down on top of me as I fell to the floor in the dark. The door slammed shut and locked from outside. I was trapped, and I drifted in and out of consciousness.

Memories flooded back out of sequence. Reality lost itself, and the dreams felt real. My mom knelt over me.

"It's time, sweetheart. Wake up. Time won't wait for you. Prepare yourself. It's coming for you! Piper…Piper, *get up!*" she rang out.

I opened my eyes, but she was gone again. "You're not here, Mom. You're dead. This isn't real. It's not real. You're not real."

Clips of memories and visions kept coming—Patrick playing ball, Dad sitting in on a conference call, Bailey dancing with Ryder, Logan and Aiden fighting. They fought ferociously with powerful fists and bloodied bodies. It was the worst fight I had ever seen. Church bells chimed, and I woke for a few seconds with ringing in my ears. Then I fell back into a nightmare. The chapel was in the distance, and I ran toward it—the same chapel Aiden had taken me to that crazy night he attacked me.

Fierce flames shot out miles high in the sky, catching all the trees ablaze. The sound of destruction surrounded me, and I felt trapped deep within the thickness of its solitude. Within a blink, I was transported to downtown Ashland, where the smell of death circulated around me. Tornados ravaged town and countryside. Earthquakes shook the ground, pulverizing buildings, homes, and churches. Large cracks split pieces of the earth in half, engulfing cars and people. Thunder pounded my ears. Lightning chased me in various directions. I dodged the remnants of Lithia Park, Mom's favorite place, as I fled for my life. Flowers, trees, and shrubs, ripped clean from the garden, still held dirty roots intact. Fountains burst and spewed water straight up into the air. I ran faster with each step, fearful of what I saw. Screaming sadness echoed an overwhelming feeling of loss. I couldn't fathom the pain and suffering all around me, and then—it stopped.

Time felt hollow and moved at a different speed. I stood in front of the Elizabethan Stage. All the actors of *Hamlet* gathered around dressed in full costume. Did they not see all the annihilation around them? The acting continued, and it wasn't a rehearsal. The audience sat behind me laughing and thoroughly enjoying the play. Nothing made any sense. I just wanted to wake up from this nightmare. The smell of fire traveled closer to us, and the winds blew horizontal.

I tried yelling at the crowd to leave, "Run! Don't look back. Just go!" Nothing came out of my mouth; my voice was stolen. I was a mime dressed in full face paint and suspenders. They were all laughing; I was part of the act. Helplessly, I waved my arms, pointing at the storms and the fires coming straight for them. Then something even more unusual happened.

Everything went still, frozen in time. The disaster movie in my head paused, and stillness covered our world. Towns, cities, and wildlife stood motionless. Ocean waves ceased, and the salty water caps turned to shimmering glass. Total calm and tranquility filled the world around me. However, I walked around able to observe this strange place—a new world eternally preserved like a tragic museum of horrors. Chilling thoughts of incredible doubt rushed over me. I sat down and sobbed into my hands while the smoke and flames grew closer. It was out of my control. There wasn't anything else I could do. I reached my hands out to the smoky heavens above me and yelled into the face of God. This time the words did come out. A loud roar of conviction toppled out from the dry air within my lungs.

"What the hell is happening? Do you see? Can't you see us? Why aren't you helping me make them see? Do you even care about us at all? What do you want from me?" My voice cracked, and the tears I swallowed burned the back of my throat. I wrathfully ran about the stage, screaming like a lunatic at the one being that could instantly spark out my existence, but it didn't matter. God didn't even care enough to take me out of my misery.

I fell to the ground, feeling beat down from emotional turmoil. I felt the blood in my muscles drain leaving me limp—almost lifeless. I sat on the stage looking up at the sky. Passively, I waited for the world to end and take me with it. Smoke filled the sky and burned my eyes, but I couldn't produce another tear to save my life. The inferno of the fires coming for me approached. I sat up and leaned forward, holding onto the whimsical wrought-iron gate at the edge of the stage. The metal sent a charging force through my skin, causing the tiny hairs on my neck to stand up straight, and a tingling sensation soothed my sadness. Then a jolt of energy knocked me several feet backward into the thick air. I fell in slow motion crashing head first into the props of *Hamlet*, but before I hit—something wonderful happened.

Everyone came back to life. Time broke free and began to tick, slowly at first, and then with precision. The actors stood stunned in disbelief, not remembering their parts. They clamored to find a way into the next scene. The audience was just a few seconds behind—because time had caught them, too. Stillness transitioned back to life as if nothing had ever happened. Smoke blew out of sight, and blue evening skies returned. The raging fires in the distance disappeared into a sunset, blazing a ball of burnt-orange overhead. I picked myself up and stepped off the stage, backing away cautiously, and everything seemed back in its place, except for me. I wandered down Pioneer Street, trying to find my way back home. The destruction had been erased, but I still felt damaged. No one should ever have to see or feel what I had.

A young couple came toward me, holding hands and smiling. I couldn't quite make out their faces. They walked hand in hand, swinging their arms in motion with each step. Sweet small talk erupted from their lips. He handed her a red rose, and she placed it in her long, shiny hair. They passed me, and I gently looked the other way. But she turned back to me and continued to walk carelessly backward, calling my name.

"Piper, it's time. Wake up, but don't forget. Love—it transcends us all." She clapped her hands twice, smiled at me, and everything turned white.

A teacher must have noticed blood pooling from underneath the door and unlocked the knob to discover the source.

I could hear her scream, "Piper, Piper, please wake up! Can you hear me? Someone call an ambulance. She's lost a lot of blood."

Next, Bailey cradled me in her arms and begged, "Piper, please open your eyes. You have to be OK. Why isn't someone doing something!" she yelled.

"What happened?" Aiden knelt down, and I could hear the depth in his voice, but I couldn't find my way through the white room.

I felt Logan's presence as he pushed his way inside and knelt down beside my friends. "Hold on, Piper. Follow my voice. Find your way back—find your way back to me," he implored.

Sitting in the corner of a room stuck inside my nightmare was a figure dressed in black. She turned her face up at me and smiled. It was Rachel. Blood trickled out of the corner of her mouth, and she wiped it away. She stroked an odd shaped necklace wrapped around her neck, twirling it back and forth. The colors circulating within the pendant lured me in for a moment. Then I noticed dried blood covering her hands as she spun the broken broomstick on the floor beside her. I walked carefully in the direction of Logan's voice. Standing in the doorway to the other side, I glanced back at her one last time. She was gone, and the wooden broomstick slammed down, smacking the ground with a sharp *thud*. My eyes opened, and clarity came back to me within a few seconds. Bailey caressed my hair as I rested in her lap. Aiden and Logan sat on the bloody ground near me. A crowd of faces looked down with expressions of fear. Wheels of the gurney squealed down the hallway and stopped in front of the doorway. Everyone was ordered out except Bailey, who refused to leave my side.

The room went dark again, and I woke up in a hospital room the next day. Rain fell against the windowpane, and thunder broke softly. I could hear my dad outside in the hallway talking to a doctor. Bailey slept in the chair near my bed. Her black formal gown soaked with blood hung on the bathroom door. Her sequined gown had been replaced by blue hospital scrubs, and I watched her sleep curled up in the chair against the wall as the rain poured a symphony of music outside.

Chapter Eighteen

Wicked Game

My concussion healed quickly after a few days of rest and painkillers. It was determined that I slipped on the scattered beads from my masquerade mask, but no one could explain the locked door. Rachel found an alibi, and I only remembered slivers of distorted memories locked up deep inside my bruised mind. But I knew she had something to do with it. Her wicked smile wrapped across her smug face gave the impression of only holding evil inside by her clenched jaw and bleached white teeth. Eventually, her mouth got her into trouble. A teacher overheard Rachel bragging about hitting me with a broomstick and locking me inside the closet at the dance. Three days of suspension and community service only angered her more.

Windy November days blew into cold November nights, ripping pages off the calendar turning day into night and night into day. No one had control over time or its relentless ticking toward the unknown. I thought of Johnny Sledge, his belief of the world coming to an end, and the possibility that something evil was released in Ashland. Or could it be possible that I was going crazy and none of this was real? I googled schizophrenia over and over again hoping I would not suffer the same condition as my mom.

I just wanted my teenage life back, not worrying about the future, just the moment. I dreamed of my first love, my first kiss, my first embrace, and all the other firsts I wanted to come and find me. I wanted to surround myself in happiness, love, and laughter. I just wanted to turn *seventeen*. Cynicism lewdly flipped the middle finger at my sweet Pollyanna outlook on life; I once had. So I pulled my rose colored glasses over my eyes and waited for the chance to blow out the candles on my birthday cake. I wasn't ready to go quietly into the night. And Logan's secret birthday gift rattled around my mind, enticing me to dream of what it might be.

It was the weekend before Thanksgiving, and we were ready for school break. Dad's business called him out of state again, and he wouldn't be back until Thanksgiving Eve. Marcella, our housekeeper turned spy, checked on us daily. Dad carried a suitcase full of shirts, slacks, socks, and ties. But no pocket or zipper could contain the missed Monday night family dinners, Tuesday afternoon errands, Wednesday night movies, Thursday evening PTA, or Friday night high school football games. Days just continued to fall off the calendar to the sound of elevator music as he cruised from place to place riding in cabs and up escalators going nowhere.

Sunday afternoon, I sat on the wooden dock at Aiden's house waiting for him to return. Staring out into the water, I watched ripples gently spin the surface as small turtles peeked up at me, momentarily escaping their private water world. A few speckled ducks tucked their heads into their feathered backs, dozing underneath the bright sun. The sound of the water lapping against the wooden platform calmed me, as a cool breeze blew over my skin. I listened to my iPod, leaned back against the wooden planks, and waited for Aiden.

Since the dance, a spiritual awakening had opened a door, deepening our relationship. Lost for words, I couldn't explain how I loved and desired to be with him every second of every day. We had spent hours together, swaying in the hammock near the pond in his backyard, picnicking at Lithia Park underneath the willow tree, and cuddling below the night sky watching Shakespeare from the Elizabethan Stage. Many memories kept me company as I waited for Aiden.

Tree branches swayed overhead. Shadows mingled with pieces of sunlight and danced the tango upon me. The sky was painted a darker shade of blue through my sunglasses. I closed my eyes and thought of the turtles paddling around the pond and entertained the idea of what it would be like to live on land and within the water. What endless possibilities if I could be an equal part of both worlds?

A dense shadow hung over me, and I opened my eyes to see Aiden kneeling down on the dock. His eyes sparkled like the turquoise water in the pond. He leaned in for an upside-down kiss, and my topsy-turvy world spun along the ripples coasting, floating, and bobbing up and down.

"How long have you been waiting?" he asked as he sat down and leaned against the wooden beams decorated with spider webs bending and swaying in the breeze.

"I've been waiting my whole life." The corny line fell from my lips without any foresight or hesitation.

"Well, I don't want to keep you waiting any longer." He twisted a strand of my hair between his fingers. "Do you want to take that canoe ride I promised you?" He pointed to the red canoe turned over on the rack.

"I would love to!" I sprang up, nearly falling into the water.

We climbed inside the narrow boat, and Aiden pushed it away from the shore with a couple of wooden paddles. The ripples changed their course, spinning the opposite direction. The ducks fluffed their feathers after dipping under the cool water. Fallen autumn leaves drifted onto the water's surface and floated beside us. I watched Aiden's muscles contract in his arms with each stroke of the paddle, and the canoe glided easily over the water.

"It's so beautiful out here. I just want time to take it all in." I paused for a few seconds. "Aiden, do you ever wonder, if this will be the last autumn we see? I mean—no one ever knows how much time we really have, but with everything going on in the news...Do you believe any of it?"

"Are you falling into that Mayan doomsday trap, too?" He smiled, trying to lighten the mood.

"I don't know what to believe, but I know something is going on." I turned my head, looking into the tree line ahead where shadows fall thick upon the ground, and whispered, "'*Something wicked this way comes.*'" *Macbeth* dug deep into my puzzled mind.

"Huh?" Aiden questioned as he pulled the paddles into the boat.

"It's nothing. Guess I'm just feeling a little apprehensive."

"Piper, you're too young to live your life worrying about tomorrow while wasting away today."

I reached my hand into the pond, pulling a fistful of water out, and splattered him across the chest. Then we fought for a paddle, rocking the boat back and forth. Moments later, we were both drenched from shoveling the chilly water at each other. Our feet were soaked in two inches of water, and our clothes clung to our cold bodies, dripping as we shivered in the November breeze.

Once back on shore, Aiden held my wet hand, trembling from the chill. Talk of the end of the world changed to laughter, sweet kisses, and the simplicity of day turning into evening. Words unspoken, thoughts without judgments, and an embrace with undefined boundaries brought the night to a closure. He walked me to my door, and I couldn't possibly think of my life without him in it.

Upstairs, I could hear what sounded like Patrick and his friends playing an interactive video game. I sat at the table with a scoop of vanilla ice cream smothered in chocolate syrup, thinking of Aiden. Out of the corner of my eye, I noticed three claw marks on Mom's table etched deeply into the wood. The claw marks cut across the table toward me. Wood shavings scattered in the air, but I couldn't move; something held me in my chair. It forced my right arm down against the table, stretched out toward the invisible claws. I couldn't move or scream out. The sharp, jagged edge rode up my wrist and arm, scratching letters into my tender skin, *ERRATUS*.

The entity freed me, and I screamed for my brother. Within seconds, Patrick was there. "Piper, what's the matter?" He saw my arm bleeding and grabbed a towel to wipe it off.

I continued to scan the room, searching for the creature that stalked me. "Something held me down. Patrick, I couldn't move. Something is after me. Look…" I showed him my arm, noticing the foreign word scratched into my skin. "This isn't the first time. I see things—I hear things. What's happening to me?" I cried.

Patrick held me in his arms, and I continued to tremble in fear. I felt somewhat relieved, finally telling someone in my family. Patrick looked deeply into my eyes appearing lost for words, and then he spoke, "Piper— you did this to yourself. There isn't anyone here that would hurt you. Do you seriously believe that something is after you? Because—that's not possible. Piper—you did this to yourself."

I shoved my brother, pushing him away. "What are you saying? I didn't do this. Why won't you believe me? You told me I could trust you—that I should tell you how I feel. And now, when I need you the most you bail!" I yelled.

"Piper, don't you see how you sound. You sound—like Mom. I think I should call Dad," he whispered while glancing at the sharp knife lying in the sink.

"Don't bother. I'm fine." I hesitated and then confessed, "You're right. I did it to myself." I couldn't worry Dad, so I lied.

Just then, Jake ran downstairs to the fridge, grabbing a few snacks to carry back up to the guys. "Hey, Patrick, are you coming back up to play? Oh, hey Piper, I didn't know you were home."

I gave a small, forced smile to Jake and then headed up to my room.

"Piper," my brother called out, but I didn't respond. "I think we should talk about this!" he yelled from the other side of the staircase.

I stumbled upstairs and turned on the shower, lathering the bloody gashes with soap. My skin was red, and the slices bled more when the water hit it. The burning sensation brought tears to my eyes, and fear shocked every sense I had into overdrive. I shook with horror of being alone.

The shower curtain blew in and out. I pushed it away, washing the soap from my body. It continued lunging toward me, clinging to my skin. I glanced down at it, and fright pushed me against the tile wall. Water from the showerhead sprinkled onto the curtain and created patterns of demonic faces and figures. Twisted forked tongues, spiked tails, sharp teeth, horns and hoofed creatures snarled and stared waiting for my fall from rational thought.

Jumping from the shower, I grabbed a towel and dressed. I thought of my dad and brother. I couldn't trust them with what was happening to me. Dad already feared for my sanity. And now Patrick was becoming suspicious. Paranoid schizophrenia had genetic tendencies, and it was possible this was the evil tormenting me. I had to confront it and eventually defeat it; I knew the exact place I should start—the place it began—the chapel in the woods.

Darkness didn't stop me while I drove into the night toward the place Aiden had attacked me one Friday night after the football game. Flashes popped in and out of my mind. I wasn't sure if any of it was true anymore. Maybe none of it actually happened. But the chapel called my name, and I'd ignored it one time too many. I needed to go back to make sense of all this confusion.

I walked the path toward the chapel. The moonlight cast its spotlight upon the bandage covering the claw marks on my arm. I pushed it from my mind and refused to feed the pain with raw emotion. I forced the door open, waiting for the creaking that had followed like last time. Wooden pews with burgundy cushions sat passionately in wait of people to accept faith before the wooden cross. The smell of fresh paint and wood polish overtook the soft aroma of the autumn blooms and pines surrounding the glass chapel.

A man kneeling near the front threw his arms into the air, pleading with words I didn't understand. The conversation unraveled from a language I couldn't comprehend—it was like nothing I'd ever heard before. I slowly tiptoed to the fourth pew, sat down, and bowed my head. But my eyes followed the stranger within the dim chapel, and my ears eavesdropped on his conversation. He spoke with a certain sadness displaying a naked, transparent love and desire to be understood. And I had no idea how I came to this conclusion since I didn't speak this language.

He made his way to his feet, wiped his face, and turned to exit the small church. I gripped the pew in front of me and buried my head deep into my lap, hiding my face. In the shadows, he didn't notice me. After the doors closed, I released a sigh of relief. A familiar roar caught my attention. It couldn't be! I ran outside through the wooden doors. Logan drove off on his motorcycle into the night, darting in and out of the forest trees. "Logan," I whispered in disbelief. I stared into the dust brought forth from his tires spinning across the path. I forgot all about myself. What was Logan bargaining and pleading for?

I drove home unaware that I'd left without facing the evil I'd set out to confront. I couldn't get my mind off Logan or the sadness he painstakingly hid from me.

The next three nights that followed, I dreamed of Logan, the chapel, and his tortured soul. His private affliction ripped him apart at the seams. Conversations with his silent creator spoke of love desired and love lost, but I wasn't sure how I knew. The tangled web twisted around him, trapping him like a hunter's prey. My secret observation held me at bay, watching the storm drag him further and further out into the treacherous sea. Each dream ended with shadowy figures chasing me. These strange evil forces hovered all around, making me powerless. I woke soaked in sweat with Logan jostling me from the nightmares. He guarded me with his presence, and then he was gone; it was just another delusion in my crazy, mixed-up world—or was he really there?

Thanksgiving morning came, and everyone had arrived for lunch, including Dad's new partner from the firm. Dad wrestled with Patrick and Jake as they warmed the homemade turkey, dressing, and sides Marcella prepared. Jake's parents were out of town visiting his grandmother. He spent more time here with our family than his own, and Dad welcomed any of our friends—especially during the holiday season. The more people around, the easier it was for him to free his mind of Mom. Logan and Aiden would both be here, and I hoped everyone could get along.

The doorbell rang constantly, and guests carried flowers, desserts, and their favorite side dishes. Dad's partner arrived last carrying a bottle of red wine. She stood tall wearing a coral two-piece business suit. The miniskirt exposed her long legs, and all the guys took notice. Her short blond hair occasionally covered her face, and she would flip it back with her fingers or a gentle head toss. And I noticed as it caught Dad's eye each time. Logan steered clear of Aiden, and Aiden politely ignored Logan. Patrick had invited, Natalie, his flavor of the month over. She sat oblivious to everything, taking pictures on her cell and downloading them to her favorite social network. Jake and Graham circulated the platters of food and piled up as much as they could. I examined it all, trying not to cringe when Alana, Dad's partner, gushed over Mom's fine china and crystal.

The Thanksgiving meal dwindled down, and everyone sat around the table conversing and laughing. I looked over at Logan, wondering where his sadness came from and how he could hide it. I wanted desperately to take his pain away. Aiden took my hand and kissed it. Across the table Alana looked over at Dad, dreamy-eyed, and used Mom's pumpkin-orange linen napkin to wipe the turkey gravy from his cheek.

Everyone started packing away the food and cleaning the dishes. The guys wanted to play a game of football in the backyard, and Dad yawned, ready for his nap. Repulsed by Alana's familiarity with my family, I jumped up to take the trash out; I urgently needed a breath of fresh air.

I carried the garbage out to the dumpster parked out front. The bag, heavy and overfilled, fought me as I lifted it. The lid slammed shut, and I turned around. A man stood in front of me.

"Oh my God!" I threw my hands into the air and stumbled backward.

The old man was unkempt, wearing layers of mismatched torn clothing. He continued to invade my personal space, cornering me between the landscaping and dumpster. His face was wrinkled and his teeth were dark with decay; his slate blue eyes focused with intent to tell me something. I thought briefly that this must have been the same man Bailey had seen last month roaming around the neighborhood.

Charades was the only language he spoke, unable to form words in his sealed mouth. He pounded on a worn black book marked with a unique symbol and became annoyed when I didn't understand his antics. Then he reached up and placed his dirty hands on my neck. His fingernails were disgusting with specks of dirt trapped underneath, and I watched in horror as he scratched at my skin.

Patrick walked around the corner, tossing his football up in the air. He saw the strange man grabbing at my neck and charged after him, knocking me free.

"What the hell? You dirty old man. Don't ever touch my sister!" Patrick yelled getting up in his face. I stood behind my brother, pulling him back.

The old man held up his hand, and a powerful force knocked Patrick up in the air, throwing him back about twenty feet.

"Who are you?" I gasped as the man continued to approach me. "Patrick! Patrick!" I called out to my brother, who was leaning against the tree knocked unconscious.

"What do you want?" I screamed at the old man as he knelt down beside me.

I closed my eyes and held out my arms, blocking him. A tingling sensation fluttered through my body, and an intense vibration caused my muscles to twitch out of control. I opened my eyes, expecting an earthquake tremor, but the ground was still, quiet, and unshaken. My arms fixed in front of me, unwillingly at this point, pushed the crazed man away as his heels cut trenches into the ground. I didn't understand it or know how to explain it. His face expressed a sense of anger and frustration, but mysteriously he didn't seem surprised by my powers.

When the old man was no longer in sight, I stood up and ran toward Patrick. He woke to my voice and began to rub his head.

"What happened?" he questioned while trying to stand.

I helped him up. "You don't remember?"

"No. But my head hurts like I was hit by a train." We walked toward the house, and pieces began to come back to him. "Hey, where did that weird old man go?"

"Um…you scared him away," I lied.

"What happened to my head? It's throbbing like a jackhammer," he complained.

"Patrick, I threw you the football, and you ran smack into the tree." The lies came quickly. He would never believe what just happened. I was there and still couldn't believe it myself.

"You mean—you knocked me out?" Patrick laughed and then grabbed his head again, trying to stop the pounding. "You're never gonna let me live this down, are you?"

I glanced back inconspicuously, searching for the man waiting—watching—wanting something. Patrick leaned his tall frame against me as we walked into the house.

"Dad!" I called out. He came from the study with Alana by his side.

"What is it, Piper?" he questioned and then responded with concern. "Patrick, what happened?"

Patrick sat down and leaned back on the couch holding the back of his head. Everyone else piled into the room after hearing the commotion. "Piper, what happened to your brother?" Dad repeated.

"I threw the football, and Patrick ran into a tree," I stated seriously. Then the room erupted into laughter.

"Are you kidding?" Jake roared with laughter and stepped closer to inspect Patrick's head.

"You guys, it's not funny," I protested. "He hit his head pretty hard and was knocked out for about five minutes. I think we should take him to the hospital."

They all looked at me for a moment with serious eyes. Then they all chuckled again at the thought of little me knocking out my athletic football jock of a brother.

Dad looked at Patrick's head and asked him questions to check his recall of the incident. Patrick began to recount the events in order. Then he stopped as if he remembered something that had just come to him. He sat up, pulled me close, and touched my neck.

"I remember now—this old man was threatening Piper. He stood in the front yard with his hands on her neck. Piper, where did he go? Dad, I think you should call the police. This guy was all over her. I guess I scared him away when I shoved him, but—I can't remember anything else. And then Piper woke me." He thought for a moment and then pulled my arm up close for inspection. "Is that the guy that came into our house, held you down, and sliced up your arm? Were you telling me the truth?" Patrick rambled with concern and confusion.

Dad looked at me and I shrugged my shoulders. "I told you he hit his head hard. He's not even making sense," I expressed with fear.

Jake and Graham ran to the front yard, searching for the old mysterious man. The door swung open, and they both stepped back inside. "We didn't see anyone out there."

Dad picked up the phone, and Alana sat down beside him. She glanced over at me and smiled. Then she took the phone away from Dad.

"Shawn, it is Thanksgiving. And he's probably long gone now. Some poor confused old man—probably a believer in that end-of-the-world crap. Maybe he thought he was trying to save you, Piper."

"Save me from what, Alana?" I questioned harshly. I didn't like her or want her around my family. "Dad, what about Patrick? He could have a concussion or a fractured skull. I really think we should have him checked out."

"Piper, your brother has been through a lot worse than this." Dad turned to Patrick, who was resting his head in Natalie's lap. "Patrick, do you want to go to the hospital? Do you feel dizzy or nauseated?"

"I'm fine. It doesn't even hurt anymore." Patrick appeared to enjoy Natalie running her fingers through his hair.

Aiden looked at the scratches on my neck. "I think we should clean this up before it gets infected." My neck was stinging, similar to the feeling in my arm. But when I peeked at my arm, the claw marks were already gone. It had healed too fast to make any sense. Then again, nothing was making sense anymore. What just happened? How did I force that old man away?

Dad and Alana had gone outside, and were studying with confusion the furrows the old man's feet had left in the grass when I pushed him away. Logan stood by the door, staring out into the unknown, with his face heavy with emotion and confusion. When Aiden left to gather the disinfectant and ointment from the bathroom, Logan glanced over at me with apprehension. His eyes spoke without the need for actual words.

"Logan, are you OK? If there's anything you need, you know I'm here for you."

"Piper, I..." He was interrupted when Aiden returned with the supplies. Logan stepped outside with the other guys while Aiden dabbed disinfectant on my neck.

"Aiden, you've been hit hard before on the field. Do you think Patrick will be OK?" I questioned, realizing the madness was now affecting my family.

Aiden continued to rub the solution on my skin. "Piper, I've had my share of concussions, but I've never been hit by you—so maybe it could be worse than we all think." He broke into a small laugh. "I'm sure he will be just fine." He leaned forward and blew his warm breath on my neck, drying the wet solution before applying the ointment. Chills formed on my skin, and I temporarily forgot about my secrets.

Chapter Nineteen

Kashmir

A week had passed by, and Dad woke up early. Alana picked him up for the drive to the airport—another business trip to New York. I sat in his home office, spinning back and forth in his leather chair. As a child, I would spend hours looking at all his books stacked high on library shelves. The smell of leather alone brought back tons of childhood memories. I always associated it with knowledge, power, wisdom, and of course, my dad—his briefcase, leather-bound books, jacket, and this worn chair.

I leaned my head down on his desk watching the metal spheres swinging in Newton's cradle. Physics was never my thing, but it was fascinating to watch. It reminded me of the old man's power knocking my brother off his feet. Confusion washed over me when I tried to contemplate where my power had come from, how I could control it, and if anyone else knew—because the old man sure didn't seem too surprised. He had all the answers; I just had questions and no one to confide in.

I turned on the television and flipped through the channels. Twelve earthquakes in the past week had devastated people overseas as well as in California, Washington, and Alaska. NASA reported daily on the Earth's rotational speed increasing by 1.8 microseconds here and 6.9 microseconds there, continuing to add up on this countdown into the unknown. Our world spun out of control, and our moon slowly crept away, making our days longer.

I continued whirling around in the chair, catching glimpses of President Obama's face displayed over each TV channel. I came across the weather channel and listened to the newscaster.

"Floods have washed out the region from Texas to Kentucky and up toward New York, and now a blizzard is rolling into the mix. Unseasonal twisters have set off a chain reaction starting in Oklahoma, and the growing cluster of tornados is heading right through these six states northbound."

I flipped the channel again and watched in utter amazement as a preacher surrounded by a packed audience screamed into his microphone. "Gone is the fear of an organized terrorist, old school vigilante, and the crazed dictator's rampage; now precarious weather patterns and Earth's instability threaten us daily! It cruises across our battlefield stomping life out one breath at a time!" I pressed mute on the remote when I felt my phone vibrate.

Bailey called, and I pulled my cell from my pocket. The connection filled with static. "Bailey, are you there? I can't hear you. I'll try calling you back." The phone went silent. I continued to dial her number, but it went straight to voice mail.

She had flown to Texas to visit her family for the Thanksgiving holiday. Bailey was terrified of tornados, lightning…pretty much storms of any caliber. Texas was swimming in massive floods from days of unrelenting rain and was now under warning for springlike twisters—in November.

I continued to spin in the chair, thinking about everything taking shape around me. The unthinkable was a real possibility. Stopping the chair abruptly, I studied the metal spheres of Newton's cradle sitting at the corner of Dad's desk. The spheres stopped as I concentrated on them. Then they slowly rotated faster and faster until they broke free, hitting the walls around me. I buried my head in my arms. The balls came to a standstill and then rolled toward me, driven by an unknown force of energy. A loud pop echoed, startling me to my feet. The light bulbs above had shattered into slivers of hot fragments, showering the glittery glass upon my skin.

Running from the room, I quickly realized all the lights in the house had turned on and were burning an intense brightness. Then they exploded, showering me with shards of glass. I ran out of the house and kept running, following the sunlight until I couldn't run any farther. Out of breath, I stood in the middle of the path with my hands braced across my hips, pacing back and forth waiting for whatever it was to catch up with me. Then I realized it was impossible to run from myself. I was trapped with this power I couldn't control or understand.

My legs folded under, and sat me down on the pathway. Staring into the forest touched by a winter's chill, I watched the stillness of the woodlands transform. Quickly, vines climbed as if on fast-forward, grabbing hold of whatever was within its wake. Before my eyes, flowers forged through the dirt, exploding into brilliant colors of red, yellow, and blue. A single blade of grass multiplied into a rolling carpet of Irish green spreading upon the dried brown ground. I was losing my mind. The wind blew the branches, swaying them back and forth. The leaves stroked my shoulder and caressed my face, catching the tears streaming down my cheeks. I got up and ran back toward my house, uncertain of what I was seeing.

A familiar sound penetrated my ears as my heart raced faster than my feet toward home. When I got there, Logan's motorcycle was parked out front, and he stood at the door pressing the doorbell. I ran into his arms shaken, unsteady, and out of breath. "I have—to tell—you something!" I stammered as I caught quick breaths in between words. "Something is happening to me—I don't..."

Logan pulled me in, pressing his lips against mine. His kiss unraveled the single thread holding me together. I let it all go as the moment lifted me into another world. Blinding bright light warmed my skin, and I couldn't open my eyes. His lips felt supple against mine as time stood completely still, and snapshots of my life traveled back in quick glimpses. Piece by piece the puzzle came together, combining thoughts, memories, and feelings. But it looked familiar and vague all at the same time. My body warmed with heat, and I feared I might burst into shiny fragments of hot glass. Time was lost, and my fear abated. My world crashed down all around me, but at that single moment each second spoke—telling me to trust him. My soul recognized him on the deepest cellular level. I knew him without figure and form. He was my...

The second split, knocking him from my arms. Aiden dove in, throwing punch after punch. Logan blocked and returned with fists, elbows, and arms synchronized in battle that appeared astonishingly equal in strength and relentless in will. I backed away, unnoticed, watching everything collapse around me. My faith faded into darkness and my warmth turned to a winter's chill; my thoughts blinded me into a pool of insanity while fists pounded muscle and bone. Blood spilled, streaming down their skin. Spit and sweat scattered as beads of liquid through the air. I screamed at them to stop, but they didn't even look my direction. I begged and pleaded to no avail. Finally I ran inside, retrieved my keys from the drawer, and sped off, unable to comprehend the growing madness. I pressed the pedal to the floorboard and imagined driving off a cliff, away from it all.

I slammed on the brakes swerving to a forceful stop. The seatbelt tightened around my chest. Out of the corner of my eye I had caught sight of a bright ball of fire spiraling through the air, landing in the road in front of me—*a meteorite*, I thought...*or the sky was falling*. I unlatched my seatbelt and walked toward the ball of flames melting the concrete it fell upon. Voices carried near the old abandoned gas station, and I walked toward the sound of blaring rock music, laughter, and conversation that sounded similar to the language Logan had spoken in the chapel. I wanted to run back to my car and drive toward Texas—toward Bailey and away from here. But my curiosity led me into the thicket covering the old abandoned shack ready to give way at any moment.

Peeking through the wooden planks nailed to the door, I saw the five bikers that had been roaming around Ashland. Dressed in dark leather clothing, each had a tattoo wrapped around his wrist and arm. They competed with precision, practicing a set of fighting moves I'd only seen in million-dollar action flicks. Gravity didn't hold them in place; they were stronger than any form of energy known by human kind. Closing my eyes tightly, I wished I wasn't there.

Stepping back slowly, I watched them through the slats of the wooden boards. A small twig snapped underneath my foot. It didn't take long before heads turned, tracking me. I ran toward my car, stumbling through the undergrowth. The thorns tore through my skin, and I tripped, bashing myself against the ground. When I looked up, they stood all around me. One knelt down and looked deep into my eyes. A tear ran down my cheek, and he caught it with his finger, broke into a warped smile, and took the tear into his mouth.

"You have no idea what is going on here. Do you, Piper?"

"No." I shook my head. "What is happening?" I whispered with fear and confusion.

They circled around me. Their tattoos took on different shapes, climbing around their arms creating sinister faces and frightening forms. I scooted across the ground, moving away from one—only to be near another; I couldn't find my way out. My keys jingled in my pocket as I trembled. I wanted to push them away like I had done to the old man, but couldn't find the source of my power.

"What do you want with me?" I questioned, but I was afraid to hear the answer.

"Should we tell her?" One of them asked the others as he used his long fingernails painted black to trace my skin. I wished Logan and Aiden would come barreling down the hill to save me.

"You know that is not the plan. She'll figure it all out soon enough."

Another spoke, "What will we do with her now?"

"Nothing!" the leader of the group commanded.

"How can this weak girl be the one? How can she be *his*?" mocked the other biker.

"Enough!" the leader snapped.

They walked away. The only female in the group formed a fireball within her hands, and threw it into the forest, igniting the old gas station. They were the ones causing all the unexplained fires in town. And within seconds, they were all gone.

I ran to my car and drove off, speeding around corners. I drove faster and faster until I felt a sudden urge to slam on the breaks. My car skidded as the tires burned rubber into the winter air. I knew this place—it was where the accident took my mom's life. Memories came rushing back as I searched for answers on that cold, dark road. I was forever haunted by the shattered glass, the crumbled metal, the ambulance lights tossed upon the towering trees, and my ballet sticker untouched on the back bumper. Blindsided, a new memory came back—one that I hadn't recalled until now. A police officer followed a pattern near the wreckage with his flashlight tracing the black symbol on the ground. It was the same symbol on the wooden box in Mom's closet where I'd found her scarf—and on the book that the crazy old man pounded on.

Quickly, I grabbed a pen and tore through the car looking for a piece of paper to sketch the emblem before I forgot it again. I looked at my arm, scratched and burning from the thorns. With no paper in sight, I turned over my forearm and drew the pattern mixing black ink and blood forming the symbol that haunted my mind. It all seemed so unreal. I knew the magic emporium would have a book on symbols. The glass case at the emporium held the answers I searched for, but I couldn't leave quite yet.

The darkness in the sky turned to streaks of light. I scanned the night sky through the window. Then I opened the door and stepped out of the car to stare up at the heavens. Stars from every direction began to fall burning a trail of light until it disappeared from my sight. The crescent moon anchored in the night sky held a faint shimmer compared to the rash of falling stars bursting out of space. My world was crumbling beneath me, and now…now my heavens were actually falling down upon me.

I knelt on the asphalt covered country road begging for forgiveness—from God. I'd blamed him for everything, and now I no longer wanted to be alone, terrified, and lost. Realizing I was at the exact place of my mother's accident, I wept into my hands. The cross my family placed for her on the side of the road was covered in vines and overgrown brush. My hands tore through the wild vegetation uncovering the wooden cross. And then a weird language, like that of Logan's at the chapel, came from my mouth babbling from my heart—not my mind. I couldn't control the words that rambled on and on. A soulful prayer was bringing a sea of tears to the surface. I waited for the rapture to come and take my soul before the heavens all fell to Earth.

I cried out for my mom to be beside me, and when it didn't happen, I cried out for my father. I could smell the leather books, his leather jacket, the leather chair…But when I opened my eyes, he wasn't the one wiping my tears. I jumped up, trembling against the car in disbelief. A strong but unbelievably beautiful man towered over me. His skin radiated a glow against the cool night. I wiped my eyes, taking another glance.

"Who are you?" I demanded, not wanting to play this game anymore.

"Piper…" His voice, deep and soothing, whispered into the night.

I interrupted, "How do you know my name?"

"Piper, I'm not going to hurt you. I would never hurt you. I'm Finley."

"Why does everyone keep telling me that they are not going to hurt me, when that is exactly what they do—they hurt me?" I blurted. "Why are you here?" I asked with my voice shaken. "Is the world ending?" The words barely broke through my lips.

"You're going to be fine." He touched my arm, turning it over, exposing the symbol I had drawn upon my skin.

"What does this mean?" I pointed to the mark. But he wasn't answering any of my questions. "Why are you here?" I tried one more time.

"Piper, where is the necklace?" He reached for my neck like the strange old man outside my house.

"What necklace? Why is this necklace so important? Why do you people think I have it, and why do you want it?" I spoke sharply, demanding an answer.

"Piper, the necklace will protect you and the people close to you. I sent it to you for your birthday." He stood silent thinking for a moment. Then he replied, "That means *they* have it."

"Who has it? Who are these people? Why do they want it? Finley!" I shouted at him. "Tell me, what do they want from me?" And then my voice fell soft. "Who am I? And what are *you*?"

He placed his firm hands on my shoulders and looked deep into my eyes. "You're very special. They want to steal you, and they will do everything within their power. Piper, you have to be strong. They will use your fears and the people you love to get what they want. I don't have much time here."

"Did you know my mom?" I questioned. "Because I found this symbol on her wooden box. Did you know her?" I repeated.

The expression on his face turned from fear to pain. "Piper, I'm sorry."

"Why are you sorry? You're going to help me, right?"

He placed his hand gently on my forehead. Bright lights exploded into a thousand fragments, and I collapsed into his arms.

Chapter Twenty

Dog Days Are Over

I woke up in my bed, and the sun hadn't yet come up. The brightness in my room only confused me. Blinking my eyes quickly didn't help; so I rubbed them intensely. A halo of light remained as some sort of freakish night vision. I turned on the bathroom light and fumbled to turn it off again. The bright light burned, causing my eyes to water uncontrollably. Staring into the mirror, I noticed my dilated pupils, round with a dark pool of emptiness. A glimpse of the symbol on my forearm troubled me. Finley—rushing memories of the strange man who had appeared from nowhere entered my mind—and then I remembered the bright light he cast upon me.

I peeked out my bedroom window, watching the hazy crescent moon fade from the night sky turning dawn into day. Everything appeared strange in this newfound light. Time was winding down, and everything on the planet was feeling its effects. I paid close attention to every detail, each breath, each beat of my heart. I knew each could very well be my last, and then my vision gradually returned to normal.

We hadn't returned to school since Thanksgiving break. Our school flooded after a pipe burst, and to complicate matters more, the electrical outages mixed with rolling blackouts affected the entire nation. Low student attendance mixed with staffing issues forced closure of schools throughout many states. Any sense of normalcy flooded, twisted, and quaked away with the intense weather patterns, holding us all captive on high ground, in basements, and hunkered down between doorways. Crazy December weather brought ice and snow one day followed by eighty-degree sunshine the next. Quakes shook the earth, floods washed land away, and the sunshine tricked us into believing it's all over. But the day after—is just another realization that more is yet to come.

Half the shops in town closed, and we had to endure a ten p.m. curfew enforced by police patrol. All the gas stations in town posted signs declaring their limited supply, and we had to drive up to an hour away to fill up sometimes. And even in these circumstances, Patrick played football in the backyard; the guys were untouched by it all. And Dad had rented a car to drive back from New York because all flights were grounded. *At least he had Alana to keep him company,* I thought as I cringed.

Aiden and Logan took turns stopping by and ringing the doorbell, but I didn't answer. Sometimes, Aiden climbed the lattice of roses outside my window and peeked into my room. I missed Bailey and wished I could get in touch with her, but she was still in Texas and not answering texts or calls.

"Piper, I know you're in there. I need you. I need you to let me in. Please, Piper, come on. I have to see you. I'm sorry." Aiden pleaded and tapped gently against the window and then jumped down from the wrought-iron lattice.

I hid out of sight drowning in music streaming from my iPod. Dealing with either of them was more than I could take. Logan's secrets and Aiden's temper broke me into pieces—practically pieces of pieces; nothing mattered anymore. Love took a backseat, and irony danced in my head. My silly life seemed pointless and irrelevant one moment, waiting for the world to disintegrate. And then blinding hope and invisible faith snapped me back together again. I bounced between moods and emotions, leaving me more lost than ever before.

Sometimes, I saw visions of Logan watching over me as I slept at night. I could smell his cologne and sense his presence, but when I woke he was gone. I didn't have any words to explain the rush of unplanned feelings that exuded from *that* single kiss we once shared, and I felt guilty if I led him on in any way. I was terribly torn between Logan and Aiden, and angry that they had placed me in this position. However, only one feeling kept coming back time after time—this intense attraction I had for Aiden only left me craving him more…and once again I failed to comprehend it all.

I drove into town and walked around Lithia Park. Burnt-orange leaves fell from the trees, rode the wind, and floated down the rocky creek as ducks bobbed up and down in the pond oblivious to the ways of the world. Red robins were busy building nests with pieces of fallen twigs and leaves. Late fall foliage turned into a sudden winter's frost, mixing shades of orange and red that casted a fiery glow upon the frozen Japanese maple sparkling underneath the ice.

I had come to the park for peace, but paranoia set in. I was convinced that people were watching me from behind magazines, newspapers, and buildings. In wait, they studied me, searching for some spark or recognition, but I refused to give in. Leaving the park, I caught the glimpse of each eye—blue, green, brown, and hazel—seeking something. I wanted to call them out and break the escapade of their stupidity, but I just kept walking.

The sky grew dark, clouds rolled in, and thunder grumbled in the distance. Leaving the park, I drove toward the magic emporium. The building was lit with candles hollowed out by the burning flames. Incense burned rich emollients, waking spirits and calming souls. Soft music played as people sat in small groups discussing the end of the world, prophesying the cataclysmic reckoning of the planets. I slid the glass door open and rummaged through the supernatural books. A few titles snagged my attention. The pages flowed through my fingertips as I looked for anything resembling the symbol on my mom's box and the symbol I'd drawn on my arm. Wicca and witchcraft boasted spells of incantations and pictures of satanic culture; I slammed the book shut disturbed that I wavered down this aisle of demonology and evil.

"Bad day?" questioned a girl that stood stocking books on the shelf behind me. Her hair was definitely dyed black with streaks of purple wisping through her bangs. Piercings to her nose, ears, and lip decorated her face, but it was her eyes that lured me in—they were the brightest blue I had ever seen. I paused, having difficulty responding. I had remembered her from before when I broke the snow globe, shattering it on the floor after buying my Alice in Wonderland costume.

"Yeah, I guess every day lately is a bad day," I replied with a smile and placed the books back on the shelf.

"Are you interested in Wicca?" she asked as she lifted the colorful stands away from her stunning eyes. "Hi," she greeted me with a warm smile. "My name is Saraphina."

"I'm Piper. Do you know much about symbols?" I pulled the piece of paper from my pocket.

"I have seen something like this before," she commented. "Where did you find this symbol?" Saraphina questioned as she ran her finger across the section of books on the third shelf one by one until she came across the one she sought. "It's not a Wiccan symbol. It's a form of angelic summoning spell. Have you ever heard of the key of Solomon?" She waited for my response as she flipped through the book and then stopped suddenly, staring at something.

"No. What is it?" I questioned, becoming lost in her facial expressions.

"The key of Solomon dates back to the fourteenth century. It was a secret book for summoning demons and listed how to perform an exorcism. Later books followed in the seventeenth century, and the combination of these books explored the ability to summon angels for strength and knowledge. The sigils, which are specific magical symbols, and the grimoires, which are the instructions, work together to create magic."

"What symbol did you say this was?" I questioned, unable to take anything other than simple at this point.

"It's a type of summoning symbol—an angel summoning symbol. I would say that the person using this symbol must be pretty special to have the power to command one of God's angels to appear." She continued to recite scattered information that she'd collected over time from her wide arrangement of mystical texts. "The books are full of demons and evil spirit conjuring, but only touches slightly on angel summoning. I'm thinking that heaven's angels don't waste their time appearing to the common man—unless…"

"Unless what?" I interrupted.

"Unless, God told them to—they are his messengers, you know."

"Have you ever heard the name Finley before?" Memories of the strong man appearing from nowhere after I drew the symbol on my arm stabbed through my mind.

"No, I can't say that I have," Saraphina replied.

"Thank you for the information," I whispered and slowly backed away trying to make sense of it all. Then I trotted quickly out of the shop.

"Wait! Did you want to see the book?" Saraphina yelled before the door slammed shut.

I drove around trying to find my place in this world literally falling apart around me. How could I possibly make sense of the uncertain powers I held, the strange evil presence haunting me, and the possibility I had summoned an angel accidently by inscribing the symbol upon my arm? The clearer picture was...I was fading into insanity, and nothing around me was real anymore. Alice's Wonderland hurled me through the air without any hope of hitting solid ground. Magical potions and symbols—that was crazy. How could they save my world?

I stopped at the market and piled groceries into the cart. The shelves were restocked, but remained limited compared to the endless aisles of consumer choices I'd known all my life. I was in the mood to bake and couldn't quite decide which flavor cake to make. So I loaded up on one of everything...chocolate, German chocolate, vanilla, strawberry, carrot, and oddly enough, devil food cake and angel food cake. The cart filled up with milk, eggs, butter, candles, and an assortment of icing. I planned to make cakes and cupcakes between electrical surges.

The house was dark when I pulled into the drive. Dad still hadn't made it home. Patrick was out. I carried the grocery bags tied tightly around my wrists and placed them upon the kitchen counter. The electricity sparked on. I turned up the music full blast and dove into the batter: cracking eggs, stirring, and blending all the ingredients together.

I kept thinking of Saraphina and her magic lesson on symbols, sigils, and grimoires: a definite recipe for disaster. But I needed to know more.

Finley burned in the back of my mind along with all my unanswered questions. Before I knew it, hours had gone by. Frosted cupcakes covered the countertop, and cakes layered the table. The sink was painted with sprinkles, glitter, frosting, and batter; it was a masterpiece in a tasty disguise. The house breathed in the sweet smell that would make any Keebler elf happy, satisfied, and most importantly full. I began to feel anxious when I got down to my last box of cake mix.

I ripped into the box top of the angel food cake mix and flipped it over, resetting the oven temperature. The instructions transcribed into a language of symbols before my eyes, transforming letters into sigil and words into grimoires. My imagination taunted me to take that ride, but I didn't get in. I closed my eyes, wishing this would all just go away. A breath went in and a breath came out, thoughts of a simple life reminded me of calmer times. The instructions returned, and I tossed the box in the trash, stirred the mixture violently, and poured it into the Bundt pan.

When I pulled the hot pan from the oven, the electricity turned off. A series of clicks fluttered through the house as lights and music geared down, erasing any sense of life. The kitchen, however, was lit up with the birthday candles I'd stabbed into the heart of each cake and cupcake. The wax melted, dripping onto the sweet, fluffy mounds of frosting. I curled up on the kitchen floor, watching the flicker of candlelight as it bounced onto the ceiling and walls. I hungered for anything other than cake at this point. I wanted Aiden.

The angel food cake sat flipped over on Mom's silver platter in front of me. I stared at its bright white color shimmering in the candlelit house. I thought of the odd symbol I had memorized. My finger traced the pattern on the cake. And I wished for Finley to come once more and answer my questions, but he didn't come.

The front door opened after a series of knocks, but I couldn't peel myself off the kitchen floor.

"Piper, are you here?" Logan's voice echoed in the dark, silent house.

He walked into the kitchen amazed by the melting bakery lit up by swirling pink, blue, and yellow birthday candles. His eyes said more than his voice ever could. My birthday was just a few days away, and I didn't know if I was counting down to becoming seventeen, or if I was counting the last days of my existence. All my wishes were lost to a blown-out candle that would never be. I wanted desperately to live.

Three simple words fell from his lips as he knelt down beside me, and I waited patiently for each one. "Piper, I'm here." He wrapped me inside his arms. "You're going to be OK. Trust me."

The front door swung open, and familiar voices echoed in the hallway. I jumped up and ran toward the entryway. "Dad, you're home." I knocked the luggage from his hand and flew into his arms. "You made it home."

"Piper, I told you I would find my way back. Nothing can keep me away from my family."

"You're not going to leave until this is all over, right? Dad, please don't go on any more trips until everything is back to normal."

"Piper, we're not going anywhere," Dad replied as Alana walked inside. Patrick carried her suitcase in one hand and Dad's duffle bag over his left shoulder.

Others came inside. Jake and Graham found their way to the kitchen with their noses. Aiden waited outside, stepping in last, carrying a single white rose in his hand. He handed it to me and whispered into my ear, "A peace offering—I'm sorry, Piper." Then three little words I'd waited a lifetime to hear fell from his lips. "I love you."

Logan leaned against the wall and caught Aiden's eye, but he stood calm and unshaken demonstrating his control.

"Logan," Aiden addressed him by name and nodded his head with a vague acknowledgment of his presence.

Dad walked into the kitchen in disbelief. "Piper, what have you done?" Cupcakes covered every square inch of the kitchen and spread onto the table as well. The candles were beginning to burn out, and the electricity clicked on, surging light and sound throughout the house. "Piper, Happy *early* Birthday," Dad proclaimed with hesitancy as he reached over and kissed my cheek, worried that I had truly lost my mind.

"Happy Birthday, Piper," Patrick rejoiced, picked me up with a bear hug, and then sat me back down.

Graham and Jake devoured the glittery treats, leaving crumbs and sprinkles on the corners of their lips. Alana picked up a silver butcher knife, about to cut into the spongy angel food cake. The silver platter mirrored the knife coming toward it. I plucked it out of her hands. "No, this one is special. I'm saving it for my actual birthday," I explained while she smiled with a confused glare in her eyes.

"OK, it is your special day," Alana replied as she bit into the devil food cupcake with chocolate frosting and red glitter.

Aiden stood to my right and Logan to my left as everyone sang, "Happy Birthday," while the candles finally dwindled into pools of warm wax.

Chapter Twenty-One

Silent Lucidity

My journals continued a day-by-day account of my life leading up to my birthday. My sketchbook filled with my latest obsessions of the mysterious angelic summoning symbol, the stars falling from the night sky, and Finley's face. The house carried more noise than it had seen in the past year combined. Life lived in laughter, and fear had no place, but within the perils of silence that crept in when I least expected it.

Graham and Jake camped out in Patrick's room night after night. Aiden occasionally spent the night and would sneak away from the group of guys to hang out with me in the garden. Logan comforted me with his kindness as he struggled in torment with his secret thoughts. Dad traded his suit and tie for a pair of jeans and a polo shirt. Patrick clowned around, turning strange sadness of the unknown into humor and pranks. Alana popped in and out with her wide eyes and countless attempts to worm her way into my family.

As I sat alone, Mom's garden bloomed before my eyes. Blossoms sprung abundantly from the winter soil as if it might be the last chance to open their soft petals. Uncertain of my growing powers, I gave into the acceptance of whatever was to come—was meant to be. After finding that single resolution, an electrical charge fired through me, waking my spirit's hibernating flame. A sudden calmness came, and I hushed the quaking energy inside wanting to burst free.

Later that night, I reclined across my bed, staring at the vase filled with my useless jewelry and dysfunctional electronics. It sat on the wooden floor a few feet away. The light bulbs in my room burned bright with an intense pulsation. Although, different this time, the glass didn't shatter. A tingling sensation swept across my skin, and a vibration gently hummed inside my head. With a steady thought, the vase began to shudder, and a few pieces of jewelry floated upward and out of the vase. I had control over the pieces of metal, breaking the heavy compounds into smaller components and finally into their simplest form; the raw material then melted, changing the form from solid to liquid above me. With a single glance of my eyes, it all mixed together into one mass of hot liquid metal circulating above me, spinning over a thousand revolutions per second. Energy electrified the air above, and a brilliant white light peeked out from the center as the lustrous liquid wrapped itself upon the thickening viscous shimmering mass. For a moment, I couldn't believe what was happening. A mere blink broke the chain, causing the transformation to fall apart. Pieces of metal rained down covering my bed with warm metallic beads.

Finding moments of alone time was difficult in a house full of people. Quietly, I sat behind my locked bedroom door scouring the Internet for telekinesis, angelic creatures, demonic evil, 2012 phenomenon, magnetic polar shifts, the power source of the Earth's core, and anything in between. The final countdown ticked away at the lower right-hand corner of my computer screen. My birthday was hours away, and the hands of time tapped at my soul—a steady beat, a somber moment, an unfathomable thought echoed without response. *Parting is such sweet sorrow.* Shakespeare's words crumbled my world, and I wasn't ready to say my good-byes. These growing powers only confused me more. Why was this happening now? What was the point of discovering these powers only to have my world destroyed by some silly Mayan prediction?

The lights flickered, and my laptop went dark. More and more satellites falling from the sky broke technology and communications, leaving the world disconnected and virtually held hostage. The electricity cut off and on, until finally the darkness remained. I lit the candles around my room. The worn wicks surrounded by a small puddle of melted wax fought to keep burning. The warm lights danced upon the walls, playing games with evening shadows. I opened the window to allow the December breeze to blow inside—*Blow, blow thou winter wind.* It was the warmest December I'd known, and the stars even looked lost up in the night sky, twinkling like beacons calling out to a wayward ship riding its last journey through rough seas.

A knock at my door startled me; if it were possible to jump out of my skin, I sure would have. "Piper, do you want to come downstairs?" Dad called through the door, and then turned the doorknob, twisting it back and forth. "Piper, can you unlock the door?" he asked. I knew it wasn't a request, but a calm demand, and I jumped up to unlock it. "Everyone's downstairs. Why don't you come down for a little bit? We can start celebrating your birthday. It's just a few hours until midnight. I miss you. And I don't like you being all alone up here." Dad was close to begging as he stood in the doorway.

"I'll be down. Give me just a few more minutes." I smiled and reassured him again, "I promise."

"Piper, you know I'll just start sending everyone up one at a time until you come down." Dad smiled, and I heard his footsteps trot down the wooden staircase. I heard music and laughter filling the first floor. I closed the door and leaned my body against it. Another knock tapped against the other side.

"Really, Dad. I said I would be down." I threw the door open as Aiden stood quietly, patiently, and beautifully in front of me. "I thought you were my dad."

"Yeah, he's really worried about you, and I have to say—I am, too. You've been locked away far too long. You're avoiding everyone who loves you—including me. Piper, I don't..."

I interrupted him with a kiss and pulled him into my room, kicking the door shut. I didn't want to think anymore. I wanted to live my life fully within the next few hours, and I couldn't think of a better way than with his touch and his lips on mine.

I rode his touch like the waves. A forever thirst unable to be quenched drove me to only want him more. A love dance without music carried me closer to him than I knew was humanly possible. Standing one moment and floating the next, we fell onto the bed, tangling into a twisted conviction on a desperate level. And during a time when nothing really mattered, *this* mattered more than ever.

"Wait—wait," I whispered into his ear.

Aiden pulled himself off and knelt by the side of my bed, staring into my eyes. "What's the matter? I thought you wanted this. I thought you wanted me." His confusion was evident in his tone, and I blamed myself for leading him on. A tiny piece of me wanted to see if he would be able to stop—unlike the time at the chapel. And a bigger piece of me wanted him more than life itself. I reached my arms around him again, closed my eyes, and pressed my lips against his, never knowing that it would be our last kiss.

I heard footsteps coming up the staircase and the sound of Patrick's voice resonating from the hallway, "Piper, Dad wants you to come downstairs," he bellowed.

Aiden pulled his shirt back on and whispered, "Come on." He reached out for my hand, and I naturally gravitated toward him. "I think I need to get a little air," he said.

"What are you doing?" I asked as he leaned out the open window, examining the route upward to the roof.

"Come on." Aiden tightened his grip, leading me up the sturdy trellis and onto the rooftop. He sat down with his back braced against the vaulted roof, and pulled me in close to snuggle underneath the stars, speckling the night sky above us. He caressed my cheek and held me in his arms. New stars were born in the night sky as others fell, bursting into white and blue flames. A rebirth of our universe spoke softly upon the brink, holding us in the present and keeping us from our nearing future.

"Aiden, I love you," I whispered into the vast universe, unable to see his expression behind me.

He leaned his head forward, touching the back of my neck, and swept my hair over to one side. I felt his warm breath against my skin. "I love you more than you will ever know, Piper." Then he kissed the back of my neck. A tingling sensation ran down my spine, and every nerve inside my body felt zapped by an electric spark.

I caught a glimpse of him checking his watch against the moonlight as meteor showers swept across the quickly approaching winter solstice sky. Time fell like pieces of sand within the hourglass glued down to the table never to be flipped over again. A wave of chills came over me, and I shivered against the cooling breeze.

"Happy Birthday, Piper," he whispered tenderly in my ear. The watch strapped firmly around his wrist had reached midnight, and my day finally arrived. I smiled as tears fell like raindrops down my cheeks, splashing onto his arms. And I knew I was exactly where I needed to be at that very moment in time. I was the speck of sand refusing to fall down into the pit of the hourglass. Secrets wrapped within perfect packages would be revealed one by one in the next twenty-four hours like birthday boxes hidden deep inside closets, under beds, and then—there was Logan's gift waiting inside the twisted tree.

Aiden held me until we both began to shiver in the cold air. We climbed down the trellis sprouting with fresh red and yellow roses that hadn't been there hours before. He didn't notice, and I didn't feel the need to explain the supernatural events taking place all around me. After climbing off the ledge and through the window, we collapsed onto my soft bed. Exhausted, we held onto one another, falling asleep in each other's arms.

Daylight broke through the open window. I reached out for Aiden and found a fresh bouquet of roses lying next to me. It was my birthday, and I couldn't stop smiling. I pulled the covers off and stepped out of bed. That was when I saw her, just staring at me with a blank gaze across her face.

"Alana, what are you doing?" I sharply questioned.

"I just wanted to be the first one to wish you a happy birthday, but I guess someone else beat me to it." She glanced over at the roses lying in my bed. "How was your night, Piper? Because mine was perfect. You know, your dad is a great guy." She sighed and sat down on my bed, beaming from ear to ear. "Is there anything you would like to talk about…maybe you and Aiden? He was up here, right? I know your mom can't be here for you when you need her the most. So, if there is anything…"

"Get out, Alana!" I screamed, shoving her off my bed and out the door. I locked it and slid down the door to my knees.

"Piper," Alana called from the other side of the door, "I don't plan on going anywhere. Shawn and I have a relationship now, and you'll have to eventually accept it—accept me. Piper, come out so we can talk about this. Everyone is gone for a few hours. It's just us two, and we have so much to talk about. You know, I always wanted a daughter," she crooned. That crazy woman assaulted every fiber of my being with her nagging voice. "Piper, they all went to clear debris from the roadside, and this would be a great opportunity for a discussion," she continued to badger.

"Discuss what? I have nothing to say to you, Alana. You'll never be my mother. How could you ever think you could replace her?" I glanced at the trellis, my only way out of the house.

I stepped out over the ledge, trying not to look down. The roses pierced my skin with their sharp thorns as I reached inside the thick foliage to find the trellis anchored against the house. I could still hear her voice taunting me. "Piper, don't you want to know why they chose you? Don't you want to know about your *powers* and who you really are?"

My eyes grew wide, my throat felt dry, my hands forgot to hold onto the trellis, and I fell, landing softly on the leafy shrubs my mother had planted. I ran to my car and raced down the country road away from the evil hiding inside my house.

A large tree blocked the road ahead, and I slammed on the brakes, realizing where I was. Logan's voice pleaded in my mind: *Promise me you'll come back on your birthday and find this tree. It's important, Piper, you have to find your way back here no matter what is going on. Promise me.*

Fear of the unknown trapped my mind into a cycle of thoughts leading to the same conclusion each time, but it was easier to tell myself I was crazy and stuck inside a nightmare unable to wake up. I grabbed the black marker and began drawing the summoning symbol upon my forearm. My skin bled while pressing down on the gashes left from the thorny rose trellis. My voice screamed out for Finley to show himself. But begging and pleading only left me weak and broken.

Stepping out of the car, I made my way down the pathway toward the twisted tree, wondering what Logan had left me and feeling uncertain of what was to come.

As I placed my hand on the branch, thunder cracked above me. It was the bluest sky without a single cloud. And then unusual streaks of jagged lightning clawed their way through the sky, and an eerie feeling encompassed me. The tree vibrated and the ground quaked underneath my feet, but I stood solid, unwavering in the face of the forces around me. A gust of wind caught my hair, blew it back, and immersed it with the smell of an earthy spring rain. A single bolt of lightning jumped from cloud to cloud, and then it struck the tree. I watched in amazement as sawdust flew up from the branch, tossing the fine wooden confetti upon my skin. It all happened so fast that I didn't have time to react. When it was over, I reached into the hollowed branch, feeling for the gift Logan hid for me. My hand burned with the warmth of a golden ray of sunlight, and I reached deep inside for the gift. I couldn't grab onto the object, but I felt it gravitate toward my fingers. A silver dagger followed my hand out of the hole and into my possession.

The silver shone in the sunlight, and my eyes continued to take in its illustrious beauty. An unusual writing was etched into the blade, and the serrated edge came to a fine piercing point. It suspended itself in thin air, rotating slowly, allowing me to inspect its divine magnificence. I carefully reached for it, and the handle forced itself within the palm of my hand. Visions barreled through my mind. Memories that were locked away in my childhood came undone…no more barriers, no guardrails, no boundaries present. Raw images came into focus, and I knew him—Logan. He was there beside me every moment of every day, guiding me, watching me, and leading me to that very moment.

As I turned back toward the pathway, I saw a man standing still, gazing at the dagger. He was dressed in black with a white collar, and I recognized him. "Father Mannelli," I called out as I tucked the dagger into the back of my jeans. The clouds darkened, and the wind tossed pine needles and dirt into the ominous air. He began to speak, and then a dark shadow spiraled through the forest air, flowing into him. I watched helplessly, stunned and shaken. Stepping backward, I moved slowly away.

Within the darkness, the man I once knew as Father Mannelli transformed into a gray wolf with golden-amber eyes. The wild animal growled and stomped at the ground. Within seconds, it transformed again into smoke. It flew around screeching a high pitched sound into my ear, reminding me of the creature that once taunted me at the Magic Emporium. It continued to transform showing its many faces of evil that tormented me the past few months. I trembled as the smoke flowed back into Father Mannelli. He came to his feet and walked toward me, but it was no longer Father Mannelli. The evil entity possessed him. He was different—the way his body moved, his hollow eyes, and then his voice cut deep into my ears.

"Do you remember me, child? I held your neck within my hands in that field while you clung to your poor little stuffed rabbit. I could have crushed you at any moment, leaving you defenseless. I've watched and waited for this time to come. Your powers are growing stronger than any of us ever knew possible. And now it's time to proceed with your destiny."

I continued backing away, and he followed with each step. "I don't know what you're talking about." I contended.

"Don't play games, child. You know perfectly well what I proclaim." His eyes caught the sight of the black symbol drawn on my forearm. I covered the mark with my hand quickly. "Do you think *he* can save you? Well, where is he? Finley, are you coming to save this poor little—little girl?"

The ground began to shake, clouds accumulated above, rumbles of thunder echoed, and the wind blew warmth unseasonable for December. The humid moisture formed beads upon my brow as a cooler wind blew from the other direction. Twisters formed and then fell apart.

"Who said I needed to be saved?" I pulled the dagger out and aimed it straight at him. "Who are you and what do you want?" I demanded.

"How can you not see—I've shown you every side of me." He approached slowly, reaching out to touch my skin, and I quickly moved away. "Piper, you have been wandering lost and weary. I found you—I sensed your presence as a child, but now that your powers evolved, I can't be without you. Finley and your mother tried to hide you, but I knew this day would finally come. They are not your true family. They have lied to you. They will never accept you. Stop pretending to be something you're not!" he yelled. I fell into the whirlpool of darkness emanating from his eyes for a second, allowing him to get close. He gently touched my face. For a moment, I wished Father Mannelli would come forward and save me, but he didn't. The creature whispered into my ear, "You're mine. I am your *real* family. Noah's flood destroyed us, but now we have you—your powers."

I held the dagger and pierced him as he continued to stroke my cheek.

His eyes widened, and he shouted, "PERDITUS...ERRATUS!" Then he shattered into a million slivers of black glass just like he had in the field near the labyrinth. The priest's white collar spun on the ground beside me, and then the wind carried it away.

I ran toward the road as a twister tore apart the forest tree by tree, forming toothpicks from broken timber. Stumbling out into the road, I froze when a car came close to plunging into me. It screeched to a halt, and Rachel got out of the car. She looked distraught and glared as if she wished she'd hit me.

"Are you crazy? You made me almost wreck my car! I should have plowed you down." Rachel contemplated out loud. "What is your problem, Piper?"

I saw a glow coming from her neck and a torn box in the front seat of her car addressed to me. It was the necklace—my necklace. The one I had seen wrapped around my mother's neck in old photographs taken before I was born. The one Finley had asked about. "Where did you get that?" I reached for it, and a light of intense emerald irradiated outward from the pendant.

"What, this old thing? You didn't even miss it, now it's mine. Finders, keepers—you stole Aiden, and I took your little trinket," Rachel spat childishly, relishing each and every word like she'd rehearsed it for hours.

Then a tornado caught her eye over the trees behind me. She slid back into the driver's seat and sped off down the country road. Within seconds, the tornado split into multiple spinning twisters and chewed up the forest, tossing debris all around. I climbed into my car, following her closely down the winding road toward the unforgiving chapel.

Feverishly, I drove with my foot firmly against the pedal, steering straight ahead. A piece of metal siding fell into the road in front of me. I swerved instinctively at the place where the dark figure ran across the road the night of the storm months back. Flashbacks of the guy running from the woods into my view broke through my mind as I slammed on the breaks. Clarity came into focus, and then I saw the dark figure—Logan.

The vision transparent and ghostlike played in slow motion becoming clearer with each moment. An out-of-body experience revealed the past to me in a step-by-step account. His face, his eyes, his movement weren't the same as the Logan I knew today. I followed the vision into the woods and watched from the cliff above as the wolves moved in. Next a bolt of lightning struck him hard, knocking him into the ravine, and I saw myself in the distance standing among the burned rubber tread, marking the wet road. I heard myself call out to the dark stranger without response and watched as I ran back to my car. The wolf with golden-amber eyes sat in the thicket watching—waiting, and then he took off to meet the pack.

A bright light fell upon Logan, and his pale skin began to glow warmth of golden tones. I climbed down the cliff, holding onto the boulders stained with his blood. Standing over his body, I saw his chest fill with another breath. Leaning closer, I knelt down beside him and reached for his hand. His eyes opened and stared into my soul. This was the Logan I'd known before time had meaning. I tried to swallow the lump clinging to my throat, but couldn't. He knew that I knew. "Piper, I'm here," he said softly. My guardian angel here to protect me fell far from Heaven, and now he was here in human flesh.

The vision left suddenly. I was alone, kneeling by the rocky ravine staring at my own reflection in the stream flowing over rough rocks. I stared into the stream, searching for something else—knowing I was more than what I was before. I gradually made my way to my feet and ran through the forest, leaving my car by the roadside. My feet felt familiar with this pathway and ran steadfast toward the chapel. I had trained for this in my dreams and knew each rock, cliff, and ravine. I ran with certainty, racing against the clock that ticked inside my mind.

Soon I could see the steeple and ran toward the wooden structure. Rachel came out of nowhere, knocking me to the ground. Her hands wrapped around my neck, squeezing me, and for a second I didn't struggle. My necklace dangled from her neck, dancing from side to side. I watched the flow of glowing particles flutter through the center of the glass pendant. And then I hit her square across her cheek and pulled the necklace from her skinny neck. She flung her fist toward my head, and the necklace flew into the forest brush. She continued ramming her fists into me with a wild look on her face. I blocked each hit as an explosion of stained glass broke into the turbulent winter air around us. Finally, I shoved her against the tree without laying a hand on her. And Rachel sank into a well-deserved slumber.

The pathway toward the chapel unlocked many memories, and I checked the dagger by running my fingers down the mighty piece of silver stashed out of sight. The dagger was the key, my hand the sword, and my heart only hoped to see what my eyes could not. I took a deep breath, felt the chapel's coarse wooden door with the palm of my hand, and swung it open.

Chapter Twenty-Two

I Don't Love You

The chapel doors creaked as I pushed them open, exposing the truth I feared. Temporarily blinded by a bright light, I squinted and held my hand up to block the burning rays of light before everything came into focus.

Aiden and Logan stood dead center of the room. Intense fury was written across Aiden's face, his jaw clenched as he threw blazing balls of fire. Logan blocked each one with a shield of bright light. Both bloody, with skin torn and bruised, they stopped momentarily to look at me. Logan's eyes grabbed me with a warm glow, and I shuddered at the intense emotions pouring over me. *If Logan was my watcher, protecting and guiding me, then what was Aiden? Could Aiden be the monster that kept seeping through a skin he borrowed like the one that took over Father Mannelli?* I forced the thought from my mind, but it kept coming back in a flutter of memories—the boy I once loved had been transformed into this wicked thing, and I didn't know what to do. As we stood within the chapel separated by the triangle of sharp corners, I didn't want to recognize what truly was...because it was too difficult to process. *Piper, choose wisely.* The words, spoken in my mother's voice, echoed through my mind, but how could I choose?

The battle to the death resumed. I felt helpless, watching it unfold. Flames shot overhead and caught the wooden chapel on fire. I begged God to send someone else to stop it all. I pleaded for them to stop and approached slowly, dodging bolts of stabbing light and round spheres of fire. Logan held up one hand without even looking my direction and pushed me away gently without human touch.

"Not yet, Piper!" he called out between blows.

My back hugged the wooden beam toward the rear of the church. The cool steel dagger, tucked secretly under the waistband of my jeans, jabbed at my hip. I wanted to pull it out, but I stood frozen, unsure of where to move next.

Aiden punched and kicked Logan to one side of the chapel, and Logan returned with moves that displayed a skill unknown to our earthly realm. The entire scene portrayed itself as my world teetered upon its shifting axis. And I couldn't forget the most crucial question—what was my part in all of this? I lost my concentration again when they both dived over me in midair colliding body to body, dripping blood down upon me—blood, I knew, they didn't even own.

The stained-glass windows sweltered from the heat inside the building. Sweat beaded against my skin, and I coughed a couple of times, clearing smoke from my throat. The sprinklers popped on, spouting off a trickle of water unimpressed by the flames dancing around it. The water hissed when it landed against the stained glass. Eventually, the colors within the glass ran into a pool of red, dripping from the ceiling and oozing down the walls—heaven was bleeding. The glass shattered into a million pieces floating through the air, and I dropped to my knees to cover my head as it all fell like diamonds and rubies all around me.

Silence screamed for me to look up. Logan fell slumped against the altar, unresponsive and bleeding profusely from his side. A steel metal crucifix clanked as it dropped to the ground next to him covered in blood. Aiden wiped the blood from his brow, leaned down close to me, cleared his throat, and stared into my eyes.

"You're already on your knees, my sweet Piper. This is easier than I thought it would be." He spoke with grandeur as I fumbled for words.

"Why are you doing this?" The simplest question purged my mouth, and I waited for his answer.

Aiden's turquoise eyes glistened in the chapel as the inferno began to rage out of control around us. "Of all the questions in the world you can ask, Piper, this is the one you want me to answer? You'll never stop surprising me." He smiled and reached for my hand, but I pulled back. "OK, you just need time to process it all. That's understandable. But, Piper, take a good look around. Time isn't exactly on your side, is it?" The fire rolled up the beams of wood, and more glass shattered in the heat.

I glanced over at Logan, and his stillness left me feeling overwhelmingly alone. Aiden stood confidently a few steps away, and I yelled, competing with the roar of the fire consuming everything within its clutch, "Aiden, why are you doing this?"

"Piper, I can offer you something that will change your life forever." He leaned down and touched my cheek, freeing the crazy strands of hair from my face. "Just think for a moment: there will be no more sadness—no more loneliness. You will have enormous power and my love forever. Piper, can you even conceive what forever means? It's a place removed from the chains of time. It's a place where we can live like gods untouched by everything and everyone. This world is ending, and there isn't anything *you* can do to stop it. When this planet is done, we can make it beautiful again. We can make it ours. There isn't even a real choice for you to make, when you think about it. You have death along with the rest of the planet, or you have forever with me—in my arms."

I swallowed the tears I refused to display for him. "What are you, Aiden?" My voice, soft and shaken, swept the smoky room as the fire raged close by. He took my hand and sat me down on the burgundy pew near the front of the chapel. It was the same place as before when I first saw his monstrosity. My lower lip ached, but it was long healed from his attack. My hands trembled. So I folded them into a single fist and hid them within my lap.

"What am I, you ask? I'm the same guy you held onto when the stars fell out of the sky last night. The same guy you declared your love to. I'm the one you laugh with—the one you talk to—the one you want to be with—the one that will never leave your side. You just have to say it's what you want, and I'll bow down to you right now, Piper."

"Aiden, I mean, what are you exactly? Are you the madness following me, the darkness waiting for me, the monsters haunting my dreams? Are you the evil she warned me of? What are you, really? Whose arms will I be wrapped up in? Could you be worse than death? What are you *not* saying?" With each question I asked, I watched the reflection of the fire blazing in his eyes. He didn't blink, didn't move, and didn't falter with his response.

"I was specifically created, much like Logan, for one of God's great purposes. I found a greater purpose, as did Logan. There's so much more I can do when I'm with you—we will be unstoppable. I was created to destroy you. Ironically, the God you love and worship designed me to kill you and everyone like you. You weren't meant for this world, Piper. God doesn't *love* you, but I do," he gloated.

"That's not possible. You're a liar!" I covered my ears and looked back at Logan, still lifeless within a steady pool of blood. I couldn't get away. Every direction I turned, Aiden was there, breaking me down further.

"Piper, I thought it would be fun and games hiding out within this disgusting human body, toying with you, but something happened during that lightning storm. When I fell to Earth and into this skin, I awoke on a wet field staring into your eyes. Feeling your touch for the first time left me wanted nothing more than you. The poor human bastard trapped inside this body only showed me the way toward human longing and love. I used him to get close to you, promising him freedom that I knew would never come. And now I can't seem to get enough of you. Fascinating, without my wings, I felt the chains of my bondage break, and I knew that I couldn't kill you—I refused my orders the moment I saw you."

"What about Logan? You didn't even blink an eye before stabbing him. So why should I trust you?"

"Logan and I are almost one in the same—both fallen angels, and more to the point, *fallen for you*. However, Logan had a disillusioned faith, and it's rather ridiculous, but he believes *you* can save this world—this world that left you disguised as a human. But Blasphemy is the real name they call you in Heaven. And your almighty God," Aiden pointed up and smirked into the heavens, "gave me the order to strike you down. Now does that sound like the precious Father you pray to each night? And that's because you don't know God like I do. I couldn't possibly spend another moment trapped in his shadows as a slave to his every whim. Take a good look around, my sweet Piper. He abandoned your kind long ago. Let's not forget—he could have saved your mother, but he didn't feel she was important enough, either. You weren't even assigned a guardian angel, but pathetic Logan secretly followed you around like a little lost puppy… watching, waiting, and wanting God to change his mind about you. And when the orders came in to take you out, he disobeyed God too. Lame little Logan never really had a chance. He could never win against me. You see, in the grand scheme of everything, I am the highest of all angels, an archangel, and no one human or otherwise will ever have the power to move past me."

The next question rolled off my tongue as I watched the fire burn hot and bright. The tail of the flame strangled the chapel as time seemed to expand, waiting for me to find my way. In my moment of deepest solitude, the simplest spark lit my path, and I followed it. "Then, what *am* I? Why does God hate *me*? What makes me unworthy of his love? Who am I, Aiden?"

"You are my greatest love. I worship your beauty, your heart, your fight, your strength, your sweetness. It burns me with hunger, and I feel I must have you beside me forever. I never knew this way of thought—invading every desire I found inside this limited human body. Emotional storms brewed for no reason, other than just to stand in your presence. Remarkable, these human feelings of endless possession take me and break me while I stand idle, wanting nothing else—but you. You ask who you are. Shouldn't you know by now?" And then he whispered into my ear, "You are mine."

I stood silent, unable to move. I secretly feared him and his power. Alice's Wonderland twisted me more, digging at my mind and heart for ever falling for him. I feared for my soul if I should fall further. The rabbit hole opened up again, and I felt myself lose my footing for a man I should have run away from and not into. My dagger dug against my numb hip, but I couldn't bring myself to wield it. Pathetically, I still longed to kiss, taste, and touch him as I had yesterday. Where was God in all of this? What had *I* done to make God abandon me—hate me—want to kill me? Still, the same question sent ripples through my mind as a pebble through a pond: *Why me?*

"Piper, this is your only chance. Come with me. Let me show you what you've been missing. Be with me." He looked around the chapel, pointing out the destruction and then redirected. "You can't stay here. The humans will find you insane and lock you away like your mother. The dark ones, lost to Noah's flood, believe you are their new hope. They've watched, waited, and will not stop until they become one with you and your powers. You see, I'm not that bad when you throw the humans and demons into the equation. What is there to think over? Free yourself. Remove the mask you hide behind and come away with me."

I sat silently near him as I counted my fate on the fingers of the fallen, fearing I was caving into his charm, his beauty, his twisted fairytale of demise. I would be stepping past a boundary I couldn't come back from—ever. Out of the corner of my eye, I saw Logan regain composure and stand, bleeding from his side, only to stumble back and fall again.

"Piper," his weak voice whispered between the roar of the golden flames, "don't believe a single word from his lips. He is the master of deceit and false charm." His voice grew stronger with fortitude and faith. "Casting doubt is his plan so he can control you and your powers. But you have the power to save us all—the power to break his chain—you have the power to say, no."

As Logan spoke, Aiden cringed in utter disbelief that a lower angel would even consider insulting his rank and authority in front of his precious love. Aiden walked toward Logan and picked up the blood-streaked steel cross. He spat upon the ground of the quaint little chapel ravaged by flames. Then he pushed Logan against the wall with a simple wave of his hand and speared the cross through the air toward Logan's chest.

"Stop!" I yelled and threw my hands up in the air. The cross floated toward me. A force immeasurable grabbed Aiden, pulling him onto the altar. His feet dangled a few inches above ground. I stood over Logan guarding him as he'd guarded me every second of my life. And then Rachel plowed through the door, screaming.

"Piper, you crazy bitch, put him down!" Rachel demanded as she ran toward Aiden, only to be forced back by my hand. My simple touch tossed her outside and pinned her against the wooden doors as she struggled to move.

The cross hanging in the heart of the chapel began to dissolve into liquid metal and circulated into a shining sphere. Other metals within the chapel verged toward the center spiraling orb of emulsified magnetic energy. Tornados twisted outside as it carried debris through the ornate broken windows, feeding the energy with raw minerals and metal as the remaining angelic faces upon the stained glass looked down in awe. The ceiling caught fire as Aiden smiled in his last attempt to lead me astray.

A break in concentration had broken the magnetic ball of energy I'd first formed in my bedroom less than twenty-four hours ago. I couldn't allow it to happen again. Sending one simple thought blew out the flames engulfing the chapel. And white residue fell down like snow. It covered my face and hair, dusting my skin and eyelashes. I gently closed my eyes, stepped back, and felt the power grow.

Wiping my face only smeared the white powder into my pores. My reflection from the liquid magma reminded me of the nightmare I had inside the janitor's closet after Rachel struck me on the head. Up on the Elizabethan Stage, where I once stood silent dressed as a mime, I warned people to run from the destruction. And now—it was truly real. It hadn't been a nightmare; it had been a premonition. *All the world's a stage,* I thought. It was practice for what was to come. The Earth's polar flip was happening, and I possessed the power to hold everything and everyone in place long enough for Nibiru, the planet Johnny Sledge swore would destroy us, to pass by. It was unbelievable; the great Mayan prophesies were true. The planetary lineup unfolded.

Logan began to struggle for breath, and blood streamed from his lips. Aiden laughed an irrevocable sound. I burned with anger at the thought of time stolen by this imposter who'd told me, "I love you more than you'll ever know." Evil claimed his face, and he was no longer my Aiden. Slipping into a dark time warp, a sudden burr of a monster's pit, I planted my feet solid and squarely within these four walls of the burning chapel. Alice found her might and drove her sword into the beast. I had to find my courage to do the same.

"My dearest Piper, '*Frailty, thy name is woman.*' What are you to do now, save the world? Really, with your tears and ball of flashy light?" he sneered. "You're going to save these people for a God that doesn't even recognize you as worthy."

I took a deep breath, and the unrehearsed words flowed from my lips without hesitation or question.

"Aiden, I realize it now. Nothing is really what it appears to be behind this masquerade. Some weak girl bound love-struck by a charming, beautiful, smart guy. A silly girl waiting around for her Prince Charming to ride up and rescue her. A fool wishing upon fallen stars to bring back her dead mom. A love story wrecked by an unhappy ending. Monsters lurch in nearby shadows, waiting to drive her mad. A world left hanging in the balance would remain, in wait for her to find her strength. A girl broken by an absurd metal allergy finds a way to transform metals into a stellar ball of energy. The truth is—I never lost it. You saw me coming a mile away. And I'm sure you thought your quest would be quick and easy. But, Aiden, maybe I'm nothing like I appear to be. A silly little girl lost to the world and a God that doesn't love her. Really, is *that* the best you can do?"

I stepped backward inside the liquid metal as it encapsulated around me. I reached back for the handle of the blade resting patiently against my hip as her words chanted back, "*Love—it transcends us all.*" The little girl in the Cinderella gown grasped within the hands of evil, the young woman walking down Pioneer Street with a rose tucked into her hair, and my mother's plea warning me to choose wisely. "*Love isn't ordinary; it transcends even the smallest of creatures.*" I loved my people, my family, Earth. I had to save her or I would certainly die trying.

Aiden remained pressed against the wall of melting stained glass, grinning, content and more in love than ever before. "You'll regret this decision, Piper. I'll have you no matter what you choose. I'll find a way, even if it means turning your family against you. Each one, if I have to. I'll find you. I'll hunt you down and make you mine one way or another." His words sealed his fate. I ran my fingers down the blade before bringing it into sight.

"Aiden, you've lost and you don't even know it!" And then I whispered one last phrase to him, "'*What light through yonder window breaks?*'" I stood inside the liquid center as it rotated full speed around me, holding time at bay and keeping Earth and everything on it intact as the galactic alignment rode into the night sky. The dagger floated above my hand, and it spiraled through the winter solstice air as it carried the magnetic substance in its tail, torpedoing toward Aiden's chest. The metallic sphere ruptured into particles, forming a silhouette of large angel wings against the wall and floor behind me. He saw my transformation and winced for the first time as the blade narrowed in.

It struck him with the fine point of the dagger and followed with the showering of liquid metal as it turned into a meteor-like strike, flinging him through the stained-glass window, down the steep cliff, and into the rocky terrain below us. Here one moment and nowhere the next.

I ran to Logan and pressed down on his bleeding wound. My hand became part of him, and his wound healed underneath with a warm glow. Rachel broke free from the other side of the strong wooden doors and ran toward the broken glass falling in pieces of rainbow flecks. She turned toward me for one last look, and then dove to her death.

"No, Rachel!" I screamed, but couldn't move to catch her because my hand held Logan together. I never expected her to give up her life to a guy that never really existed. But then again—I knew all too well how love, whether true or not, could blind you.

Logan opened his eyes, looked up at me, and then closed them gently. And I would wait patiently for him to regain consciousness. I owed him that much. His faith in me never wavered, and he gave up his wings to save me. I was exactly where I needed to be to see, to truly see. The rabbit hole, seared shut and patted down, was no longer able to swallow me up.

Memories kept me company while I waited for Logan to wake. I pictured the painting hanging in the atrium of Schneider Museum titled *Watch*. The gears and numbers frozen in time in rich oil-on-canvas weren't mocking me or winding down my last seconds. They were preparing me for my destiny, my fate, my journey. A glimpse of the *David* sculpture crept into my mind, but I buried it deep inside Alice's rabbit hole. I couldn't bear to think of the Aiden I once knew.

Logan woke, and his eyes gravitated around the room, taking it all in—the broken glass, the badly burned wooden beams black with smoldering steam, pellets of metal beads rolling upon the ashen wooden floor, and the giant hole at the front of the church. The pulpit was intact with a carved impression of a cross upon the wooden podium stand. Logan glanced back at me, wiped the blood from his lips, and tried to speak.

I covered his mouth with my finger, and his silence remained a part of me. Then I repeated the words—his words. "Logan, I'm here. You're going to be OK. Trust me."

Chapter Twenty-Three

Wish You Were Here

Logan stood in the puddle of blood that once poured from his side, now healed with the faintest scar. He took my hand, pulling me up and into his arms. Over his shoulder, I stared out the broken window expecting Aiden to crawl out from the depths of the pit. Unusually, the longest night of the year disappeared into a crisp morning horizon.

We didn't say a word. Logan held me tightly in his arms. Steam and smoke radiated from the hot pillars. Broken stained glass crunched beneath my feet as I gently swayed inside his embrace. I still didn't believe it all really happened. I mean, I didn't want to believe. I missed him already—the Aiden he'd pretended to be; I didn't want to let *him* go.

I stopped at the doorway, turned toward the broken view once more, and spotted the shiny steel dagger balancing over the ledge. The slightest motion of my hand moved the dagger toward me and straight into my palm. I tucked it back into my waistband, knowing I would need it again someday. Aiden wasn't alone in this. There were others waiting for another chance, and I had to be ready.

Logan broke the silence with his motorcycle, and then he spoke. "Piper, I have to take you somewhere. It's something I've wanted to tell you, but couldn't until now."

Another mystery wrapped up in the unknown. I just wanted to sleep a thousand years. I felt numb to life. I nodded and climbed onto the motorcycle behind him.

I stopped him from taking off by pulling on his shirt. It was killing me. I had to ask. "Is it true, what Aiden said? Did God send Aiden to kill me? Did you leave Heaven to save me? Where do I fit into all of this? Who am I?"

"Piper, there's still a lot I have to explain. Trust me, I will tell you everything, but I have to take you somewhere first. I need a starting place to break it all down, and you need a place to hear the truth."

"Logan, I saw you here before. You were praying, pleading for something. You spoke a language I didn't understand. The words were foreign, but the meaning felt universal. Your sadness shook me to the core as I watched you fall apart. Will you ever be able to go back to Heaven...to God?"

He revved the engine and spoke one last phrase before driving off. "All in good time. I promise—I will tell you everything." The motorcycle lunged forward, and I held on tight as he wove around the destruction that was scattered about the battered forest.

Three bolts of lightning struck through the sleepy morning sky, crashing into one large bolt. I refused to look back. My arms wrapped around Logan's waist as I watched dirt turn to gravel and gravel turn to pavement, counting the miles between me and the unimaginable madness back at the chapel.

On the drive out of Ashland, I caught a glimpse of meddlesome Kate sitting stone faced on a bench outside her house wrecked with debris. For once, she sat quietly inside the chaos that she didn't create. The drive steered us out of Ashland and toward a place I'd visited as a child. People stood in their yards looking up at the sky in disbelief at the tragedy all around them. I closed my eyes and continued to hold onto Logan while flashes of Aiden plagued my mind. A disease, an addiction, an obsession nibbled away at the very essence of who I was, breaking me into pieces of pieces. How long would it take for time to heal the wound rubbed raw with each thought of him?

"Here we are," Logan declared as he slowed down and turned into the drive.

"Where is here?" I questioned, investigating the property with my eyes. The two-story stone-on-log building resembled a resort mixed with the charm of a bed-and-breakfast. However, the recent destruction didn't discriminate. Cracks had leveled the parking lot and rippled across the green lawn. Pieces of stone were scattered around the grounds, and the roof had caved on the east side of the building. But a simple beauty pulled me in. A large pond in the front held lily pads with purple flowers, and rose petals blew across the field from the broken bushes that had once lined the valley from hill to rolling hill. A wrought-iron gate secured the residence, and a security guard waved us through the gate.

"What is this place?" I asked. In the back of my mind, I dreamed of room service, a warm bed, and a hot shower. He parked, slid of the motorcycle, and took my hand leading me toward the main entrance.

"Miss O'Leary, we've been expecting you," said the lady at the front desk. She wore scrubs, and her badge jingled as she walked toward me to shake my hand. A ring of keys dangled from her wrist when she punched in the code to open the locked double door ahead. "We knew one day you would make it here. I'll tell her you're here." She paused, wiped some dirt and blood from my cheek, and gazed into my eyes. "Really, the resemblance is uncanny."

I felt like I'd stepped into the twilight zone, but at this point, I didn't care. My shoulders ached, my head throbbed, and then—my heart sank when I saw her. I saw her sitting at the piano, playing the melody I longed to hear just one more time. Her hair caught the natural light from the multitude of windows all around. Her skin radiated with warmth, and her cheeks blushed to the sound of the music pouring out into the air around us. Her fingers swept across the piano keys, and her foot danced across the pedals.

I fell to my knees, weeping into my hands. She turned toward me, and slowly her fingers ceased to find the keys. Lost in her own world of confusion, her eyes fought through all her doubt and despair. And then she found me, smiled, and returned to playing the piano—the same melody over and over again.

"Mom," I whispered. "Mother!" This time I called out to her louder. She continued playing. A ghost, come to life, sat before me, and now I was the one invisible to her.

Logan lifted me from the floor. I glanced around at the other people tuning out the world with paints, clay, pencils, and music.

"What's wrong with her?" I asked one of the caretakers as Logan held my hand tightly in his.

"Piper, is it?"

I nodded as she directed us over to a small table near the window.

"Piper, your mom's last psychotic episode left her in an altered state of mind. She's here physically, but her mind has drifted away to another place—a place that gives her comfort from all the demons in her mind. Mental illness is difficult to understand. But one thing for sure, when assaulted, the mind will travel to a place of comfort, a place of safety, a place far from reality. I do feel she recognized you, your voice, and your presence. It's more than your father has seen, and he's been here almost every week since the car accident. He really wanted to tell you two, but he felt it best to protect you from heartbreak." She paused to take a look around the room, "I'm surprised your father didn't come with you."

I turned to Logan in disbelief. "She's been here all this time, just a few towns away—all this time."

The woman excused herself to check on another staff member.

"Logan, how long have you known?" I demanded. "I told you things. I told you how much I missed her. And how I wished she would come back to me. I sat on her grave begging her to speak to me, to guide me, to keep me from the darkness that claimed her, and she was *here* all along."

"Piper, please understand, I couldn't tell you. I wanted to…desperately, but I had to wait until now. So much had to line up to get us here to this very moment. It had to be this way," he contested.

"Who do your orders come from? Why wait until now? What's so important about this moment, this second?" So many other questions raced through my mind.

Logan leaned forward and began to explain. His lips kept moving, and I forced myself to keep up with everything flowing from his mouth. "You have a gift passed down from your *real* father. Your mother fell in love with him a long time ago, before the dad you know today. He was a fierce fighter, an archangel, sent on a secret mission. He crossed the line when he fell in love with her and made a choice to disobey God. His choice angered many. And when you were born, he hid you away from it all—a new life, a new father, a way to give you a chance to grow. You are a Nephilim, part human and part angel, and a survivor to everyone's dismay. Ashtriel was a great archangel that took over Aiden's body. He was ordered to kill you, but then he got a taste of you, your powers, and your freedom as he fell from God. He changed the course and set out to turn you dark, keeping you as some sort of trophy. Piper, you have amazing powers unlike anything I've seen in human form. Even in biblical times, the Nephilim were giants, but you—you are different. Your powers don't reside in your size, but your heart, your mind, and your desire to love."

"Why did they hide me? What were they hiding me from? Who told Ashtriel to kill me?" Then, in utter disbelief, I answered my own question, "God—God told him to kill me. You told me that Ashtriel was lying in the chapel, but he was really telling me the truth."

"No, Piper. Ashtriel is deceitful and wanted you for himself—to use your powers for evil. You are better than that. Give God a chance to see what I see. He doesn't know you like I do because of how you were conceived. He didn't take the time to know you as a person. Your human side is just as important as your angel side. In time, I know, he will grow to love you. Rules were broken, and you were caught in the middle. These are strict rules…angels should never become intimate with humans." He gently pulled away as he glanced down at his own hands. Again, I felt he was hiding something—maybe feelings he held for me.

My eyes cut away from him in disbelief. "This is too much to take in all at once," I whispered. He placed his hands on my cheeks and pulled me closer. Finally I ventured, "My father…my real father is Finley?" I knew the answer before he even formed the words to agree. "That's where my powers came from?"

My mother, escorted by her personal caregiver, had overheard the bold angel's name. "Finley," she sighed and smiled while walking back to her room. I reached out to touch her, hoping I could cure her of the darkness that surrounded her mind. Logan grabbed my hand, led me back to the table, and sat me down.

"You cannot save her like you healed my wounds at the chapel. It's not mental illness, but demons chasing her. Only Finley can save her. He afflicted her with the darkness when he made his choice to defy God. He has to be the one to make it right," Logan explained.

It was the first word my mom had uttered since the accident—the name of her one true love—Finley. He was the one she looked desperately for in her dreams, in her gardens, and in the back of her mind. I watched her walk away, and I was determined to find Finley and free my mother from these demons tormenting her every thought.

"It's his dagger you gave me," I acknowledged. "I felt something the first time I touched it. I think I knew all along, but couldn't make sense of it. So where can I find a lost archangel who doesn't want to be found?"

"I thought you would never ask, Piper." Logan held my hand tightly, and my strength seemed to replenish. "But there is more," he continued. "There are different sides of evil. The spiritual forces haunting you are the lost Nephilim of the past destroyed by God. They grow more and more desperate in search of freedom for the life they once had. They believe you are the way. You know them as Demons. They will stop at nothing to have you, your light, and your powers. You are their lost wanderer oblivious to see them for what they are. They believe you are family and it angers them because you do not understand this connection."

"The lost Nephilim were the ones destroyed by Noah's flood—the giants I learned about from the Bible. So when they died, they couldn't go to Heaven or Hell—they just roamed the earth as demons. Is that what will happen to me?" I questioned in horror. I shook my head, wanting it all to stop. "I'm their family," I whispered, finally figuring it out.

"Piper, I won't allow that to happen to you. Trust me. You have to trust me."

I nodded fearing I had nothing left, but to trust him. And then I remembered the old man that roamed my neighborhood and knocked Patrick into a tree on Thanksgiving. "What about the old man that was after my necklace? The necklace Finley asked me about—the one I found wrapped around Rachel's neck. And the fires—what about the mysterious fires breaking out all over Ashland?" I questioned, gathering as much information as I could.

"The old man was cursed to walk the earth forever and wants your necklace to free himself. The necklace is of great importance—in the wrong hands, it would be catastrophic. We have to find it and get it back." Logan quickly glanced around the room and then scooted his chair a little closer toward me. He lowered his voice and continued his explanation.

"The fires were started by a crossbreed of Cerberus. They are wolf like creatures that can also shape shift into human form. You saw them as a group of thugs on motorcycles roaming around town, but they are hellhounds called by Ashtriel to track you and wait. Once they found you, they grew bored and began to cause destruction."

"And you Logan—why do you care? What do you see in me that they all do not? Why do you have so much faith in *me*?" I pressed.

"In the heaven's, there was talk of a girl born from an angel—not an ordinary angel, but a powerful archangel. You were denied a guardian to protect you. They never expected you to make it this far. You were hidden well from everyone, but you seemed to call out to me. I knew you needed help, and I couldn't refuse. It was almost—almost like we were meant to be together. Once Ashtriel found you, I gave up my wings to come here to protect you. Don't worry, Piper, they will see that you're good and deserve to be here like everyone else."

Pieces were coming together. Gaps of knowledge began to fall into place. An unsettling thought caught me off guard, and I wondered, *what about the one he was meant to protect—his assigned child to watch over.* "Logan, if every human is assigned a guardian angel to protect them from harm, then what happened to the one you left unguarded—the one you left for me?"

I watched as his shoulders fell forward, his eyes grew heavy, and his mind traveled to a secret place outside the window. I knew I struck a nerve that burned beyond words. For a moment, he fell silent. And then he cleared his throat and spoke, "Another time, Piper."

I quickly changed the subject back to another unanswered question— one that burned deep inside me. "Why did I have to fall in love with Aiden? If you came to protect me, then why didn't you save me from heartbreak, knowing that he had possessed the body of a boy I loved? What if it wasn't Aiden I fell in love with? What if I fell in love with Ashtriel?" I struggled for answers as a tear ran down my cheek. "Why would you allow me to become so close to a monster?"

He regained his composure, singing my praises once again, "Love is your most impressive power. You had to find it, feel it, and release it in order to find yourself in the process. It was the only way," he explained.

The fortune cookie answer would have to be enough for now, I thought, because time was ticking, and I couldn't possibly take anymore. I led him out of the locked room, away from the lady with jingling keys, and into the sunlight of a new December day.

"I'm ready," I said firmly. "I think I've always been ready for something. But now—I'm just more aware of what's at stake. I'll find Finley, and he will bring my mom back from the darkness."

Chapter Twenty-Four

Starts With Good-Bye

The motorcycle pulled into my driveway as memories of my childhood wrestled through my mind. Time felt different; everything I knew about my life had changed its path. There were many unanswered questions I would have to deal with later. Right now, the simplest questions haunted my spirit; I was still learning who I was and what I would ultimately become.

The blue motorcycle vibrated with an occasional popping sound as I stepped off and glared intensely at the home I'd known all my life. This time, I knew I didn't belong here. I felt like an imposter in more ways than one.

Logan reached out and grabbed my hand pulling me back. "Do you want me to go in with you?" he asked with concern.

My connection to him brought me back to a familiar place…a place I needed. I took a quick breath and stepped forward. "No, I think I should do this on my own. Just give me ten minutes."

Leaning forward, he reached over and released a strand of hair stuck to my bruised cheek. His warm, soft kiss pressed against my forehead, and I knew what I needed to do.

Releasing his hand, I walked toward the house that had been severely damaged by the storms. Cracks riddled the yard, and roofing shingles mixed with wooden beams scattered about the neighborhood. The remnants of the tree house rocked side to side in the cool December breeze, waiting patiently to fall to its demise. I couldn't help but feel I'd left my mark here among the damage and destruction. Earthquakes and twisters had violated the heart of our home, leaving our lives in shambles. And suddenly the sadness filled me. Taking a deep breath, I walked up the steps to the porch and stepped inside.

The house was empty. Making my way up the staircase, I studied the collage of photos from my life with people I knew as my family. I touched the glass and remembered how my prayers had been answered. But then again...I pondered the thought, *where did my prayers go?* Logan said God didn't know me. I shook it off because it was too much to take in. I guess it didn't really matter because my mom was alive. And now I had to devote all my energy into finding Finley, my real father. He was the only one that could pull her out of insanity. And I had questions that only he could answer.

The floors creaked more than usual, and the second floor felt unstable. I gathered what I needed into a small backpack. Quickly, I pulled a pair of jeans over my bruised legs and threw on a blue T-shirt; it just happened to have a pair of white wings across the back. Once again karma found me and kicked me in the teeth.

The blue Tiffany vase seemed to be the only thing in my room untouched. I lifted it up into the sunlight that filtered gently into the room. The jumbled pieces of metal floated up until the vase sparkled. The metal pieces dangled above me. As I walked through the doorway, metal beads gathered into the spinning mass rotating into hot liquid. Bright lights beamed out, and then the objects vanished. My powers were becoming sharper and stronger.

I carried the vase outside. It tasted water for the first time in years as the faucet leaked a spewing stream of water. The garden, torn from the earth, left trees uprooted and flowering bushes beaten down. I reached out for the battered rose lying in the dirt, and a thorn pricked my finger. The stem, crushed and peeled back, held on tight to wilted flower petals. The pink rose reminded me of someone. Battered, bruised, broken, and brought back to life—it was me.

A golden shimmer spread through my skin, starting at my arm and blending toward my wrist and then my fingers. The rose strengthened before my eyes, restored to its finest state. It seemed my touch was sensitive enough to bring life back, but it still wasn't powerful enough to bring my mom back from darkness. I had to find Finley.

I placed the single rose in the vase on the wooden table where it was destined to be. Reaching into my pocket, I pulled out my phone and sent a brief text to Dad, Patrick, and Bailey, making sure they were OK. I gave them an abbreviated version of what I had discovered—my mom was alive. Obviously, I left out the supernatural aspects—it's not likely they would believe I faced my demons, found out I'm half angel, killed my egocentric fallen archangel boyfriend, and saved the world. However, I did tell them I was leaving to figure a few things out in time to save Mom and my own sanity. And how could I forget Dad's part in all of this; he had a lot of explaining to do. But most of all I was sad to be running out on Patrick when he needed me.

My phone erupted with text and calls, but I didn't reply. A tear ran down my cheek and dropped into the small stream running across the floor. I missed my family, even if they weren't mine to have. I closed my eyes, sat the phone down next to the vase, and then walked away.

As I turned around, I saw Dad—I mean Shawn O'Leary, the man that only pretended to be my father, standing in the doorway. His crumpled suit was soaked and stained with destruction, but I couldn't get past the destruction I felt brewing in our father-daughter relationship.

"How could you!" I yelled. And then I tossed my backpack over my shoulder in an unsettled fashion informing him that I had no desire to stay.

"Piper, where are you going?" he said as he blocked the door. "We have to work through this. I know you are angry at me for lying to you about your mom." He paused for a second—possibly trying to come up with other lies, but I refused to listen. "I did what I thought was best for her, best for you and Patrick, best for all of us," he confessed.

My temper blew, and I thought the house might actually come down on both of us, "How dare you say that—say it was best for all of us! What you actually meant to say—was that it was best for you; so that you could move on. You should think twice about your new girlfriend, Alana. She's not what she claims to be." I felt myself growing more hostile just thinking about Alana, my dad, and my poor mom secretly locked away in a mental hospital. And then I shouted, "You're a coward! I don't even know who you are anymore." And then I calmed for just a moment to deliberately give one last blow because I felt he deserved it in some way. "You're not even my father," I sneered.

"Piper, what does that mean? Who gave you that information? Piper!" he yelled my name one last time as I walked out the door, leaving him alone. And it broke my heart into pieces that continued to stab, scarring my heart for a lifetime.

Seconds later Marcella's car veered into the drive, and Patrick jumped out with Marcella following closely behind. He yelled, "Dad is it true? Did you lie to us about Mom? Did you hide her away from us?" Patrick's hands struck the December air in anger as Dad tried to console him. "Is she alive?" he cried out.

Marcella appeared stunned and covered her mouth, releasing a gut wrenching sigh. Then Spanish erupted from her lips, and the only phrase I caught was, "Oh God, why?"

I knew my brother needed me, but I couldn't stay. I had to find Finley. I wiped the tears from my cheeks, climbed onto the back of the motorcycle, pulled my hair into a quick ballet bun, and Logan drove us away—away from my life, my town, and my family. My arms held onto him tightly, and it wasn't until we made it down the road and around the curve that I relaxed. I caught the wind, closed my eyes, expanded my arms, and flew. The motorcycle vanished into thin air. The only thing remaining were the metallic beads rolling down the county road, and we were gone.

The motel sign outside flickers a stream of red into the cool, dark room between the broken blinds, hanging in the window; a crazy Morse code entices me to find answers hidden within the pattern of lights, keeping me from sleep. Everything around me feels unfamiliar. We found this seedy hotel late at night after hours of driving and took the only vacant room out of desperation, hoping to catch a few winks of sleep. I miss my family, my friends, my school, and my life—my life, the way it was before.

On the flickering television, the media continues to report the failure of the great Mayan prediction, chalking the recent destruction up to a violent streak of freakish weather. My people still don't know the truth. The Mayan's knew something was coming—something that would change our world forever. I just never realized that I am a piece of the puzzle. The Mayan's didn't believe the world was coming to an end, but to a new era—a new chapter—in fact, the last chapter. I open the drawer to the nightstand and pull out the Bible. I flip it open to the last book—the Book of Revelations. I dive into the passages, recognizing the beast, the destruction, the horror. The gates of Hell push open, and I wait—I wait to prove myself worthy.

My bruises ache as I lie down against the hard mattress, and I want to drift away to another place. I catch a glimpse of Logan staring at me, but silence is the only communication between us tonight. Logan turns away, pulls his shirt off, and stares straight ahead at the wall. Then he kneels to the floor and gradually lowers his head in prayer. I notice the same red scar across his back, reminding me of Aiden. Both had been stripped of their wings as they fell from Heaven. But both were different—Logan has given up everything for me, and I have no idea how to repay him. The weird thing is, I haven't asked for any of this—it just happened so fast.

I close my eyes briefly as memories come flooding back. My body is so tired, and I just can't fight it any longer. I begin to gently drift off, and I see him in the distance. We're at school, walking in the hallway toward each other. He's tossing the football hand to hand. I stand breathless, watching his every move—how he plants his feet on the ground with each step, how his football physique gravitates toward me like a heavenly body deep in an unknown universe. His wavy hair and warm sun-kissed skin enhance his turquoise eyes. My hands sweat, my heart races, and my mouth dries up. I wish my eyes could speak for me in some sort of telepathic connection, screaming out—*See me, hear me, fall for me!*

We pass each other, and I turn back to yell, "Aiden, I love you!" But he's gone. I'm alone, standing in the hallway at school. Everyone's gone. Time has passed me by again, and I've lost my only chance to… A crashing sound jolts me from my dream to my feet. I peek out the window as cops in SWAT gear force their way into the next room, arresting a group of thugs. I sling my backpack over my shoulder, and we drive away from the screaming sirens and flashing lights. It's time to run again, and we run like hell. We are running from a place where reality twists and bends, only to be consumed by darkness—a place I only know as *oblivion*.

Epilogue

I Miss You

The wind blew through the leaves near the pathway of the once-beloved chapel, uncovering the necklace Rachel had stolen. It shimmered in the morning sunlight. Then her fingers, stained with blood and crusted with dirt, grabbed the necklace and fastened it back around her neck.

He smiled as he admired the necklace with his turquoise eyes. He knew he still had a chance, and a new plan was close at hand. Rachel, different than before, smiled a wicked grin, twitched with a crazed look in her eyes, and reached out for his hand. They both disappeared into the forest. He vowed to do whatever was necessary to find his love—his true love—his Piper.

About The Authors

Tonya and Todd Hollers live in the Lone Star State of Texas. Todd attended the University of North Texas and received his bachelor's degree in education. He eagerly dreams up new exciting visions for current and future storylines. Tonya graduated from nursing school in 1995 and is actively employed as a pediatric registered nurse at a local hospital. After a week of caring for patients and saving lives, she saves her sanity by jumping into writing in the land of fantasy, romance, and paranormal literature.

They live in a quiet town with their teenage son, dog, and three cats. When they are not immersed in writing, they spend their time walking the dog, going to museums, watching movies, bowling, playing putt-putt, people watching, geo-caching, camping, fossil finding, and watching their favorite TV show, *The Walking Dead*.

Oblivion: the Masquerade is the first in a series of YA books featuring Piper, Logan, Aiden, and their eternal quest for love, acceptance, and forgiveness as the world continues to teeter in the balance.